Robert Sinker, Ion Grant Neville Keith-Falconer

Memorials of the Hon. Ion Keith-Falconer, M.A.

Late Lord's Almoner's Professor of Arabic in the University of Cambridge, and

Missionary to the Mohammedans of Southern Arabia. Sixth Edition

Robert Sinker, Ion Grant Neville Keith-Falconer

Memorials of the Hon. Ion Keith-Falconer, M.A.
Late Lord's Almoner's Professor of Arabic in the University of Cambridge, and Missionary to the Mohammedans of Southern Arabia. Sixth Edition

ISBN/EAN: 9783337033965

Printed in Europe, USA, Canada, Australia, Japan

Cover: Foto ©Raphael Reischuk / pixelio.de

More available books at **www.hansebooks.com**

MEMORIALS

OF THE

HON. ION KEITH-FALCONER, M.A.

Yours affect^{ly}.
Ion Keith-Falconer

MEMORIALS

OF THE

HON. ION KEITH-FALCONER, M.A.,

LATE LORD ALMONER'S PROFESSOR OF ARABIC IN THE UNIVERSITY
OF CAMBRIDGE, AND MISSIONARY TO THE MOHAMMEDANS
OF SOUTHERN ARABIA.

BY THE

REV. ROBERT SINKER, D.D.

LIBRARIAN OF TRINITY COLLEGE, CAMBRIDGE; CORRESPONDING MEMBER OF
THE ROYAL BOHEMIAN SOCIETY OF SCIENCES.

WITH PORTRAIT AND MAP.

"Ἄτινα ἦν μοι κέρδη, ταῦτα ἥγημαι διὰ τὸν Χριστὸν ζημίαν.—PHIL. iii. 7.

SIXTH EDITION.

CAMBRIDGE:
DEIGHTON, BELL AND CO.
LONDON: GEORGE BELL AND SONS.
1890.

CHISWICK PRESS :—C. WHITTINGHAM AND CO., TOOKS COURT,
CHANCERY LANE.

PREFACE.

A CAREER of exceptional promise was early closed in the death of Ion Keith-Falconer. The beauty of his character, his ardent missionary zeal, his great learning, form a combination rarely equalled; and the feeling was very generally expressed last summer, especially in Scotland, that an attempt should be made to portray the many-sidedness and goodness of that life. It was represented to his family that it was a duty "to make the story of such a life the possession and the stimulus of the Church and the country."

When I was honoured with the request to write the Memoir of my late dear friend, I could but feel it was too sacred a trust to be refused.

How noble a life his was, how unselfish, how worthy to be loved, those who knew him know well; how hard it is adequately to set forth, on the one hand, its harmonious beauty, on the other, the rich variety of its aspects, I am very fully conscious. Still even the simple record of his life is its truest encomium. Its essence may be summed up in St. Paul's words, "I count all things but loss for Christ."

The numerous letters with which I was entrusted by the members of his family and others, to whom my grateful thanks are due, give a fulness to the narrative which it must otherwise have lacked. Many will learn, perhaps to their surprise, how many were the interests of one whom they knew or heard of in one aspect only.

My especial thanks must be given to my friend of many

years, the Rev. H. C. G. Moule, M.A., Principal of Ridley Hall, Cambridge, who has aided me with his counsel and help at every stage of my work, and to whom I owe many valuable suggestions, while the book has been passing through the press: and to Dr. George Smith, C.I.E., Secretary for Foreign Missions in the Free Church of Scotland, who has kindly allowed me to appeal to him constantly for information as to the details of the South Arabian Mission.

In conclusion, I humbly commit this book to God's blessing. May He, Who has called His servant home to Himself, grant that some hearts may be quickened into a fuller love towards Him, a deeper zeal, by the record of a life devoted to His service.

R. S.

TRINITY COLLEGE, CAMBRIDGE,
February 2, 1888.

NOTE TO THE SIXTH EDITION.

IN the second and subsequent editions, a very few details have been added to the account of the Shaikh Othman Mission. No change calling for any remark has been otherwise made.

I cannot send forth this new edition without expressing my thankfulness for the welcome accorded to the earlier editions of this book. That welcome both marks a widespread appreciation of the noble character I have sought to portray, and is a symptom of the remarkable growth of interest in the cause of Foreign Missions, which the last few years have witnessed in our country.

The portrait in the present edition is a reproduction of a photograph taken by Mr. Vernon Heath.

March 6, 1890.

CONTENTS.

CHAPTER IX.

CHAPTER X.

CHAPTER XI.

ILLUSTRATIONS.

MEMORIALS

HON. ION KEITH-FALCONER, M.A.

CHAPTER I.

INTRODUCTION.

> " The rest of Scotland's war-array
> With Edward Bruce to westward lay,
> Where Bannock, with his broken bank
> And deep ravine, protects their flank.
> Behind them, screened by sheltering wood,
> The gallant Keith, Lord Marshal, stood :
> His men at arms bear mace and lance,
> And plumes that wave, and helms that glance."
>
> SCOTT, *Lord of the Isles.*

IN the reign of Malcolm II., King of Scotland, a battle
was fought at Barry in Forfarshire, in the year of our
Lord 1010, with an army of Danish invaders, who were
signally defeated. Their leader was slain by a young
Scotch nobleman, Robert Keith, as the name would
now be spelt, who for his valour was created by the
king Hereditary Great Marischal of Scotland, and was
rewarded with lands, some of which, in East Lothian,
still bear the name of Keith. The king is said to have
dipped his fingers in the blood of the Danish chief and to
have drawn three vertical bars on the shield of his follower ;

B

and these enter into the family arms to this day. The king at the same time pronounced the words *Veritas vincit,*—"Truth overcometh," afterwards the motto of the Marischals.[1]

From this warrior sprang a family memorable in the annals of Scotland. His descendant, Sir Robert Keith, was one of the supporters of Wallace, and afterwards joined the standard of King Robert Bruce. He aided largely in gaining the battle of Inverurie, A.D. 1308; which led to his receiving a grant of lands in Aberdeenshire, and henceforward it was with this part of Scotland that the family was specially associated. Sir Robert commanded the Scotch cavalry at the battle of Bannockburn, A.D. 1314, and his attack on the English archers in flank had an important effect on the fortunes of the day.

About the year 1380, Sir William Keith built Dunnottar Castle near Stonehaven in Kincardineshire. In the course of building this, long the chief seat of the family, he was excommunicated for encroaching, as was alleged, on consecrated ground. The grandson of this Sir William was in 1458 created Earl Marischal by James II. At Flodden, A.D. 1513, the two eldest sons of the house fell in their father's lifetime: and William, the fourth earl, a staunch supporter of the Reformation in Scotland, fought at the battle of Pinkie, A.D. 1547.

More generally known, however, than any of these is George, the fifth earl. In his youth, he was sent abroad with his brother for his education, and studied for some time at Beza's house at Geneva. He was highly esteemed by James VI., who sent him in 1589 as ambassador to Denmark, to conduct the Princess Anne, his betrothed queen, to Scotland: and subsequently, when James VI. had become King of England, Earl George was appointed,

[1] Douglas, *Peerage of Scotland*, ii. 184. Davidson, *Inverurie and the Earldom of the Garioch*, pp. 15, 435.

A.D. 1609, Lord High Commissioner to represent the king in the Parliament of Scotland.

Some years before this (1593), he had founded at his own cost a college at Aberdeen, for a Principal and four Professors, which, under the name of Marischal College, long did useful work to the cause of religion and learning; till in 1860 the University system of Aberdeen was re-modelled, and Marischal College lost its independent exist-ence.[1] Carlyle, writing at a time when the College still existed in a separate form, speaks of it as a place "where, for a few, in those stern granite Countries, the Diviner Pursuits are still possible (thank God and this Keith) on frugal oatmeal."[2] Earl George died in 1623, having throughout his life taken the warmest interest in the cause of learning.[3]

The seventh and eighth earls fought for the king in the Civil War, and the former was imprisoned in the Tower of London from 1651 to the Restoration.

In the unfortunate rising of 1715, the tenth Earl, George, was seriously implicated; and an act of attainder having been passed on him, he fled from Scotland, accompanied by his brother James, who was also involved, though only nineteen years of age at the time.

The latter, afterwards the famous Marshal Keith, entered successively the Spanish, Russian and Prussian services, became a highly-trusted friend of Frederick the Great, and fell at the battle of Hochkirch (1758), where he commanded the right wing. He was buried with all honour at Berlin. Some words of his epitaph may be cited: they are relevant

---

[1] One of the last professors, at the time of this absorption, was the late Prof. Clerk Maxwell of Cambridge.

[2] *History of Friedrich II. of Prussia*, v. 624, ed. 1865.

[3] In the Signet Library at Edinburgh, is a rare tract, the lament of Marischal College on the death of its founder, "Lachrymæ Academiæ Marischallanæ, sub obitum Mæcenatis et Fundatoris sui munificentissimi, nobilissimi et illustrissimi, Georgii Comitis Marischalli, Domini de Keith et Altrc." Abredoniæ, 1623.

to other heroes and other warfare, " suorum aciem mente, manu, voce et exemplo, restituebat; pugnans, ut Heroas decet, occubuit."[1] Carlyle gives the letter written by Frederick to the surviving elder brother, then and for some years after, governor of Neufchâtel, " loved by him almost as one boy loves another."[2] The king begins by saying " If my head were a fountain of tears, it would not suffice for the grief I feel ; " and subscribes himself, " Your old friend till death."[3]

After this, through the intervention of Pitt, the Earl Marischal was pardoned (1759) and allowed to come back to Scotland, but before long he returned to Prussia, and died in 1778. With him the title of Marischal became extinct.

We must now look back to the time of the great Civil War of the seventeenth century, and to an event which indirectly led to the creation of the Earldom of Kintore. In the year 1651, Cromwell's troops were besieging Dunnottar Castle, whither the Regalia of Scotland (the crown, sceptre and sword of state) had been taken for safety after the battle of Dunbar. The castle was of exceptional strength, standing as it did upon a rock protected on one side by a deep ravine, and on the other by the sea. Still great anxiety was felt by the defenders of the castle for the preservation of their treasures, on which it was known that the English set an inordinate value.

Accordingly, the governor's wife, Mrs. Ogilvie, concerted an ingenious scheme, with her parish minister, Mr. Grainger, of Kinneff, and his wife. One day the latter lady rode past Dunnottar Castle to Stonehaven, accompanied by her maid, to procure flax for spinning. On her return she obtained leave from the commander of the English forces to visit Mrs. Ogilvie in the Castle, and was followed by the maid with the flax on her back. The maid having been sent away

---

[1] Carlyle, *u. s.* 373.   [2] *Ibid.*   [3] *Ibid.* 386.

to talk to her friends, the Regalia were concealed in the flax
by the two ladies.

After a while the unconscious maid resumed her burden,
and she and her mistress again passed through the English
lines, the English general actually helping Mrs. Grainger
to remount her horse. That night the minister and his wife
buried the Regalia under the pulpit of Kinneff Church, and
here the treasures lay safely hid till the Restoration.[1] In
the meantime, to divert suspicion from the true state of the
case, a letter was allowed to fall into the hands of the be-
siegers, purporting to be from Sir John Keith, the fourth
son of the sixth Earl Marischal, which stated that he had
reached France in safety with the Regalia, and would give
them to the king.

At the Restoration, Sir John Keith received a grant
of the lands of Caskieben, now Keith-Hall, in Aberdeenshire, and was afterwards (1677) made Earl of Kintore,
assuming the appropriate motto *Quæ amissa salva,*—
" What were lost are safe."

The second earl fought for the old Pretender at the
battle of Sheriffmuir, but no very serious consequences
befell him. His two sons died childless, but his daughter,
Lady Catherine, who was married to Lord Falconer of
Halkerton, had a son ; and on the death in 1778 of the last
Earl Marischal, to whom the estates, though not the title[2]
had passed, Lady Catherine's grandson became fifth Earl of
Kintore.

The great-grandson of this nobleman was the father of
the subject of our present sketch.

The late Earl of Kintore, the eighth holder of the title,
succeeded his father in 1844 at the age of sixteen, married
his cousin in 1851, and after a life spent in the faith and
fear of God, and in the furtherance of every good work

---

[1] For these details, I am indebted to the interesting account
given by Dr. Davidson, *op. cit.* p. 367.

[2] This was in abeyance from 1761-1778.

"mente, manu, voce et exemplo," passed to his rest in 1880.

Many were the schemes for shedding the light of gospel truth in the dark places of the earth, which lost in him an earnest and eloquent advocate. Specially had the Free Church of Scotland cause to mourn at his death one of its most loyal and munificent supporters.

Of his four sons, two passed through the golden gates before him, and now, in the spring of the present year (1887), Ion Keith-Falconer has rejoined his father and brothers.

CHAPTER II.

" Whose high endeavours are an inward light
That makes the path before him always bright."
                                        WORDSWORTH.

THE river Don may be said to divide Aberdeenshire into
two approximately equal parts, and to separate the Highland half of the county from the more level country to the
north and north-east. About twenty miles above the place
where it falls into the sea a little north of Aberdeen, and
in a north-westerly direction therefrom, stands the small
town of Inverurie, within the angle made by the union of
the rivers Don and Urie, whence its name. Still closer to
the place where the rivers meet, there rises abruptly a
mound of considerable size, perhaps of artificial origin and
intended for sepulchral or the like purposes, perhaps a relic
of the glacial period. This is the so-called Bass of Inverurie, on which, in the twelfth century and doubtless
earlier, stood the Castle, commanding the fords over the two
rivers. It is referred to in one of the so-called prophecies
of Thomas of Ercildoune, " the Rhymer," [1]

> " Dee and Don shall run in one,
>   And Tweed shall run in Tay ;
> And the bonny water o' Ury
>   Shall bear the Bass away."

[1] Davidson, p. 1 ; Thom, weaver of Inverury, *Rhymes and Recollections*, p. 98. The latter states that the old rhyme is in every
one's mouth in the district.

Spite of this, however, the Bass still remains a very picturesque object in the rather flat country.

The town of Inverurie has a thriving and comfortable look, but can hardly be called picturesque ; and the white granite of its buildings gives to it, as to its great neighbour Aberdeen, a look of decided coldness. Level though the immediate neighbourhood is, hills can be seen in the distance, and six miles away to the north-west rises Benna-chie, one of the outlying summits of the Grampians.

It is of a tributary of the Urie, the Gadie, which falls into it a few miles above Inverurie, that the well-known and beautiful Scotch song " Whar Gadie rins " was written.[1] I venture to quote the first stanza,

> " I wish I were whar Gadie rins,
> 'Mang fragrant heath and yellow whins,
> Or brawling doun the boskie lins,
>   At the back of Ben-na-chie !
> Ance mair to hear the wild birds' sang ;
> To wander birks and braes amang,
> Wi' frien's an' fav'rites left sae lang
>   At the back of Ben-na-chie."

Of the lands between the Don and Urie, anciently and still known as the Garioch, the lord, in the latter part of the twelfth century, was the celebrated David, Earl of Huntingdon, the companion of Richard Cœur de Lion in the glories and perils of the second Crusade. A charter is extant of Earl David, of about the date 1202-1206, one of the witnesses to which was Matthew the Falconer, ancestor of the Lords Falconer of Halkerton, and of the later Earls of Kintore.[2]

These latter became in their time the holders of much of what had been Earl David's land, and their chief seat Keith-Hall stands close to the town and Bass of Inverurie, but on the other side of the Urie. It is built on the site of an older house, already mentioned, Caskieben, some portions of which are perhaps included in the present

[1] Thom, p. 143. Also, with some variation, Davidson, p. 167.
[2] Davidson, p. 26.

building. This is largely the creation of the first Earl of Kintore, who was the planter moreover of numerous fine avenues of trees, of which the stately remains still partly surround the house.[1]

The house itself is of the square massive type of building characteristic of so many Scotch mansions of older date, and in the stern whiteness of its appearance, seems to lack the rich warmth of colour of an English house of equal date. In the well-wooded park surrounding the house, and at no great distance from it, is a small and very picturesque lake, and the line of hills, among which Ben-na-chie is prominent, forms the distant view seen from the park and garden.

Such were the surroundings amid which were passed the early years of the subject of this memoir.

Ion Grant Neville Keith-Falconer, the third son of the late Earl of Kintore, was born at Edinburgh, on the 5th of July, 1856.

His early years were spent at Keith-Hall, varied by long visits to Brighton and elsewhere, but the annals of childhood are of necessity almost uneventful. His mother speaks of two marked characteristics even of those early days, his intense and as it were innate truthfulness and his unvarying thoughtfulness for others. The chivalrous, self-sacrificing, warm-hearted man could not possibly have been developed from a different boyhood than this.

With tender, earnest care did his God-fearing mother instil in his earliest years the simple, unquestioning faith in Christ, which throughout his life seemed, while growing with his growth, never to lose its fresh, deep simplicity.

Some interesting reminiscences of this part of Ion's life are furnished by Mrs. Blundell, who when he was between four and five years old, came to Keith-Hall as one of the children's nurses.

[1] Davidson, p. 402.

I give the narrative just as it has been communicated to me : the perfect simplicity and life-like character of the details are more than apology.

She describes how from the very first she was struck with his extreme unselfishness and consideration for others. He was always eager to give up to his brothers and sisters; —if anything was to be shared among them, he would say, " Give it to the others first, I will wait." For his elder brother Dudley in particular, there was nothing he would not do or give up; he delighted in being his slave, his wish was absolute law to him. He brought everything to Dudley for his judgement, and delighted in telling others how much Dudley was superior to himself.

If Ion had been anywhere when Dudley could not go, he would immediately on his return give him a minute account of everything, and be full of regrets that Dudley had not been able to share his pleasure. They used to draw and paint and carve a great deal together, and once, under Dudley's directions, Ion and his eldest brother made a little model railway-line, on which a small engine ran.

His devotion to Dudley remained the same all his life, and he felt his death most acutely. He used afterwards to go to the nursery and talk about him for hours with the nurse, and everything in any way connected with him was sacred in his eyes.

He never required to be amused like most children, but was always full of resources in himself—reading was at all times and above all things his delight. From the time when he was about five years old, he used on Sunday afternoons to read the Bible to the other children and explain it ; and Dudley and he were in the habit of reading and praying together. When he was about seven, he began to go and read the Bible in the cottages, and the people were perfectly amazed at his knowledge of the Bible and his power of explaining it. He did this entirely without suggestion from any one, and never talked of it to any one ; it was only from the people themselves that it was found out. His old nurse used then to say that she was sure he would one day be a missionary. He was so much loved by every one, that he went by no other name in the household than that of "the angel."

He was as generous then as he was in later years. When out walking, he could not pass ragged or hungry-looking persons, without emptying his pockets for them; and when all his money was gone he would save up biscuits and the like and give them away. Before he received his allowance of pocket-money, he always carefully planned how every penny was to be spent, and faithfully adhered to his scheme. He once saved up to buy some ginger-nuts, which were his favourite weakness, for himself, and went down to Inverurie to buy them; but on the way back, he met a hungry-looking boy, and promptly bestowed them all on him. Of such things too he would never speak, and it was only through the nurse watching him continually that his acts of kindness were found out. He did it all, as the nurse said, "just as if it was his ordinary work."

He was always full of life and merriment, and after he grew older there was nothing the younger children enjoyed more than when he came, as he often did, to romp with them in the nursery.

At the age of nine, he began to work under a tutor. This gentleman, Mr. Redknap, at first gave daily lessons to Ion and Dudley at Brighton, where Lord Kintore was then living, and subsequently became resident tutor at Keith-Hall, and accompanied the family abroad when for nearly a year they resided at Vico near Naples, or in Naples itself. Mr. Redknap writes:—

"The work of God the Holy Spirit was clearly mani-sested at an early period of Ion's life: grace wrought in his heart, and deeply was he interested to listen to the story of the Cross, and of the life and ways of the Lord Jesus in His path of love and grace. During the many walks and rambles that we had together, he would often say to me, 'I wish you would talk to me,' which I knew meant to say, Will you speak to me of the Saviour and of the incidents in the life of the Lord Jesus? . . . . He was a thoroughly conscientious and noble-hearted boy."

At the age of eleven, he was sent to the large preparatory school of Cheam, near Epsom, in Surrey; then as now, under the management of the Rev. R. S. Tabor. Here he gained a considerable number of prizes, and seems to have been thoroughly happy.

In 1869, being now thirteen years of age, Ion went up to Harrow to compete for an Entrance Scholarship, which he was successful in obtaining.

Mr. Arthur Watson, the master in whose House he resided while at Harrow, has written the following note describing their first meeting and his subsequent impression :—

"I well remember my first meeting with Ion Keith-Falconer. At the beginning of the Easter holidays in each year, an examination is held at Harrow for the election of entrance scholars. It was at that time in 1869 that two visitors were announced to me, who proved to be Ion Keith-Falconer, then a bright, fair, intelligent looking boy not thirteen years old, and a master from his private school. Ion then and there informed me that he was coming to be a boarder in my House, and did not seem disconcerted when I assured him that there must be some mistake, as no previous communication on the subject had been made to me. Eventually we came to a compromise. I was greatly attracted by the open guileless face of my young visitor, and I promised that if he obtained a scholarship I would find a place for him. He was duly elected a scholar; and thus it happened that I had the happiness of seeing and watching him throughout his too short, but always blameless and distinguished, career at Harrow.

"His boyish life was noticeable from the first for marked individuality and determination. The public school system, great as are its merits, has at present too great a tendency to repress idiosyncrasies of taste and temperament, and to impel those who come under its influence to adopt a more or less common type of manners and pursuits. It was therefore refreshing to meet with one who was by no means disposed to swim necessarily with the stream; and who though in no wise self-engrossed or unsociable, would not flinch for a moment from saying or doing what he believed to be right, at the risk of incurring unpopularity, or being charged with eccentricity. He was one of those boys, not too common, who are not afraid to have the courage of their opinions. Always high principled and religious, he never disguised his views. I remember how, when almost head of my House, he displayed conspicuously on the wall of his room a printed roll of texts from the Bible—an open avowal of his belief, which was far less common, and more noticeable, at the time I speak of, than it would be now. Not that he was anything of a prig or a Pharisee: far from it. He was an earnest, simple-hearted, devout, Christian boy.

"He had not been very long at Harrow[1] before, under the belief that he would make more progress in Mathematics than in Classics, he was transferred to the Modern Side. He rose to the head of it before he left the school, which he left at an earlier age than usual, to read with a tutor preparatory to entering Cambridge: I perfectly recollect how in presenting him with his last prize Dr. Butler, then our head master, expressed his regret that he was not to remain his full time at Harrow.

"He was no trifler or dilettante, but always energetic, manly and vigorous. As far as I remember, he was not remarkable for any success in games: and of course there was no opportunity of developing that special skill in bicycling for which he was afterwards so conspicuous. He showed however great proficiency in shorthand writing, and succeeded in inspiring one or more of his companions with an enthusiasm for it. In fact, either he himself or a pupil was in the habit of taking down whole sermons in shorthand that were preached in the school chapel.

"My own intercourse with him was always most cordial and happy. Nothing ever occurred to overcloud it: and I feel sure that his lofty consistent character, and scorn of all that was low and base, must have had influence over his companions. When his Harrow days were over, it was always a great pleasure to me when I was able to meet him again. I was delighted to hear from time to time of his Cambridge distinctions, and increasing fame

---

[1] He had, as a matter of fact, been there three years.

as an Oriental scholar, and greatly shocked and distressed when the news came that a life of so much promise had been, in the Providence of God, so prematurely, as it seemed, cut off. With me the pleasant memories of his bright and God-fearing boyhood will linger as long as I live."

With the above it is interesting to compare the reminiscences of a school-fellow, Mr. G. W. E. Russell, formerly M.P. for Aylesbury. Mr. Russell thus writes of him :—

"Ion Keith-Falconer came to Harrow in September, 1869. Earlier in the year he had won an entrance scholarship, an honour gained by open competition among all the best taught boys of the private schools. He was therefore already known as a clever and industrious boy, and I remember being interested by what I heard of him before I ever saw him.

" I was older than Ion : I had been nearly two years in the school, and I was not in Mr. Watson's House, where he was ; therefore my opportunities of seeing him were few : but I well remember my first sight of him. Mr. Watson gave a breaking-up supper before the Christmas holidays (1869), and asked me to it. Ion was then pointed out to me, and I perfectly recollect the engrossed expression of his face, and the pose of his head as he leant back in his seat, in complete and intense enjoyment of some humorous speeches and songs. I have a photograph of him as one of a group of Mr. Watson's House, in which this attitude and this expression are exactly reproduced. I cannot remember anything of Ion during the year 1870, beyond the general impression that he worked hard, particularly at Mathematics, and rose rapidly in the school. . . . .

" In 1871 I went into Mr. Watson's House, and then for two years I saw a great deal of Ion. My recollection of him at this time is perfectly distinct. He was not like other boys : he was essentially the reverse of commonplace. In every action and quality—in look and voice and manner and bearing—he was individual. In the first

place as to religion: Ion's was not the simple goodness of
an uninstructed but well-meaning boy, though that in its
way is beautiful.   He was already an advanced, and, if
the word is permissible in such a context, an *accomplished*
Christian.

"It goes without saying that his moral standard in
speech and action was the highest.   And this in him
was the result of a heart filled through and through with
the love of God and Christ.   But besides this, he had
thought carefully and gravely about religious problems,
and had defined and even rigid opinions.   Thus when a
Confirmation was about to be held in the school chapel,
and many of his friends and contemporaries were candidates for it, Ion astonished his tutor by declaring himself
in heart and intention a member of the Free Church of
Scotland, and on principle opposed to episcopal rites.
His religion was by no means self-contained, personal and
passive.   He longed to make others better; and he took
an earnest, and, as he rose in the school, an authoritative
part against those forms of 'evil communications,' which
are always present in a greater or less degree in every
assemblage of boys.

"Then again as to his work, Ion was not like other
boys.   Most boys who work at all, work chiefly from the
wish for distinction.   This motive never seemed present
to him.   He worked often at odd and out of the way subjects, such as shorthand, not for the sake of prizes or
promotion at school, but either simply to improve his
own mind, or with a view to future usefulness. . . . ."

Perhaps the foregoing remark as to the absence of any
wish for distinction as such, though in the main true,
must not be absolutely pressed.   There was indeed a
total absence in Ion Keith-Falconer of the petty vanity
which can see in each school or college success an end in
itself, rather than the stepping-stone to a fresh advance
and a means towards higher usefulness; but he was by
no means without the healthy ambition which enjoys a
keen intellectual contest, rejoicing heartily if success attended him, though ready with most genuine sympathy

to congratulate the victor, if the result were otherwise.
It may be worth noting that his chief distinctions at
Harrow, besides the Entrance Scholarship, were the
Ebrington prize for German, the Flower prize for German
prose, and the prize for Problems, all of which were
gained in 1873.

Mr. Russell has referred to Keith-Falconer's practice of
writing shorthand while at school. Of this we shall speak
more fully in the following chapter; it will suffice here to
say that he learnt it quite unaided, and before he had left
school he had acquired a very high degree of proficiency.
His favourite amusement too of bicycling had begun in
the Harrow days, when he was about fifteen.

Truly the boy was father to the man in this case, if
ever. The lines of reading, the bent for languages, the
keen interest in the study of Scripture, the simple, rest-
ful, yet thoughtful faith, the eager desire to be of service
to others, the deep warm affection he gave to those whom
he called friend,—all these characterised Ion Keith-Falconer alike as schoolboy, undergraduate, and to the last.

The following interesting note, written by Mr. E. E.
Bowen, the master of the Modern Side at Harrow,
strikingly brings this out. Both this note, it is true,
and that which follows it, written by the present Master
of Trinity, who was Head-Master of Harrow during the
whole time that Keith-Falconer was at the school, extend
into a period beyond the Harrow days; but the present
seems the fittest place for both the accounts. It will be
remembered that at the end of the summer term of 1872,
Keith-Falconer passed from the Classical to the Modern
Side at Harrow, mainly with the view of devoting increased attention to Mathematics. Mr. Bowen writes:

"It was for only one year, 1872-3, that Keith-Falconer
was in my Form at Harrow—the Modern Sixth. He did
well as a schoolboy, but short of the very front rank.

Though industrious, he had some caprice. . . . . It would
be difficult to find a pleasanter boy to deal with; he was
always interested, always cheerful, with an eye for the
picturesque side of things, and a delightful way of running
off the rails in any direction that happened to suit his
fancy. He took a good deal of pains with his lessons;
his note-books were master-pieces, and he shewed a remarkable refinement and delicacy in all that he did; but
his views of the proportion of things were often different
from those of his teachers, and he would devote himself to
some side issue, or spend hours on writing out some shorthand notes, when other boys were passing him by.

"I saw him often when he was at Cambridge, and was
happy enough to retain his friendship till the last. His
bicycling feats were one subject of common interest between
us. Bicycles were just coming into fashion when he went
to the University: he was an enthusiast in the use of them,
and an admirable performer; and when he appeared in
riding costume at Harrow, with his tall figure mounted on
the enormous machine that he rode, it was a sight to see.
He kept up the amusement for many years: for two or
more he was certainly the best bicyclist in England, and
his delight in success only shewed in more than common
relief the charming modesty with which he carried his
honours. He had a real delight in feats of strength and
endurance for their own sake. He seemed to have found
the same quality in one of the professional bicyclists with
whom he became acquainted; and again and again he
would tell me how John Keen was a man whose soul was
above prizes—a man to be made a friend of.

"It is about eight or nine years ago that under the impression, which may have been a mistaken one, that he was
in danger of squandering his powers for want of some definite object, I remember writing to him at Cambridge,
urging that on the one hand he should lay himself out to
edit some book—I suggested one—which fell within the
line of his reading, and set to work at it for the next year
or two; and that on the other, while his physical powers
were still at their best, he should perform some bicycling
feat which it would be a pleasure afterwards to remember.
He came down to Harrow more than once to discuss these

plans, but especially the latter; and we spent the evenings over maps of England, and argument about roads and routes. Finally it was settled that he should go down to Cornwall with his bicycle and start from the Land's End, to ride, if he could, to John o' Groat's House within a fortnight. The experiment was a failure; bad luck in roads, and abominable weather, stopped him. But the idea was not given up: and in 1882 he accomplished the feat in thirteen days. It has since been done by shorter routes and in much shorter time: but six years ago the roads were worse made and less familiar than now; and machines have since then been built in special view of performances of the kind. As it was, and with the difficulties that were encountered, the ride was a splendid display of strength and endurance. He carried post-cards and telegraph forms, and two or three times a day he would despatch one of these to give me an account of his progress. There still lingered a memory of him in the Harrow Modern Side; and we hung up a big map of England in the class-room, and marked his victorious career with a tiny red flag day after day throughout the fortnight till we landed him safe at John o' Groat's. He did 215 miles in his last two days. He was very much pleased at his success, and came and gave us an hour's talk about it—a sort of informal lecture—a few weeks later.

"The other subject on which I used to hear from him from time to time was the special line of study to which he had devoted himself. He had always been particularly interested in the Old Testament lessons at school: and he had also, as it seemed, a Scotchman's delight in questions of theology. I suppose it was this which attracted him, by means of Hebrew, to the other Semitic languages. The study was one in which I was unable to follow him: but I can form some estimate of the vast amount of labour that he must have gone through when once he had adopted this line of reading. Of one thing I am sure, that whatever he learnt he made his own; for I never knew anyone so clear-headed, I had almost said so candid, about what he knew. The way in which he could state an unsolved difficulty seemed almost as good as a solution of it. He was no less a consummate expounder of subjects known to few than he was a delightful companion on ground which was common to all. I remember writing to him once to ask about the method and time of the adoption of the Western Aramaic among the Hebrews. There are very many scholars who could have answered the question; but I am afraid some would have left the questioner at the end much where they found him. Keith-Falconer's reply, on a couple of sheets of note-paper, was a model of simple and clear-headed statement; it said just what was wanted, and told it without any display of learning or attempt at style. I think this clear-headedness in matters of intellect was after all only a reflection of the moral simplicity which was his highest and most beautiful gift. I have often known young men who were candid, many who were devout, and many who were pleasant: but I can hardly remember any who united the three qualities so fully. He approached the world of ideas as great observers approach the world of nature, with wonder, with reverence, and with humility. His earnestness of feeling seemed to grow more large-minded and wider in sympathy as he developed into manhood; and even in the things about which he cared most a sort of boyish playfulness—freedom—trustfulness—never left him."

The following letter, from the pen of the present Master of Trinity, will fitly close the series of reminiscences of Keith-Falconer's Harrow life.

"TRINITY LODGE, CAMBRIDGE,
Nov. 30, 1887.

" DEAR MR. SINKER,

" You have asked me if I can give you a few recollections of our dear friend Keith-Falconer when he was a boy at Harrow. They must be but few, for he came comparatively little under my own personal notice. He was not a member of my House, and his stay in my Form was, for reasons which I will soon explain, very brief.

" He came to Harrow, as you know, in 1869, winning one of our Entrance Scholarships in open competition. It was a Classical Scholarship, and as a matter of course he was placed on the Classical Side. He rapidly passed up the

Forms on that Side till he reached my own, the Upper Sixth. I was struck at once by his intelligence and steady work, and was surprised when I learned that he wished to be transferred to our Modern Side, with a view, if I remember rightly, to a fuller training in Mathematics, French and German. In consequence of this transfer, I saw much less of him, our intercourse being almost limited to a weekly lesson in Modern History.

" While a member of the Modern Side, he won, in 1873, our two school prizes for knowledge of German ; soon after which he left us for Trinity, carrying with him no special distinction, but the highest character for manly sterling goodness.

" Later on came the good news of his University successes in Theology and the Semitic Languages, proving that he was working with a definite purpose as a professional student. Soon too we began to hear of his feats as a bicyclist, including those rapid progresses from south to north which were telegraphed by him to Mr. Bowen, and at once carefully indicated by pins on a map for the edification of Mr. Bowen's boys.

" It must have been, I think, in 1884 that I received from him an unexpected but welcome offer to continue certain Prizes for the study of the Scriptures at Harrow, Prizes which had hitherto been provided from another source. The correspondence which then took place between us, followed by a long interview for the discussion of details, shewed me how warm was his affection for his old School, how deep his conviction that the study of the Scriptures at school might be made fruitful at once and interesting, and how thoughtful and well considered were his suggestions for making the Prizes efficient for their purpose. I say nothing of their money value. It was very considerable ; but, as you know, it was not in his nature to spare himself or to do things by halves. He instituted them not in his own name, but in memory of his father, the late Earl of Kintore. He followed up this signal service to the School by consenting to be the first Examiner for the Kintore Prizes ; and he sent me, when the work was over, a thoughtful report, giving his impression of the performances of the boys.

"My departure from Harrow in the summer of 1885 put an end to official intercourse of this kind, and I do not think we had any further communication with each other till the end of last year (1886), when I received from him at Davos-Platz a most kind letter of congratulation on my appointment to the Mastership of Trinity. He told me also of the plan which he had formed for going to Aden, and there employing his knowledge of Arabic for missionary purposes.

"The result of this generous enterprise we know but too well. The work was scarcely begun before it reached its earthly end. To those who believe in the abiding results of devotion to the cause and the Person of Christ, his short life will not seem a failure. His image will remain fresh in the hearts of many as of a man exceptionally noble and exceptionally winning, recalling to them their own highest visions of unselfish service to God and man, and helping them to hold fast the truth that in the spiritual world nothing but self-sacrifice is permanently fruitful, and that the seed of a truly Christian life is never quickened except it die.

"Believe me to be,
Dear Mr. Sinker,
Most truly yours,
H. MONTAGU BUTLER."

Some extracts from letters written by Keith-Falconer during the Harrow days may now be given, and will help considerably to shew what manner of boy he was. The first extract is taken from a letter to his old tutor, Mr. Redknap, written at the age of fourteen, and the remainder from letters written to Lady Sydney Montagu, afterwards his sister-in-law, now Lady Kintore.

"KEITH HALL, *July* 31, 1870.

"I arrived here yesterday morning. I started from Harrow at about a quarter to 8 A.M. on Tuesday, and proceeded thence to the Langham Hotel, Portland Place, where I met Mr. Karney and Inverurie.[1] At 12 o'clock

[1] His eldest brother, now Lord Kintore.

the same day we started for Cambridge from King's Cross station, and arrived there about 1.30. Having lunched at an hotel, we went to look for lodgings for Oddo,[1] which was soon effected, and then a jolly row down the Cam. Then we went round the colleges, &c., and came back to London in the evening.

"The next day we separated, I and Oddo departing by the 'City of London' boat for Aberdeen, ... The 'City of London' is clean and comfortable, but very slow; we took 54 hours to make the journey, labouring against a wind dead against us for a good part of the way, and rocking about like a cork. I was not, however, sick, but once or twice very near it, which is almost worse.

"When we arrived before Aberdeen, it was past time for the last train for the north; at least we could not have caught it, being only seven minutes to the time. The tide was unfortunately out, so that we could not cross the bar; we then signalled for a tug-boat, which, in accordance with the proverbial slowness of Scotchmen, came, in about half an hour, or more, with a small boat in tow. This was to convey passengers from one boat to the other. The latter occupied a very long time, as only about 15 could go at once. So we had to wait till four boatfuls had been deposited safely on the tug, which in itself was not over safe, on account of the swell. Getting into the tug-boat required a little presence of mind, as one had to wait till the swell lifted the small boat on to a level with the deck of the tug-boat, and then take a spring in; a false step would probably have proved fatal.

"Well, at last all the passengers were got safely on to the tug, and we started for the harbour, where we arrived about half-past eight P.M., and I was not at all sorry to sit down to dinner at Douglas's. We started next morning by the first train, arriving at Inverurie at eight; the rest you can guess.

"So much for the journey, now for Harrow. I am now in the third fifth, V. 3 in fact, Mr. Watson's Form, in whose House I am. In Classics, out of 37, I came out altogether 9th, in Mathematics 1st, and in Modern Languages 3rd; placing me altogether 4th in the total, which

---

[1] His old boyish name for his brother.

I think good. I got a prize for Mathematics, Smiles's *Life of George Stephenson*, which I read on the voyage and which was very interesting.

"I must see if I can't come out *first* in Form next term, in the V. 2 (Mr. C. F. Holmes). . . . . I am now in the Harrow Rifle Corps *Band* as drummer; I had some rare lark at Wimbledon where we vanquished the other public schools, and won both the Ashburton Shield and Spencer Cup. I will write again.

"Your affectionate friend."

The letters to Lady Sydney Montagu dwell largely on his thoughts on religious subjects, and bring out at once the depth of his love for Christ, and his great humility. His allusions to his friend Mr. Charrington's work in the East End of London will be better understood when I shall have spoken of that work at some length in a subsequent chapter.

"HARROW, (no date, but *May*, 1873).

". . . . Do you know the hymn beginning, 'The sands of time are sinking, the dawn of heaven breaks'? It is my favourite one. A verse of it is quoted in *Forgiveness, Life and Glory*,[1] as follows:—

'O Christ, He is the fountain,
  The deep sweet well of love;
The streams on earth I've tasted
  More deep I'll drink above.
There to an ocean fulness
  His mercy doth expand,
Where glory, glory dwelleth
  In Emmanuel's land.'

I wish I had tasted more deeply of that stream than I have. . . . . I have very nearly decided to become a Free Church Minister. If so, you will have to look over my Hebrew Exercises and hear me the Shorter Catechism. . . . . I have been reading the *Shadow and the Substance* to-

---

[1] Both this work and the other mentioned in this letter are by Mr. (now Sir) S. A. Blackwood.

day, annexing a remark here and there. . . . . I am grinding away awfully hard at my German, for the Ebrington prize. The exam. comes off on the 10th of next month. . . . .

" The last of my texts for to-day on the roller is ' Surely, I come quickly. Amen. Even so, come Lord Jesus.' I don't feel as if I was *ready* for that. I mean I am so bad, but ' I have blotted out as a thick cloud thy transgressions, and as a cloud thy sins.' "

" HARROW, (no date, but *June*, 1873).

" I have had my German examinations : did I tell you ? I did very well, I don't think anyone better. I am not proud, but I don't mind telling you exactly what I think. I did good *prose*, which counts very high. . . . . I am also writing for the Flower Prize : not a prize for botany, or anything about flowers, but for a prize offered by Mr. Flower for the best bit of German *prose*. The exercise is to be sent in on Saturday, 21st June. I hope to do well . . . . I did it nearly all to-day, and I can't find out any mistakes. What is the German for ——. No, that is unfair. I suppose I must do it all myself. (Don't think that I wrote the last three lines to shew off my honesty ! I was really going to ask for something, but it wouldn't be quite fair.) . . . . Your shorthand was much better than the preceding one—but you have forgotten the vowels, please learn them up. . . . . ' Don't let your desire to write fast exceed your desire to write well,' as you have probably seen in Pitman's book."

" HARROW, *July* 6, 1873.

" . . . . . I want you to answer this question. Do you think a person can be saved without knowing how he is saved, that is only by acknowledging Jesus as the one person who *can* and *is willing* to save him and by asking Him to do so (*i.e.* to save him somehow, *how* he knows not) ? I say, Most decidedly. For He says, ' Come unto Me, &c.,' ' Behold I stand at the door and knock ; if any man, &c.' Now if you asked me how Jesus saved me, I could not tell you. I know He died for *my* sins . . . . I have often asked God for Jesus' sake to make clear to me everything

I don't understand. But He won't. (Why?) I often nearly cry because everything is so confused and dark. Yet whenever I see a person who loves Him, I immediately feel *drawn* towards him. However I sometimes feel very happy when I think that the Lord Himself hath said, ' Come unto Me, and *I* will give you rest ; ' and · If ye then being evil know how to give good gifts, &c.' and texts like them, which are all contained in that little book you sent me. . . . . I send my character : tell me if it is true, and whether it is not too good."

" HARROW, *July* 16, 1873.

". . . . I must say something about Jesus Christ, because I think *He* ought never to be left out ; and that is the fault I find with parties and balls and theatres : Jesus Christ, Who is the All in All, is utterly left out. It seems very curious, when one comes to think about it, what power the devil has over people, has not he ? But that shall not always be so—Lord, hasten the time when Thou shalt reign altogether, and when Thy servants shall serve Thee, and Thy Name shall be upon their foreheads, and when they shall *see* Thy face—for Jesus' sake."

" HARROW, (no date, but *July*, 1873).

". . . . Charrington sent me a book yesterday, which I have read. It is called *Following Fully*, ... about a man who works among the cholera people in London, so hard that he at last succumbs and dies. But every page is full of Jesus Christ, so that I liked it. And I like Charrington, because he is quite devoted to Him, and has really given up all for His glory. I must go and do the same soon : how I don't know."

The concluding letter from which I cite was written from Mr. Charrington's house.

" STEPNEY GREEN, (no date, but towards the end of *July*, 1873).

". . . . After dinner we went the rounds to inspect the tent for preaching, and Charrington lent it to a little missionary to hold a midnight meeting in on Thursday.

We also visited the Mission-Hall, where they were making a pool for baptizing people in. . . . . In the evening a well attended meeting at the tent; foul air. After the meeting (the speakers were Dr. —— an old, but very energetic and godly Scotchman, *broad accent*, a soldier from Wellington barracks, a Mr. Kerwin, and a Mr. ——), we went to have some tea, and then to the Hospital, to see a man supposed to be dying, but found to be recovering.

" I have lots to do here. I did not get to bed till nearly one o'clock, having been up nineteen hours. We visited the Boys' Home, which I think a capital place. The dormitories are perfect; ventilation, cleanliness and comfort could not have been better looked after."

At the end of the summer term of 1873, Keith-Falconer finally left Harrow, it being settled that he should spend his last year before entering Cambridge with a tutor, and devote himself exclusively to Mathematics.

Accordingly in October he went to reside in the house of the Rev. Lewis Hensley, Senior Wrangler in 1846, and formerly a Fellow of Trinity. This gentleman was now vicar of Hitchin, a small town in Hertfordshire, half-way between Cambridge and London; and here Keith-Falconer spent the ensuing twelvemonth, save for various short vacations. Soon after he had begun to reside in his new abode, he writes to his sister-in-law:

" There are three other fellows here: we work six hours a day. I do mathematics exclusively, trigonometry and analytical conics at present . . . . To-day is Sunday: I and Mr. Hensley walked over to Preston this morning, a small village at a distance of about three miles, where he preached. The Church here is an enormous building. The vicarage is just between the Market-Place, or the town-square, and the Church railings. My window, at which I am now sitting, looks out on a sort of walk which runs half-way round the Church, and which is the resort of all the little boys in the neighbourhood; so that I hear nothing all day but 'Oh, 'ave you seen the Shah !' varied by a continual ringing of the Church bells. Then there is

the Church clock which strikes lustily every quarter of an
hour, giving forth 636 strokes per diem, which is a great
excitement for us in this little place."

Although Keith-Falconer worked, as his habit was,
conscientiously at the task set him, it cannot be doubted
that neither for Classics at Harrow, nor for Mathematics
at Hitchin, did he feel any special enthusiasm. Partly, as
Mr. Bowen has pointed out in his note on the Harrow
days, he had various side-interests which absorbed a certain amount of time and energy, so that he was sometimes
passed by students, who, with less originality of thought
than he, and often probably with less brilliancy, did however stick with greater persistence to the subject in hand.

Still there was a further reason and a weightier one.
In neither of the two lines of study to which as yet his
mind had been directed, had he found anything on which
his zeal could be thoroughly aroused. When his mind at
last found its true field of work, no student could show a
more enthusiastic or more unchanging zeal.

Mr. Hensley has kindly furnished me with some interesting reminiscences of his former pupil. In these
while one reads as a matter of course :—' I soon found
that he would be diligent and conscientious in his work,
and that I had in him a satisfactory pupil, whom I could
trust without fear, indoors or outdoors' ; one is not surprised to find the further remark, ' In neither Classics nor
Mathematics was he an *intense* student.' Mr. Hensley
continues :

" He was full of all sorts of by-occupations and hobbies,
and it was in following these that his eager character expended itself. He took up Pitman's Shorthand, which he
practised diligently, and frequently treated us to disquisi-
tions on its advantages. He was at all times full of some
matter of this kind, and overflowing in talk about it with
others, and generally in very high spirits and full of fun.
Then he brought with him a bicycle, and rapidly devel-

oped, whilst at Hitchin, that mastery of the machine which
made him afterwards the champion rider of England. I
suppose his tall figure was an advantage to him, but more,
I should say, the 'perfervid' resolution, with which he
threw himself into whatever interested him. Or he would
rise at seven to take lessons in the Tonic Sol-fa System, or
at other times might be heard singing to himself as he lay
in bed, at the same early hour. In short, he was always
doing something : if he had but a quarter of an hour before
work-time, he would be busy with his Shorthand, or would
spring on his bicycle and dash round the town and be home
again at the appointed hour.

"I have mentioned his singing. This was connected
with plans for doing good, which likewise occupied much
of his thoughts. One of these was the promotion of the
Temperance cause, to which he devoted himself by assist-
ing in the entertainments and addresses of a Temperance
Brigade of young men, which was under the management
of Mr. Arthur Latchmore. With him also he would frequently, after attending the Parish Church in the morning,
gather together a meeting of poor people in the open air or
in a schoolroom in one of the outlying parts of the Parish,
and conduct a little service with Moody and Sankey's
Hymns, or would visit the sick and infirm on a week-
day.

"He had been brought up in the Free Church of Scotland, and although this did not prevent him from attending our Church services, he was in many ways independent
in his views, at times startling strictly orthodox and
regular Churchmen, and no doubt kept in his heart and in
his convictions a strong attachment to the Church of his
early education. . . . .

"I have already touched on his labours amongst the
poor, and a few words may perhaps be added, contributed
by Mr. Arthur Latchmore, with whom he shared in these
labours, and to whom he expressed his most intimate
thoughts :—'Keith-Falconer was very fond of visiting the
cottages of the poor, especially at the Folley, speaking a
kindly word to try and rouse them to think more of their
souls' salvation ; and often by the bedside of the sick and
infirm would he sing and read to them, cheering and com-

forting many a weary soul, and not forgetting to help
those in distress with his purse. He was a strong believer
in the power of prayer, for nearly always before going out
either to the open air services, the visiting the poor, or
conducting the Bible Class in connection with our Young
Men's Brigade, we used to have a few minutes in prayer
together.' "

Mr. Hensley concludes :—

" He became much attached to Hitchin, and frequently
in after years ran over from Cambridge, and twice in
vacation time came to lodge here with friends for the sake
of reading, and once in 1875 came back to me for a week's
special help. Taking all this into account, I can still
hardly believe that his residence with me was so brief, so
deep is the impression which he has left with us all."

It was during his residence at Hitchin, that the first
great sorrow of his life befell Keith-Falconer.

His elder brother Dudley, two years and a half older
than himself, had always been of a more delicate constitution than his two strong young brothers, one older and the
other younger than himself. The departure of the eldest
brother for school, and the gap in years dividing the others
from their youngest brother Arthur, tended especially to
associate Ion with Dudley.

The delicate health of the latter forbade his being sent
to school, and thus he continued to study at home with
the tutor with whom Ion worked. In their amusements
too they were inseparable, and spent much time together
in a room allotted to them at Keith-Hall for carpentering
and the like.

In spite of Dudley's lack of physical strength, he was at
all times a leader in his brothers' various boyish pursuits : to his judgement various points were referred for
decision.

At last the mere delicacy of health began to assume

a graver form, and Dudley became more and more a confirmed invalid.

He had from his earliest childhood been one in whom the love of God had been of the very essence of his being; and now with gradually increasing weakness, the pure flame only shone out brighter and fuller.

At times, though very weak, he was capable of taking the fullest interest in all that was going on around him, and would throw his whole soul into the endeavour to speak words of peace to others; at other times, intense pain allowed him but to lie still and suffer in silence.

In the autumn of 1873, Dudley's increasing weakness warned his parents of the expediency of removing him to a warmer climate. Accordingly, as on previous occasions, he was taken to Cannes, his mother accompanying him. Here for a time some improvement seemed to shew itself; but it was the last flicker of life, and gradually it became plain that the end was near, and the father and Ion were summoned from England. Still death came not as speedily as he had been looked for. Day after day the dying boy awoke to the consciousness of the fact that this world was around him yet. No fear of death disquieted him; he had loved his Saviour with too deep an intensity to feel aught but earnest longing to meet Him. Nor was there at all a desire for death simply as the release from keen bodily anguish.

With brain clear to the last, with heaven opened to his enraptured gaze, he waited, eagerly but submissively, till the time should come for him to cross the river.

On the 27th of November, Dudley Keith-Falconer died. His death caused the first gap in the bright family circle, since so sadly thinned.

CHAPTER III.

" Whose powers shed round him in the common strife,
Or mild concerns of ordinary life,
A constant influence, a peculiar grace."

WORDSWORTH.

In the October term of 1874, Ion Keith-Falconer began his residence as a Cambridge undergraduate, having been entered on the books of Trinity College on the 24th of September preceding.

To this great College, with which so many illustrious names of the past are associated, he was warmly attached, and his letters in later years contain frequent remarks shewing cordial love both to College and University.

He did not occupy rooms within the College walls at any period of his undergraduate life, save in the Long Vacations, when, by the rule of the College, such residence is obligatory. With this exception, he occupied the same set of rooms during his whole Cambridge life until his marriage in 1884. These were on the north side of the Market Square (21 Market Hill), facing the Guild-Hall. Here he worked resolutely at his books, utterly unaffected by certain distracting sounds, which might have disturbed a less diligent or less equable student. On market days, a noisy hum from the busy square pervaded his room; all day long and all night the clock of the University Church of St. Mary chimed the quarter-hours, and at nine each evening the great curfew bell rang, as it had done for centuries, and this was followed by the tolling of the number of the day of the month.

To all these disturbances, Keith-Falconer was supremely indifferent: he liked in the intervals of work to look out on the busy scene of life below. The late Bishop Hampden was said to have written his *Bampton Lectures* while his children were playing around him in his study. The same kind of concentration over work, irrespective of surrounding disturbances, was always a marked characteristic of Keith-Falconer.

In dealing even with the undergraduate career of a man so many-sided in his interests, it is necessary to aim at giving its due importance to each element to be described. Here was a young Christian man, whose Christianity prompted him to use every faculty for the furtherance of the Gospel,—a student as careful and painstaking as any of those to whom the highest goal of human ambition is a distinguished place in the class-list,—a writer of short-hand, whose pace and accuracy could hardly be excelled,— a bicyclist, whose prowess and endurance won him innumerable triumphs.

We propose in the present chapter mainly to dwell on the student side of Keith-Falconer's life, from the time of his first entering Trinity in 1874 up to that of his last examination in 1880 ; and also to speak of those secondary interests which served him for relaxation of mind and body. We shall reserve to the following chapter some account of certain schemes for benefiting others with which he was associated even at this early period.

His intention had been in the first instance to compete for Honours in the Mathematical Tripos, Mathematics being a subject to which, as we have seen, he had paid special attention at Harrow, and with Mr. Hensley. With this intention in view, he became a pupil of the late Mr. Thomas Dale, Fellow of Trinity, one of the most distinguished of the then Cambridge Mathematicians.

Early in his first term he writes to his sister-in-law :—

"I have lots to tell you, but I don't know where to begin. Yesterday was the ten-mile bicycle race—three started. I was one. I ran the distance in 34 minutes, being the fastest time, amateur or professional, on record. I was not at all exhausted. The road was splendid, and a strong wind blowing from behind. . . . . To-day I am going to amuse the public by riding an 86-inch bicycle to Trumpington and back. There is a little scale of steps up it, up which I am helped, and then started off and left to myself. It is great fun riding this leviathan : it creates such an extraordinary sensation among the old dons who happen to be passing. If I fell off it, I should probably break an arm or a leg—so I shan't repeat the performance after to-day. . . . .

"I have been going in for Sol-Fa lately with vigour. I have got two of the certificates given by Curwen, and astonished mother by singing some tunes at sight correctly.

"The Little-go begins on the 5th and ends on the 17th, one paper only each day. . . . . I like my lodgings very much. My landlady can almost remember Adam, and tells me stories about Dr. Whewell and people dead long ago. . . . . I have a class in the Choir School on Sunday mornings."

The "Little-go" referred to in the preceding paragraph is, it perhaps need hardly be said, an examination which all undergraduates must pass, whether candidates for Honours or for an Ordinary Degree. He again refers to it in another letter to the same : —

"*Jan.* 3, 1875.

"Did you see the Little-go list ? . . . . The papers were absurdly easy. About forty men were plucked, and seven for *cribbing*. The man next me wanted me to give him a few hints, but I could not do it ; so he was plucked . . . ."

This last incident deserves a somewhat fuller mention,

as illustrating alike Keith-Falconer's keen sense of honour
and his kindliness. On the day before the examination
began, a man going in for it wrote to him saying that he
had found they would sit side by side during the examination, and that as he was not very well prepared in some
of the subjects, he hoped Keith-Falconer would give him a
little surreptitious help. To this Keith-Falconer replied
that he would not dream of such a thing, but if the other
cared, he would devote every minute of time till the examination began to ' coaching ' him for it. Nothing, however,
was seen of the man, and the result happened that might
have been anticipated.

A few days later he again writes to his sister-in-law :—

"*Jan.* 8, 1875.

" The bicycle race at Lillie Bridge has been postponed
till the 23rd . . . . I went to stay with my antagonist for
a few days, and took him and his mother and his aunt to
Spurgeon's on the Sunday. They were slightly astonished
to see such a mass of people all *rivetted* for nearly an hour.
Moody and Sankey will probably hold a meeting in his
Tabernacle. I shall go to hear them, I hope. I expect it
will be glorious."

Three terms in due course passed away, and at the annual
College examination in June, Keith-Falconer obtained a
First-Class, and was a Prizeman.

All this time he seems to have entertained a certain
amount of doubt whether the course he was pursuing was
the best for him ; whether, in spite of the mental training
which the study of Mathematics gives, he was not perhaps
making an end of the means ; instead of following a line of
study in which he could feel a higher degree of sympathy
with the work itself.

It was not without careful thought, in which reasons for
and against were anxiously weighed, and not without the
fullest search for help and guidance, that when one-third of

his undergraduate course had passed, Keith-Falconer resolved to give up his previous plans, and to begin to read for Honours in the Theological Tripos.

No one who knows the English University system needs to be told that to change from Tripos to Tripos is an altogether unusual proceeding, and is, as a rule, one to be decidedly deprecated. In Keith-Falconer's case, there can be no doubt that the change was a wise one. If viewed merely on the comparatively low ground of academic distinction, it might be urged that Harrow had given him a sound, scholarly knowledge of Greek and Latin (languages which of course hold an important place in the work of the Theological Tripos), and his first year at college had taught him the student's first great lesson, how to read. If viewed on the higher ground of permanent interest in the work for its own sake, then too there could be no doubt. He shewed the keenest appreciation of his new line of work from the first, and kept it to the end.

A man, in whose heart was the desire to serve God—and how fervent the desire was the Harrow letters have shewn —and therefore the desire to aid others to serve Him, and who felt that great powers had been entrusted to him by God so to be used, might well feel in these new studies as though he were humbly seeking to carry out, so far as in him lay, God's purpose concerning him.

I first became personally acquainted with Keith-Falconer, when, on his deciding to read for Theological Honours, he became my pupil in July, 1875.

His appearance at this time, his manner, his tastes, were all strikingly like what they were in later times. He had a remarkably tall, well-shaped figure, whose symmetry seemed to take off from his height of six feet three inches. Physically very strong he certainly was, in one sense, or his wonderful feats of athletic endeavour, of which we must speak presently, would have been impossible. Yet for all those feats, which were partly due no doubt to the sustaining power of a strong will, he could not really be called robust.

His kindly voice and genial smile will live in the recollection of his friends ; like good Bishop Hacket of Lichfield, he might have taken as his motto, "Serve God and be cheerful." Side by side, however, with his geniality there was in Keith-Falconer at all times the most perfect and, so to speak, transparent simplicity. Never was a character more free from any alloy of insincerity or meanness. No undertone of veiled unkindness, or jealousy, or selfishness, found place in his conversation. From the most absolute truthfulness he would never waver ; his frank open speech was the genuine, unmixed outcome of the feelings of his heart.

A certain slight, very slight, deafness in one ear made him at times seem absent to those who did not know this, and unknowingly had sat or walked on the wrong side.

A characteristic habit of his seemed now and then to give a certain degree of irrelevance to his remarks. Sometimes, when in conversation on a topic which interested him, he would, after remaining silent for a short time, join again in the conversation with a remark not altogether germane to the apparent point at issue. He had been following out a train of thought suggested by some passing remark, and after working out the idea on his own lines as far as it would go, made his comment on the result. Yet whenever the conversation had to do with the interests or needs of those to whom he was speaking, no one could throw himself more completely, heart and mind, into the matter. Talk for talking's sake he cordially abhorred, that talk which is simply made as though silence were necessarily a bad thing in itself.

This interest in widely different topics of conversation was not, however, simply the result of mingled good-nature and courtesy, a mere complaisance, where it was but a careless good-nature that saved the courtesy from hollowness.

Far from it.   No one who knew Keith-Falconer well needs
to be told how thoroughly, how constantly, and in what
varying ways, he could make the business or cause of
another his own ; whether it were a friend in need of help,
from the most trifling to the most momentous matters, or
the absolute stranger whom apparent chance had sent
across his path.

His old landlady, Mrs. Emmerson, between whom and
himself the warmest cordiality always existed, writes :—

" During the nine years he was in residence with me, his
sole aim seemed to be, to benefit all needing help, whether
friends or strangers.   He would frequently bring in those
he met accidentally in his walks, give them refreshment,
better clothing, or money, and start them in fresh spirits."

Still with all this, his kindliness was by no means one
lacking its proper counterpoise of discretion; his strong,
clear-headed, Scotch common-sense was constantly mani-
fested, even in his schemes of beneficence.   Yet even thus
it must be remembered that his was a character in which
the warm heart was guided in its action by the clear head,
not one in which the clear head did but allow itself to be
swayed more or less by the loving heart.   Love was the
dominant power, discretion the corrective influence.

It may be well to add a few words at this stage as to
what I have called above his secondary interests.   Of physical exercises, his favourite, and indeed the only one in
which he habitually indulged, was bicycling.   To this he
had first taken at Harrow, when he was about fifteen, on
what was popularly known as a " boneshaker."   The level
Cambridgeshire roads afforded him admirable scope for
this amusement, and the great pace at which he could run,
and the long distances for which he could endure, were extraordinary.   A dozen years ago, it must be remembered,
the bicycle had not come into nearly such general use as at
present, and great feats of pace and distance were corres-

pondingly more noticeable.   On one occasion, he went on
his bicycle in one summer's day between dawn and darkness all the way from Cambridge to Bournemouth, where
his family were then staying, a distance of nearly 150
miles.   It will be desirable to give a brief sketch of some
of his athletic successes, but this may best be postponed
until we have spoken in detail of his work as a student.

Another favourite pursuit, which can hardly perhaps be
called an amusement, but which certainly often furnished
recreation in the true sense of the word, was shorthand
writing.   This he had taught himself at Harrow, according to the system invented by Mr. Isaac Pitman, known
as phonography ; and kept it by constant practice in a high
state of efficiency.   It proved of course of immense use to
him in various University and other lectures, and count-
less sermons were thus taken down, not simply for practice
only, but often with some kind intention to be of service.
Thus the Rev. P. W. Minto, for many years the Free
Church Minister at Inverurie, writes:

"As showing his readiness to be helpful, I may mention
that he frequently gave me the benefit of this useful ac-
quirement.   When I wanted to preach, as far as language
is concerned, extempore, he took notes of the sermon, word
for word, and then would spend three or four hours next
day in writing it for me in longhand, so that I might have
it for use on future occasions." [1]

Lastly, I may mention music.   While his tastes were
not keenly musical, of certain forms of sacred music he
was very fond.   He had acquired a competent degree of
skill by means of what is known as the Tonic Sol-Fa system, which he maintained to be far more easy of attainment by the ordinary learner, though the notation itself
was one in which the most difficult music could be accurately expressed.

[1] *Free Church of Scotland Monthly*, July 1887, p. 213.

With this digression as to Keith-Falconer's various side-interests at this time, we must now attempt to give some account of his work as a student of theology. This, from July 1875 to January 1878, was guided, as I have already said, by the requirements of the Theological Tripos.

These pages may be read by some to whom everything connected with the development of such a mind as Keith-Falconer's must be full of interest, yet to whom the details of this particular examination may be altogether unknown. I therefore venture to give a short description of it, as it was constituted at the time when Keith-Falconer was a competitor in it.

At that time, it lasted for seven days, two papers being set each day, and three hours allowed for each. The last four days were devoted to more advanced or more specialized work.

There were thus fourteen papers set; or fifteen, if an additional paper in Hebrew be included, the marks for which only had regard to the Hebrew Prize. Of these fourteen papers, one was a general paper on the Old Testament, three were devoted to the Hebrew subjects, three to Greek Testament, and the remaining seven to miscellaneous Divinity, Church History and the like. Some of the subjects were unvarying, some were changed from year to year.

The general Old Testament paper consisted of questions on the criticism and exegesis of the various books, on the history of the Hebrew text, and of the Greek and English versions; as well as on the history of the Jews down to the Christian Era.

The three Hebrew papers in 1878 were respectively on Genesis, on Isaiah, and on Zechariah and Ecclesiastes. In the third of these papers, questions on the Septuagint version of the books named were also set. Into all these, in addition to pieces for translation from the Hebrew, and critical and exegetical questions, there entered, more or less largely, what is technically known as "pointing"; that is, pieces of Hebrew are set in which the student has to supply the vowel and other marks known as the "points." This exercise is one which tests the soundness and accuracy of a student's Hebrew knowledge thoroughly. In the additional Hebrew paper, pieces of English were also set to be turned into Hebrew, answering to the Greek and Latin composition of the Classical Tripos.

Of the three papers on the Greek Testament, one was of a very general kind, including questions on the history of the New Testament Canon, on the criticism of the text, on the language, and on the contents of the several books. The other two were respectively on the Gospels, with special reference to one, that in 1878 being St. John; and the remaining books of the New Testament, again with special portions, those for 1878 being Acts i.-xii. and the First Epistle of St Peter. Questions were set in these two papers analogous to those on the Old Testament subjects.

Two papers were set on Church History, the first a general one on the first six centuries of the Christian Church, and the other on special subjects, varying each year, those in 1878 being the life and times of Pope Gregory VII. and of Archbishop Cranmer.

The five remaining papers were, one on the Ancient Creeds and the Confessions of the Reformation period; one on Liturgiology, purporting to deal with the structure of the chief ancient Liturgies, and with the history of Christian worship; two on selected Patristic works, Greek and Latin respectively, those for 1878 being, in Greek the first *Apology* of Justin Martyr, and three of the polemic treatises of Athanasius; and in Latin, a book of Irenæus's work *Against all Heresies*, and two books of Bede's *Church History*.

Lastly, there was a paper on certain Modern Theological

writings, those set for 1878 being the first part of Butler's *Analogy* and the first two sections of Bishop Bull's *Defensio Fidei Nicenæ*.

It will be obvious to any one, whether professed student or not, that the above represents a mass of work to do which creditably might well occupy two years and a half.

As a matter of fact, very few men took up quite all the work, though very few on the other hand quite restricted themselves to the first six papers, on which alone the question of passing or failing hinged.

Keith-Falconer made it his set purpose to cover the whole ground, and to do it thoroughly and carefully; and this he succeeded in doing, though the amount was enough to keep him busily occupied during the two years and a half, except for one digression into another piece of work of which we shall speak presently.

While, however, he worked most conscientiously at the whole allotted scheme of subjects, he took distinctly more delight in the Biblical than in the non-Biblical work, and from the very first shewed pre-eminently the keenest interest in the study of Hebrew.

The Talmud says, in a well-known passage: "There are four sorts of pupils, the sponge and the funnel, the strainer and the sieve. The sponge is he who spongeth up everything; and the funnel is he who taketh in at this ear and letteth out at that; the strainer is he that letteth go the wine and retaineth the dregs; and the sieve is he that letteth go the bran and retaineth the fine flour." Among the last of these four classes any one to whom Keith-Falconer had been a pupil would assuredly place him.

It goes without saying that he was neither careless nor unappreciative, but he was not simply the careful, plodding student, who in his utmost zeal does but more or less imperfectly reproduce his teacher. The scholar, whose study is really to bear worthy fruit, must not only " read, mark and learn," but also "inwardly digest" and make in the highest sense his own what he is taught. The teacher of such a pupil need be no chopper-up of intellectual food into small doses, there is certain to be a sufficiency both of receptive and of assimilating power.

Such a pupil was Keith-Falconer. Docile he was in the true sense of the word, at the same time he certainly was ·

Nullius addictus jurare in verba magistri,

and this not from captiousness or any contrariety of spirit, but simply because the true scholar's instinct was strong within him, to seek ever for the truth and that alone. Thus it was the sterner, severer form of study, specially associated with Cambridge, with its traditional loyalty to Mathematical science and pure scholarship, that attracted him, rather than something perhaps more seemingly inviting, but less uncompromisingly exact.

Hebrew, we have said, was a subject to which Keith-Falconer took kindly from the first, and in a comparatively short space of time he was able to compose with accuracy and elegance in that language. It hardly needs to be said that, as contrasted with a language like Greek, Hebrew has an exceedingly small vocabulary, and is largely lacking in the power of marking delicate distinctions and modifications of thought characteristic of the former. In this seemingly rigid, inelastic medium, Keith-Falconer early found a peculiar delight in composing, not only by rendering suitable pieces of English into Hebrew, but also by writing letters in it as a means of communication. A bundle of post-cards now lies before me written by him in that language from 1876 onwards, on every conceivable subject, which shew a power I have not often seen equalled of bending the inflexible idioms and making the scanty vocabulary suffice for the needs of nineteenth century English.

We spoke above of a slight digression from the main stream of his work, if it can fairly be called a digression. This was his competition in December, 1876, for one of the prizes founded by the late Dean Jeremie, of Lincoln, for proficiency in the Greek of the Septuagint. The special subjects appointed in the year when Keith-Falconer was a candidate, were the first book of Samuel, Daniel in the two existing Greek versions, and the apocryphal " Gospel of Nicodemus." Although his Tripos work was heavy, he spared no pains in this competition, and even acquired, with a view to the more thorough treatment of his subject, a sufficient knowledge of the so-called Chaldee language, in which part of the book of Daniel is written.

He succeeded in obtaining one of the two prizes, and was also a prizeman at the two annual college examinations in June 1876 and June 1877.

On his way up to Cambridge for the October Term of the former year, he broke the journey at Stockton-on-Tees, with the view of helping for a few days in a certain good work that was then being carried on in that town. At this time, Mr. G. J. Holyoake, the secularist lecturer, was holding a series of meetings in Stockton, and after one of his lectures challenged public discussion. Keith-Falconer, who had been present at the lecture, immediately went upon the platform, and brought forward certain objections with such force, that on the particular points at issue he completely silenced his opponent.

In December, 1877, the month preceding his Tripos Examination, a great blow befell him in the death of his youngest brother Arthur in his fifteenth year.

Always delicate and lacking the robust strength which thrives amid the rough vigour of a public school, Arthur had been educated almost entirely by tutors at home.

The heathen poet declares that they " whom the gods love die young"; and the thought may be consecrated to a Christian use. In looking at Arthur Keith-Falconer one

could not help feeling that the exceptional sweetness and
gentleness, so absolutely simple and engaging, and the
depth of love for Christ which seemed so completely part
of his nature, and to carry one as though into a quiet
resting-place away from the world's rough din—all pointed
to a life which the Master would early call back to Himself.

His absorbing delight was music, for which he had as
distinct and special a gift as his brother Ion for language,
and to this, his time, so far as it was not taken up with his
studies, was largely devoted.

During the summer of 1877, he had been, though not
robust, seemingly in very good health; but in the autumn
signs of increasing weakness began rapidly to shew themselves, and as the winter approached it became clear that this
world's sunshine was for Arthur almost at an end. It needs
not to be said that the two brothers were tenderly attached
to one another, and at the beginning of December, Ion
Keith-Falconer hurried away from Cambridge to Keith-
Hall to be with his brother for such short remaining time
as God might will.

Besides the desire to see his brother once more, he needed
change also for himself, for he was by this time feeling by
no means well under the long-continued strain of work and
anxiety; indeed during the examination itself in the following month, he was sufficiently unwell to require to have
recourse to a doctor.

He found his brother simply fading away. He suffered
no pain, and was perfectly conscious to the last, looking
on to the future with the peaceful unquestioning calm of a
child who is going home.

He died on December 9, and changed the hymns of this
lower world for the song of the Seraphim.

With the shock of this great loss upon him, and in by
no means good physical condition, Keith-Falconer went in
for his Tripos on January 4, 1878. On the 24th, the list

was published, and his was one of the six[1] names in the first class, the prize for Hebrew being also awarded to him. On the Saturday following he took his B.A. degree.

For some months after his degree, Keith-Falconer did not reside much in Cambridge. He certainly needed rest, and found it largely in change of occupation, though his letters shew that the studies at which he had made so satisfactory a beginning by no means languished. Most of the time till June he spent at Brighton, where his family were then residing, and devoted himself largely to preparing for an examination at Cambridge an undergraduate friend who needed exceptional help.

In August he was at the Broadlands Conference. This is the name given to a meeting gathered by the Right Hon. W. Cowper-Temple (now Lord Mount Temple) at his seat in Hampshire; a meeting which has for its end the strengthening and deepening of spiritual life. Here his powers of writing phonography came into play to report the addresses. To the published account of the proceedings was prefixed an Introduction by Keith-Falconer as to the object, scope and results of the Conference. This Introduction exhibits not only considerable power of language, but also a greater depth of thought than could ordinarily be looked for from a young man of two and twenty. The absolute earnestness of the religious conviction underlying it is manifest, and it fully deserves to be reproduced here in full. In order, however, not to break our thread, we give it as an Appendix to the present chapter.

In October, Keith-Falconer settled again into residence at Cambridge, in his old rooms looking out on the market-

---

[1] It is interesting to note that of these six, two others besides Keith-Falconer devoted themselves to the cause of missions abroad; Mr. Lefroy becoming one of the members of the Cambridge University Mission at Delhi, and Mr. Williams an S. P. G. missionary at Rewari, near Delhi.

place. He was now definitely working for two examinations, both more or less on the same lines, though by no means absolutely identical. These were the examinations for the Tyrwhitt University Hebrew Scholarships, to be held in May 1879, and that for the Semitic Languages Tripos, in February 1880. The former of these, founded in 1818, represented, then as now, the highest distinction to be obtained for Hebrew in Cambridge. Among the scholars who have won it in the past are to be found such names as Bishop Harold Browne of Winchester, the late Bishop Ollivant of Llandaff, Dean Perowne, and the late Dr. F. Field. The direction of the founder was that the examination should turn primarily on the Hebrew Bible, and in a secondary degree on things directly tending to illustrate it. Accordingly, passages are set for translation from any part of the Bible, both in the Hebrew and that which is called Chaldee; and, moreover, extracts are set from Rabbinic, or in other words, post-Biblical Hebrew, Commentaries on the Scriptures by the great Rabbis and the like; and also from the Targums, or paraphrases of the various parts of the Bible into the vernacular language of Palestine, such as it was in our Saviour's time, such language as St. Paul used when he addressed and stilled the noisy mob of Jerusalem from the steps of the "Castle." Pieces of Syriac also are occasionally set. In addition to all this, there is "pointing," such as I have already explained, and also pieces of English to be turned into Hebrew. These last are often of considerable difficulty.

There lies before me now a rendering into Hebrew, made by Keith-Falconer at this time, of Cardinal Newman's beautiful hymn, "Lead, Kindly Light." The hymn is written in strong, idiomatic English, by no means easy to reproduce adequately. Yet the rendering is most happy, and, for a student at the stage of progress at which Keith-Falconer then was, gives warrant of very high promise.

In this term, he began to read Syriac with Dr. Wright, the well-known learned professor of Arabic at Cambridge, and, in the interests of both examinations, though mainly the Semitic Languages Tripos, he worked at it very regularly in 1878 and 1879.

Thus occupied with his reading, now directed to a sufficiently large field of new work, and with his heart undoubtedly very much in earnest as to his coming examinations, the time passed by till the following May, when the first examination was held, and he was elected a Tyrwhitt scholar.

From what I have already said, and from much that will follow, it will be clearly understood that at the times of his busiest occupation, his heart had the fullest room for interest in anything by which God might be glorified or man benefited. Still, to prevent endless breakings of continuity, I have felt it undoubtedly best to let the student-life stand as a continuous story.

After the examination, he went for a time to London, where his family then were, and his letters are full of his hopes as to the contest just over, and yet more, of his plans for the other yet to come.

It may be well perhaps at this stage if I briefly sketch the nature of the Semitic Languages Tripos for which Keith-Falconer was now working. The examination was one of recent foundation, being first held in the year 1878, and was designed to give encouragement to a wider range of Oriental study than was provided by the Tyrwhitt Scholarships. The examination is one lasting for seven days, of which the first two are devoted to Arabic, then two to Hebrew, then two to Syriac, and on the last day two papers are set on the Comparative Grammar of these languages, and on their Literary History respectively.

At the time when Keith-Falconer entered for this examination, he had not acquired more than a slight knowledge of Arabic, and did not take up the first two days' papers. The remaining five days, however, provided ample work. A knowledge was required of the whole Hebrew Bible, with special reference, as in the case of the earlier Tripos, to certain books; those for 1880 being Genesis, Ruth, Job, and Amos. Rabbinic Hebrew was represented by selected books from such writers as Maimonides and Rashi, that greatest of all exponents of Scripture in the eyes of an orthodox Jew.

Syriac, in which, as well as in Hebrew, composition is set, was represented by selected books of both Old and New Testament in the various ancient Syriac versions of Scripture, Curetonian, Peshito and Harklensian; by non-Biblical works such as the Doctrine of Addai, parts of Aphraates, and Joshua Stylites; as well as by a paper containing pieces from unspecified books.

The professed scholar and an unlearned person can alike feel that all this is a very serious mass of work. Keith-Falconer faced it in his customary methodical way. Writing from London on June 26, he remarks:—

"I have revised pretty carefully Isaiah 1-39, and after Isaiah will do Ezekiel (harder than Jeremiah) and a few chapters from Leviticus; and then will return to Psalms, Proverbs, Minor Prophets, &c. (old ground). I have very nearly finished the Joshua Stylites, the hardest of all the Patristic Syriac. Peshito, &c. will be very plain sailing."

Moreover, he read his books not in the undiscriminating way of one to whom everything which is printed must of necessity be true, but with a very clear idea of the value of what he was reading. Thus of a certain well-known text-book, he makes some very just remarks:—

"I have read through ——. Knowledge which every-one possessed long ago is here put in a nice, handy shape. He has however done his best to make everyone believe it is all a new discovery, but there is very little of really new information contained in the book."

One topic which interested him much, then as in later times, was the relation of the Septuagint to the existing Hebrew text. The Septuagint, venerable as being the oldest of existing translations of the Old Testament, and most valuable in many ways both for the criticism of the text, for exegesis in many difficult passages, and in a very high degree for the light it throws on the Greek of the New Testament, is a book for which extravagant claims have been put forth by some of its advocates.

It may suffice here to say that whether or no there are passages where the Greek translation has preserved a purer text than the Hebrew, still there are beyond all doubt hundreds, literally hundreds, of places where the variation is simply due to a blunder on the part of the translators. When to such a blunder there has been further added a corruption of text due to a transcriber's carelessness or wilfulness, the case is often one which calls for a considerable degree of ingenuity and scholarship combined to solve it, if indeed it is soluble at all.

Points of this kind always excited a keen interest in Keith-Falconer. In a letter written about this time, he says, "Send me some Septuagint nuts to crack if I can." I cannot refrain from giving a specimen of one of these, where I feel convinced that Keith-Falconer's proposed solution, thought out by him in the summer of 1879, is the undoubtedly true solution of a very curious difficulty, as to which numerous theories have been put forth.

In Psalm xc. 9, the beautiful wording of the English, "We bring our years to an end, as it were a tale that is told," is, perhaps, not an absolutely literal, but is certainly a faithful rendering of the Hebrew. The Septuagint, however, gives a curiously different rendering, which is represented by the translation as given in the Douay version of the Bible. In this version, the only English version, be it remembered, sanctioned by the Roman church—an English translation (so far as the Psalms are concerned) of a

Latin translation of a bad Greek translation of the Hebrew, the clause runs, " Our years shall be considered as a spider." Of the various hypotheses put forward by various scholars to explain this curious difference, I have no hesitation in saying that I consider Keith-Falconer's theory, which sees in the passage a translator's blunder complicated by a scribe's further corruption, wilful or otherwise, as undoubtedly the true one.[1]

In the course of the summer, Keith-Falconer felt the need of being braced up somewhat for his work, and went away for a few weeks to Ramsgate, taking his books with him ; and from thence to Scotland, first on a visit near Loch Luichart in Ross-shire, and then home, until he returned to Cambridge for the ensuing term.

The examination for which he had long been working was held in February, 1880, and resulted in his being placed in the first class, his work having been distinctly brilliant and of decided promise. It is interesting to remember that one of the four examiners on that occasion was Mr. E. H. Palmer, at that time Lord Almoner's Pro-

---

[1] It may be desirable to put this definitely in a note. The existing Hebrew is כְמוֹ הֶגֶה "like a passing thought" (or "passing speech"). The *existing* Greek is τὰ ἔτη ἡμῶν ὡς ἀράχνη ἐμελίτων (" I thought upon our years as doth a spider "). It must be noted, however, that the two oldest MSS. of the Septuagint, the Sinaitic and Vatican, agree in reading, not the nominative ἀράχνη, but the accusative ἀράχνην. Keith-Falconer's suggestion was that ἀράχνην was a scribe's error for ἀχνην (" chaff "); and we may compare Psalm xxxix. 11 (" like a moth fretting a garment "), where the עָשׁ (" moth ") of the original was misread as קַשׁ (by both Septuagint and Peshito), and rendered ἀχνη in the former, which was corrupted into ἀράχνη. But whence has ἀχνη been derived in the 90th Psalm? In all probability, the Greek translators misread כְמוֹ (" like "), for כְמוֹץ (" like chaff "). Thus the resulting idea of the Greek verse would be, " I mused upon our years as though but chaff." The ἐμελίτων is of course got by only a slight alteration from הֶגֶה.

fessor of Arabic, destined at no distant date to die a violent death at the hands of Arabs, members of a race among many tribes of which he had lived as one of themselves. The massacre of the Wady-Sudr does but add another to the list of lives of the highest value wasted amid the so-called exigencies of party warfare.

With the Semitic Languages Tripos, the first portion of Keith-Falconer's student-life found its natural end. He had essayed his weapons, he had now won his spurs. He was henceforth to prove, through such length of life as God might vouchsafe him, what use he would seek to make of his exceptional gifts.

In subsequent chapters it will be my duty to speak fully as to the form in which Keith-Falconer's further devotion to learning shewed itself. I propose now to look back once again to the beginning of his undergraduate career, and see in what secondary interests he chiefly found delight.

I have already said that his chief, and in some respects his only settled amusement, was bicycling. In this his powers were so exceptional, and his successes so striking and so numerous, that I feel bound to speak of this aspect of his life in some detail. It might otherwise have seemed somewhat surprising that after such a narrative as that of Keith-Falconer's student-life, I should now proceed to dwell, with some fulness of detail, and using of necessity a certain amount of technical phraseology, on a chronicle of athletic successes.

Although the great majority of hard reading men are not as a rule famous as athletes, which is very different from saying that they do not freely indulge in vigorous bodily exercise, for this indeed they must do if the brain is to perform its duty properly; still there have been not a few men who have combined in a striking way the highest academic distinctions with marked success in various forms

of athletics.   Thus Bishop Selwyn, "of Lichfield and New
Zealand," who took the degree of Second Classic in 1831,
rowed "seven" in the Cambridge boat in the first race
with Oxford in 1829.   The Hon. Mr. Justice Denman, who
was Senior Classic in 1842, rowed stroke of the First
Trinity boat when it was head of the river ; and also rowed
in 1841 and in 1842 in the race with Oxford.

So too Keith-Falconer, while never allowing his bicycling
to interfere with his reading, and indeed habitually declaring that the chief value of it was the help it gave to
men in doing their duty so much the better, stood, in this
his own favourite form of athletics, quite in the forefront
even of those who made it their chief ambition in life to
win a race, or " break a record."

It would take too large an amount of space to give a full
list of the various bicycle races in which he competed, and
of the various successes he won, and would serve no really
useful purpose to do so ; we propose merely to give sufficient details here to enable the general reader to see how
remarkable his powers were in this respect.

He had begun the practice, as we have seen, at Harrow,
and had carried it on while with Mr. Hensley at Hitchin ;
and so decidedly had his fame preceded him to Cambridge
that he received the unusual compliment of being elected
Vice-President of the C.U.Bi.C.[1] on June 6, 1874, although
he did not come into residence till the following October.
On November 26, he rode and won his first race at Cambridge, doing ten miles of road in 34 minutes, then considered unusually quick time.   His own reference to this
race has already been given in a letter to his sister-in-law.
He was in December elected Secretary for the ensuing
term, and subsequently at intervals held office in the club,
of which he was a Life Member.

In the following year, he was victorious in a C.U.Bi.C.

----

[1] Cambridge University Bicycle Club.

Lent term race from Hatfield to Cambridge, a distance of 42 miles; and on May 10, he won the race for the University against Oxford, the course being from St. Albans to Oxford, a distance of 50 miles.

In the April of the following year, 1876, he won the Amateur-Championship Four-miles race at Lillie Bridge, in what was then the fastest time on record; and on May 15 following, he won the C.U.Bi.C. Fifty-miles trial race, at Fenner's ground, at Cambridge, in 3 hours, 20 minutes, 37 seconds.

On May 1, 1877, he was elected President of the London Bicycle Club, and to this office he was annually re-elected for nine years, retaining it until his resignation of office at the annual dinner of the Club, on October 29, 1886, shortly before he left England for the last time.

In the C.U.Bi.C. races this term (May 23, 24), he was successful in the Two-miles, Ten-miles and Twenty-five-miles races, accomplishing the last-named distance in 1 hour, 30 minutes, 25 seconds. He was very successful too in the Inter-University races held at Oxford, when he rode the Two-miles race in 6 minutes 1 second (the first mile having been done in 3 minutes) and the Ten-miles in 32 minutes 25 seconds, all of which were then the best amateur times on record.

The Rev. W. d'A. Crofton, of Worcester College, formerly captain of the O.U.Bi.C., who rode for Oxford in the Inter-University races on each of the occasions when Keith-Falconer rode for Cambridge, tells me that in 1877, at the start for the Two-miles race Keith-Falconer's step broke, racing bicycles being in those days provided with steps. When the starter gave the warning, "Are you ready?" Keith-Falconer's voice was heard saying, "No, I'm not ready, I want a chair." A chair was brought and he duly mounted, as calm and unruffled as if nothing had happened at so critical a time.

In May 11, 1878, he competed successfully, at Stamford

Bridge, near Fulham, in the Two-miles race of the National Cyclists' Union, for the title of "Short-distance Champion:" but at a race held at Cambridge, in the October of that year, will be remembered as one of his best performances. This was one of Five-miles between amateurs and professionals, and ultimately resolved into a contest between Keith-Falconer and John Keen, the then professional champion, in which the former was victorious by five yards.

I annex an amusing account of this race from a letter addressed by Keith-Falconer to Mr. Isaac Pitman, the veteran inventor of phonography, in reply to a letter of the latter, urging him to give up smoking. After thanking him for a subscription which he had sent to the Barnwell Mission, he proceeds :—

" As for smoking, I think that the following will gratify you. Early in the year I consented to meet John Keen, the professional champion of the world, in a five-mile bicycle race on our ground at Cambridge on Oct. 23. But I forgot all about my engagement till I was accidentally reminded of it nine days before it was to come off.

" I immediately began to make my preparations and to train hard. The first great thing to be done was to knock off smoking, which I did. Next, to rise early in the morning, and breathe the fresh air before breakfast, which I did ; next to go to bed not later than 10, which I did ; next to eat wholesome food and not too much meat or pastry, which I did ; and finally, to take plenty of gentle exercise in the open air, which I did.

" What was the result ? I met Keen on Wednesday last, the 23rd Oct., and amidst the most deafening applause, or rather yells of delight, this David slew the great Goliath : to speak in plain language I defeated Keen by about 5 yards.

" The time was by far the fastest on record.

			mins.	secs.
" The 1st mile was done in			2 .	59
2nd	,,	,,	3 .	1
3rd	,,	,,	3 .	7
4th	,,	,,	3 .	12
5th	,,	,,	2 .	52$\frac{2}{5}$

Total time 15 . 11$\frac{2}{5}$

"The last lap, that is, the last circuit, measuring 440 yards, we did in 39 seconds, that is more than 11 yards per second.

"The excitement was something indescribable. Such a neck and neck race was never heard of. The pace for the last mile was terrific, as the time shews; and when it was over I felt as fit and comfortable as ever I felt in my life. And even when the race was going on, I thought actually that we were going slowly and that the time would be bad, and the reason was, I was in such beautiful condition. I did not perspire or 'blow' from beginning to end. The people here are enchanted about it; so that it is gratifying to me to think that, notwithstanding my other work and other business, I can yet beat, with positive comfort and ease, the fastest rider *in the world.* . . .

"I am bound to say that smoking is bad, bad for the wind and general condition. . . ."

In May 1879, races were again ridden between amateurs and professionals on the ground of the University Club at Cambridge. On May 21, he met his old adversary John Keen in a Two-miles race, defeating him by 3 inches! The time in this was 5 minutes 36$\frac{1}{5}$ seconds; and this, I understand, was not beaten for several years. On Saturday, May 24, he won the Twenty-miles race by 16 yards, the time being 1 hour, 4 minutes, 15$\frac{1}{5}$ seconds, which at that time was the best on record.

An eye-witness, describing the scene, and referring to a time when all Keith-Falconer's competitors had dropped out save one, says that he " was contented with riding just behind until 200 yards from home, when, with a spurt which the Cantabs were expecting, but which simply astonished all others, he came right away and won as he liked." [1] From the same source I extract the following anecdote, which certainly bears sufficient internal marks of genuineness:—" On the day of the 20-miles race, it was stated that he was studying hard all the morning, and forgot that he had to race ; and it was not until all the other competitors were at the starting-post, ready to start, that he rushed into the dressing-room, changed his clothes as quickly as possible and mounted for the race. He rode several miles before he recovered his breath." [2] It may most fairly be added here that at the time of these races, a week had barely elapsed since Keith-Falconer had been engaged in a heavy examination, of which we have already spoken, that for the Tyrwhitt Scholarship. Six hours' examination work *per diem* for four consecutive days forms by no means a good preliminary training for a keen physical contest.

Although it is beyond the period covered in the earlier part of the present chapter, it will be desirable to include here, as probably his last race, or at any rate the last of any importance, the 50-miles Bicycle Union Amateur Championship race, at the Crystal Palace, on July 29, 1882. This was won by Keith-Falconer, who beat by nearly seven minutes all previous records, the time being 2 hours, 43 minutes, 58¼ seconds. An account of an interesting ride the whole length of the island, made by Keith-Falconer in that year, will be given at length in its proper chronological place.

Another great interest, as we have seen, was shorthand. This was undoubtedly a recreation in one sense, but it certainly was constantly turned to very practical account. Great as was his skill in it, he had never received any in-

[1] *London Bicycle Club Gazette* for May 27, 1879.
[2] *Ibid.*

struction, but had simply taught himself the art at Harrow, as is mentioned by Mr. Arthur Watson.

Mr. Isaac Pitman, who I sincerely trust will pardon me for changing " the reformed English spelling " of his letter to that in current use, says in a letter :—

" He learnt shorthand simply by reading the instruction books, and was a good writer in May, 1874, when I first made his acquaintance during a three weeks' stay at Bournemouth. He took a deep interest in phonography, wrote it swiftly and accurately, and had a thorough knowledge of the minutest part of the system ; and that not merely as a stenographer, but as a judge of its value as a part of a harmonious whole. He must have learnt it some years before this date, but I do not know how many."

When I first knew him in 1875, I was astonished at the ease with which he could keep up with a rapid speaker, and the equal ease with which he could read his MS. a considerable time after.

To a beginner in the art, he was not only willing, but positively wishful to be of use. His constant advice to those seeking to learn, used to be, "Mind you practise every day, and don't be in a hurry to write quickly."

A vast quantity of note-books on his work were filled with this writing, and his correspondence with Mr. Pitman was entirely in phonography.

Student, athlete, phonographer,—in all three aspects, Ion Keith-Falconer took a foremost position among experts in three very different lines ; in all three, his excellence was avowed and undoubted.

Yet there was something more, something beyond all this power and skill of brain and muscle,—a heart which the love of Christ constrained to work for Him, a heart filled with the old faith, fervent still after all the turmoil of a great public school, and the more subtle temptations of a great University, as when in childhood he learnt its first rudiments by his mother's knee.

The two principal works, but by no means the only ones, in which he was engaged, during and after his undergraduate career, in Cambridge and in London, will form the subject of the following chapter.

APPENDIX.

See above, p. 51.

BROADLANDS CONFERENCE, 1878.

FOR the information of those who were not privileged to be present at the Broadlands Conference of 1878, we preface our report by an introduction, in which we hope that the salient points of the Conference, its object, scope, and results, are fairly brought out.   The subject for consideration was—

PENTECOSTAL BLESSING,

or the

PROMISED OUTPOURING OF THE HOLY SPIRIT.

(1) The promises of which the realization may now be expected.
(2) The conditions that assist, and the hindrances that impede, the reception of the promised blessings.
(3) The use to be made of the gifts of the Spirit.

In the very early days of Christianity, the believer could not do otherwise than keep separate from the world, for the world would have nothing to do with him.   He was shunned, maligned, and persecuted.   On the other hand, for this very reason, his faith was bright and clear, and he expected very shortly the second coming of Christ.   He was indeed a burning and a shining light in this dark world.   But after a time when men began to recognize the splendid morality of the Gospel, and when the false charges of Atheism, inhumanity, and vicious practices, which were commonly circulated, began to be disbelieved, certain advances were made by the State and the world. Philosophers began to choose and to pick from the Christian system what they thought beautiful or true, and to introduce the same into their own systems; and the State commenced to look on the new religion with a certain amount of distant toleration, and, in time, to assume towards it an attitude even of respect. On the other hand the Church was gradually losing some of its first love, and its old ardour was cooling. The Lord delayed His coming. Heresies began to spring up, grievous wolves entered the Church of God in sheep's clothing and tore the flock. The evil, we cannot help thinking, was consummated when Constantine, early in the fourth century, laid his diseased hand on the Church, and united it with the State. We do not express any decided opinion on the vexed question of Church and State. It would be out of place here to attempt to decide whether the abstract theory of union of the Church with the State is warranted by the Bible. We are dealing with the practical question, viz., How has that union affected the attitude of Christians towards the world? The mass of people now flocked in, were baptized, and professed Christianity. It was now the religion of Rome, and so the religion of the whole civilized world. It is true that under Julian, relapse to heathenism was attempted; but the power of the old religions of Greece and Rome was gone for ever, and the attempt was all in vain. Christianity was henceforth, to speak in a general way, the religion of the civilized world. This was glorious in one way, and when we contemplate the wonderful progress which Christianity had by this time made, and remember the despised Nazarene, and all His low estate when here below, we are bound to exclaim, "This is the Lord's doing, and it is marvellous in our eyes" (Matt. xxi. 42).

But still one bad result seems to have followed. The Church and the world became more than ever united, and the solemn command to come out from among them and to be separate, more than ever difficult of performance. And passing over the long expanse of centuries, which intervened between then and now, we see other influences at

work, which render this our separation from the world
increasingly difficult.   The conditions of life in the present
age are entirely unfavourable to any kind of seclusion.
The multifarious interests of this toiling, rushing, fevered
day, have so banded men together, and the vast increase
in railways and telegraphs, and all other means of communication, have rendered the exchange of thoughts, the
"collision of mind with mind," and the social intercourse
of individuals, so easy, that a certain amount of mutual
advance, of interchange of thought and feeling, is now
demanded where none was expected before.   Yet the command is plain—"Come out from among them, and be ye
separate."   But a consideration of the evil will suggest the
remedy, and a contemplation of the difficulty will point to
the solution.   It is evidently quite impossible for the
Church to be absolutely separate from the world in this
sense, that the believer is to be a marked man, shunned
and ousted by all.   Civilization has thrown a garb of seeming friendship over all, and the "white ashes of social
hypocrisy" choke anything like open hostilities.   Nor is it
the Lord's will that the believer should be entirely shut
out from the world, for if the leaven never come into contact with the meal, how and when will the whole be leavened?
The difficulty is at once recognized and solved by our
Lord when He says, "I pray not that thou shouldest take
them out of the world, but that thou shouldest keep them
from the evil.   They are not of the world, even as I am
not of the world" (John xvii. 15, 16).   "In the world, but
not of it," is to be our motto.   Still though we know what
the mind of the Lord is with respect to this, the practical
difficulty remains, how to maintain this separation, and
how, while discharging those manifold duties of life in
which we are necessarily brought into contact with others,
yet to maintain our purity, nor ever to touch the unclean
thing.   We cannot do it, except we be endued with power
from on high.   And to this end, a gracious provision has
been made for us.   The Shepherd truly is no more in
bodily presence with the flock, and the wolves abound;
but the sheep are not defenceless. The Comforter has been
given to them.   In other words, it is by the mighty power
of the Holy Ghost working in us, with us, and through us,

that we are to overcome the world, to resist its allurements, and to hurl back its every encroachment. And here the question naturally suggests itself: How is it then, that though the Holy Ghost has been imparted to the believer, he is yet liable to danger from sin and the world ? (not to speak of danger from within). The answer is, that Christianity never did, and never will, do away with human responsibility. We are indeed in a state of probation. We have a warfare to fight, and how are we straitened till it be accomplished ! The Holy Ghost hath in very truth been given to us, but (humanly speaking), its manifestation depends on ourselves. We are responsible for its manifestation. " Stir up the gift of God that is in thee." This is the command ; and the Conference spent much of its time in considering what conditions assisted, and what hindrances impeded, this manifestation. The subject seems to us a very important one, for the simple reason that in proportion as Christians live in the power of the Spirit, in that proportion will their influence be felt in the world that surrounds them. When spirituality is at a low ebb, then the believer is weak, and dares not come into contact with the world, lest he be drawn away and enticed ; and if he does, woe to him. And it seems to us that the reason why infidelity, scepticism, heresy, and schism are so alarmingly on the increase in our day, is that the only light which illumines the world's darkness is so faint and dim. " Ye are the light of the world " (Matt. v. 14). The truth of Christianity may be proved by the most incontestable evidence, internal and external, but unless this evidence be mightily confirmed by the consistent walk, and the holy conversation of its professors, the world will never be convinced. Precept is well, but without example 'tis a mockery. Preaching is good, but practising is a *sine qua non.* " Christian character is a more magnificent apology for the claims of Jesus, than all Christian preaching and talking e'er can be." We may now enumerate some of the principal conditions of, and hindrances to, the manifestation of the Spirit within us, which were dwelt on at the Conference.

CHAPTER IV.

" Heart and soul
A very man, tender, and true, and strong,
And pitiful."

MORRIS.

To Cambridge men of a quarter of a century ago, the
name of Barnwell bore an ugly sound. It was that part
of the town to which seemed to gravitate a mass of various
ills; a large, poor, rapidly growing suburb, whose name
seemed synonymous with squalor and vice.

Yet this state of things was one which had only risen
comparatively recently; old men who have not long passed
away remembered a very different Barnwell. The late
Professor Sedgwick, who died in 1873, once described to
the present writer a ride he had taken when a young man
from Trinity College to Newmarket, in which he would of
necessity pass through Barnwell.

The long street which is still called Jesus Lane, from
the College which has stood near it for four hundred
years, was then really a lane. Beyond the College, where
now is a continuous street of houses for a mile and a half,
came a distinct break with green fields and a plantation of
trees, followed by a small straggling village, with a very
pretty, though somewhat dilapidated little church, which
once had been the church of Barnwell Abbey. Half a mile
further on, was a yet smaller chapel, with some exquisite
Norman work, which was intended for the use of lepers,

who might not come to the service with the rest of the congregation. Then came the open moor all the way to Newmarket.

This small village was Barnwell, and was the inhabited part of the large parish of St. Andrew the Less. Close to this was the river Cam, which formed the northern boundary of the parish.

It may be not without interest to call attention to the fact that, in the space between the old Church and the lepers' chapel and the river, there has been regularly kept each returning September for centuries,[1] a fair, popularly known as Stourbridge Fair, once one of the most important business meetings in England, I had almost said in Europe; and even in the last century a very busy scene of real trafficking,[2] now a gathering that might very well be done away with.

Various causes co-operated vastly to increase the population of this part of Cambridge, not only absolutely, but also relatively to the rest of the town. Among the foremost of these causes is doubtless to be placed the railway. The quiet University town, in the heart of a thinly-peopled agricultural district, was quickened into a noisier and more stirring life by the advent of the railway, and four competing lines now meet in Cambridge. Both the construction and working of these led to a large influx of men of the working class. Again, the discovery of great beds of fossils, known as coprolites, and rich in chemical constituents tending to the fertilization of land, brought also large numbers of navvies, who lodged in Barnwell and in many cases permanently settled there.

The steadily increasing numbers of the University also

[1] Probably instituted by a charter of King John in 1211 A.D. (Cooper's *Annals of Cambridge* i. 34.)

[2] For an interesting account of the fair as conducted in the last century, see Cooper, iv. 318 sqq.; Gunning, *Reminiscences* ii. 148 sqq. ed. 2.

brought about a corresponding increase in the number not
only of College servants, but of irregular hangers-on, men
ready to make themselves useful in connexion with the
various amusements of the undergraduates.

Whatever the various causes may have been, an immense
rate of increase in the parish is most marked. Thus in
1801, the population of the parish of St. Andrew the
Less, or, as it was then called, St. Andrew in Barnwell,
was 252; the number of inhabited houses in the parish
being 79. The population of the whole town of Cambridge
in that year was 10,087. In 1881, the population of the
parish was 21,078, that of the whole of Cambridge being
35,363. The number of the inhabited houses in the
parish had now risen to 4,342. I subjoin in a note the
population of the parish and of the whole town at each of
the censuses since the beginning of the century, to shew
how continuous and how rapid has been the growth.[1]

It is true that, as the town of Cambridge is at present
constituted, the popular name of Barnwell is not applied
to the whole of the huge parish. It denotes, however, a
large part of it, and pre-eminently of the poorer districts.

It is thus abundantly clear that the provision adequate
for the spiritual needs of the small village would soon be
found insufficient for so rapidly growing a population. For
some time apparently things were allowed to drift, with
merely sporadic efforts to give help. The beginning of a
more systematic attempt to cope with the needs of the

		Parish.	Town.
[1]	1801	252	10,087
	1811	411	11,108
	1821	2,211	14,142
	1831	6,651	20,917
	1841	9,486	24,453
	1851	11,776	27,815
	1861	11,848	26,361
	1871	15,958	30,078
	1881	21,078	35,363

case was the establishment by a party of undergraduates, in the year 1825, of a Sunday School, which speedily assumed large proportions; and which still, under its original name of the Jesus Lane Sunday School (though it is many years since it left its first abode which gave it its name), exercises a most important influence for good. This, though not strictly a parochial agency, was distinctly designed for the benefit of Barnwell; and in 1839, largely through the instrumentality of the Rev. C. Perry, afterwards first Bishop of Melbourne, a large Church was opened in the parish under the name of Christ's Church.

Since that time other Churches have been built, and several chapels of various dissenting bodies testify to much hearty zeal for the furtherance of the Gospel.

In the present generation great improvements have taken place in the character of the parish, due, under God's blessing, to a succession of earnest, hard-working Vicars, and to no one more largely than to the late Rev. J. H. Titcomb, afterwards Bishop of Rangoon, and the Rev. E. T. Leeke, now Chancellor of Lincoln. No one who remembers Barnwell twenty-five years ago can fail to realize an immense improvement.

Still the labourers were very few for so great a mass of people, mostly poor and ignorant, including even yet a large number of persons following vicious courses; and while the Gospel teaching of a band of devoted men was gradually leavening the mass, yet while the workers were slowly gaining on the task which faced them, hundreds were dying.

It was this state of things which led to the special effort of which I have now to speak.

On the high road through Barnwell, not far from Christ Church, stood a rather disreputable-looking theatre, with the high-sounding name of the Theatre Royal, Barnwell. This was not so valuable a property as it might otherwise

F

have been, for by immemorial law, no plays could be performed in Cambridge without the permission of the Vice-Chancellor; and this permission was never conceded except in vacation time, when the great mass of undergraduates have left Cambridge.

In May, 1875, in anticipation of a visit of Mr. D. L. Moody to Cambridge, a few gentlemen, both members of the University and townsmen, decided to hire the theatre, then of necessity closed, for a month, and hold evangelistic services in it, to break the ground, as it were, for his visit. Although Mr. Moody was prevented from paying his visit at that time, the theatre was taken notwithstanding; and a vigorous effort was made to reach that still large element of the population which never by any chance went to any place of worship whatsoever, to all intents and purposes as heathen as if the name of Christ had never been proclaimed in England.

With all this, Keith-Falconer associated himself most heartily. Still, it must be noticed, his interest, however great, co-existed with his studies, yet did not interfere with them. He fully recognized, then and subsequently, a truth which not all young men when seeking to be of use to others do sufficiently realize, the truth namely that for a time duties which may seem the highest, and in one sense certainly are such, ought to be subordinated to others which seem to them less important. Yet there can be no doubt that to an undergraduate living in a University, and therefore presumably a student, the highest duty of all is for the time his study. The legitimate claims of that being satisfied, let him be useful in every possible way so far as his opportunities permit.

To confine ourselves to Cambridge men alone; such names as Henry Martyn, Bishop Selwyn, and Bishop Mackenzie, shew how noble may be the outcome in the service of God of an undergraduate career *primarily* devoted to steady University work. Such too was Keith-

Falconer ; he never neglected his simple everyday duty, to attend to one apparently higher, yet not so distinctly and directly assigned him as his proper work.

When the month for which the Theatre had been hired came to an end, the building reverted to its ordinary condition for a time. So great, however, had been the success attending the services in the Theatre, that it was determined to carry on the same kind of work elsewhere in Barnwell, and for about three years and a half mission services went on at a Ragged School in New Street.

All this time, Keith-Falconer was a steady and consistent helper of the mission, by his purse, by his personal co-operation, and we may well feel sure by his prayers. An old friend of his has remarked that in his active share in evangelistic work may probably be found the explanation of the fact that Keith-Falconer was so little assailed by speculative doubts as to the Faith. For a mind so keen and so inquiring as his was, to have been so free from such attacks, is a thing which must strike one as remarkable in an age like ours.

On one occasion, I think in 1876, I accompanied Keith-Falconer to a meeting at the Ragged School. The gathering of people, of whom there were several hundreds, displayed a remarkable contrast to an ordinary Christian congregation. They represented as a whole a stratum decidedly below that of the decent working man of the poorer sort. Many were ragged, most were dirty and unkempt, and before the service began, many of them behaved most outrageously. Yet when the service began, I rejoice to say, the conduct was orderly enough ; evidently many, while coming in the first instance simply from curiosity, bore in their way a friendly feeling enough for their visitors. Yet it may be noted, as shewing the stratum from which the bulk was drawn, that on one of the speakers remarking, " A great many of you, I know, have been, and I fear some are still, thieves ! " he was greeted, in tones which shewed that no offence had been taken, with ready cries of, " Yes, Sir."

It was at this meeting that I heard Keith-Falconer speak in public for the first time, and on the somewhat unusual subject of Zelophehad's daughters. What had specially led to this topic I forget, but he worked up in a very practical way the ideas suggested by the petition of these maidens, not afraid to speak out boldly and ask for the object of their need. ' Have faith to draw near to God, and ask for help just as you feel the needs of your own soul, be they what they may,' was the thought throughout. His speech was evidently that of one who had thought over carefully what he was going to say, and meant most deeply and sincerely every word he said. One felt that he would grow in time to become a weighty and effective speaker, though not what would popularly be called a brilliant one; never to the last did he seek after the ornate eloquence of the rhetorician.

The work went on in this quiet, unpretentious way till the autumn of 1878, when it became known that the owner of the Theatre was about to sell it by auction ; and at a meeting of the band of workers it was resolved to buy it, if it could be got at a price not exceeding £1,200. After this meeting Keith-Falconer, feeling that the building was sure to fetch a decidedly higher sum, at last prevailed upon his colleagues to increase their bid to £1,650; but to their great disappointment, the bidding rose to £1,875, at which price it became the property of the late Mr. Sayle.

This gentleman, however, on hearing the above facts, consented with great generosity to give up the Theatre to the Mission workers, for the price they had been willing to give for it, the extra £225 being viewed as a subscription undertaken by Mr. Sayle and his friends.

Even as it was, a considerable sum had to be provided, and a glance at the subscription list shews that more than half was raised out of Cambridge. This was mainly due to the untiring advocacy of Keith-Falconer, who not only contributed largely, but also used his utmost efforts with his friends; his father, Lord Kintore, and his future father-in-law, Mr. Bevan, each subscribing £100, the former ultimately giving a second like sum.

The requisite amount was rapidly raised, and, after the necessary cleaning and repairing of the building, it was formally opened for its new purpose as a mission-hall (though the old name of Theatre was still retained) on Sunday, November 17, when very large audiences were assembled. On the Monday evening the house was crowded, and on the Tuesday, when there was a social gathering for tea, followed by a public meeting, every available seat in the Theatre, from the pit to the gallery, was filled.[1] On the stage were about 300 persons, and the corridors were blocked by an eager crowd.

After more than 600 persons had partaken of tea, a public meeting was held. The chair was taken by Mr. W. R. Mowll of Corpus Christi College, with whom were gathered the various gentlemen, who, with the subject of our present memoir, had striven manfully at the work; Mr. H. D. Champney, also of Corpus, Mr. Vawser, Mr. Flitton, and others. Besides these, other friends were present from a distance, among whom were the Rev. W. Hay Aitken, and Mr. F. N. Charrington, each of whom gave a very effective address.

Keith-Falconer also spoke on this occasion. The speech was so characteristic of the man, so peculiarly appropriate to the occasion, and was marked by such sterling common sense, that I feel fully justified in giving it nearly in full, as reported in a local paper:—

" I am not given to much speaking. But this occasion is so extraordinary, and the sight before my eyes so exhilarating and inspiriting, that if I were a stone I should

---

[1] The Theatre can readily hold 1000 people.

be forced to throw in my note of praise and thanksgiving with the rest. What a marvellous transformation this place has undergone! Well may we exclaim, 'Look on this picture, and on that.' Our theatrical friends are familiar with transformation scenes, but they have got a novel one to-night, and I hope they have all come to look at it. And who can deny that it has been a transformation from bad to good? It is all very well for the supporters of the theatre (especially when they have a pecuniary interest in the popularity of the drama) to say that theatre-going is educating and elevating and ennobling. I will only remark that if this place has been the means of educating, elevating, and ennobling a fallen humanity, in Barnwell at least, it has not got on with its work particularly fast, and the results do not exactly stare one in the face, and the sooner a more efficient system comes into play the better. There is one point about this transformation scene worthy of notice, and that is that the place is open, free to all. And this is like the Gospel of the great God. It cost so much, and the sum to be paid was so vast, that we poor sinners, slave and struggle hard as we might, could not possibly make up the sum, and so we have been let off altogether, for the Saviour of the world has paid it for us. Now our prayer to God is that this transformation scene may be the earnest and precursor of many a transformation scene in the hearts and lives of men and women now careless and without God. I hear that an actor, quite unworthy of being named, who was performing here in the summer, on his benefit night, made an oration to an admiring audience, and told them in effect, that the poor players, who had so long striven by their elevating and instructive performances to raise the tone and purify the morals of Barnwell, were at length to be supplanted by a company of religious hypocrites. 'Acting,' he said, 'has not ceased in this place: there will be acting still.' His opinion apparently was that religion is another name for hypocrisy. But he spoke the truth unwittingly. We trust that there will be some grand acting in connection with this place. It requires no prophetic eye to see the time when men and women, now sunk low in sin and vice, will be constrained by the mighty power of a Saviour's love and the solemnities of a coming eternity proclaimed from this place, to act the magnificent part of the champions of God, and the followers of Christ. For, remember, this life of ours may be viewed as a great drama. The God that made us has assigned to each his part, and written it in letters so plain and patent that he who runs may read. And soon the curtain must fall, and the players must depart to return no more. It is a play once acted, and only once. It has no rehearsals, and one false step can never be made right, and one slip of the tongue can never be recalled. A numberless audience watches the performance, and, with intense interest, witnesses the characters as they develop, and the plot as it thickens. Now there be two prompters on this stage. The evil one stands on this side and the Holy Ghost broods over us on the other. Many there are who, casting aside with the folly of contempt or the blind-ness of indifference the part that God has bid them play, speak and act that which is prompted by the evil one, ' and live lives deservedly wretched, because they make them de-liberately base.' But there are others who, taking heed to the commands of God and to the promptings of the Holy Ghost, live lives of splendid morality and of glorious wit-nessing to the despised Nazarene. These are the salt of the earth, and to these doth England owe her greatness, and in proportion as these diminish, in that exact propor-tion will our nation sink among the nations of the earth. To whom, then, will ye hearken? To the Spirit of truth, or to the spirit of lies? Will you be one of those to whom, in the words of the great preacher, ' Life is a mere collec-tion of fragments, whose first volume is a noisy and obscene jest-book, and whose last is a grim tragedy or a despicable farce?' or, will you be numbered with those to whom ' Life, however small the stage, is a regal drama played out before the eyes of God and men?' There be some here who have come out of idle curiosity and the love of novelty— would that you were curious enough to inquire into the things of God, and to taste and see that the Lord is good; would that you were sufficiently fond of novelty to try the new life, which is as different from the old one as light is from darkness. God, in mercy, turn the idle curiosity into earnest seeking, and the love of novelty into a longing for a new life, and then you will be able from your own experience to testify that the new act is better than the old ; for the old was selfish and brought you misery, but the new act is Christ-like and brings joy unspeakable and full of glory."

Since that day, nine years ago, the Barnwell Mission has done a great amount of work for good ; and, I understand, the Theatre has never been closed for a single Sunday throughout the whole of that time. Though Keith-Falconer frequently attended the meetings, he gave but few addresses, and, unfortunately, none of them were reported. He was always most cordially welcomed, and his zeal for the furtherance of the work continued quite unabated. Some further examples of this will be given in a later part of our story ; we must now shift the scene from Cambridge to the East End of London with its thronging myriads.

In the widest part of the Mile-End Road, that great artery leading from the heart of London eastwards, the attention of the passer-by is irresistibly caught by a very large, imposing building, of great breadth and commanding height, over the central door of which is the name, under a large clock, ' Great Assembly Hall.'

This building is the final outcome of the resolve, gradually developing during many years, of Mr. F. N. Charrington, to bring the Gospel and every good subsidiary influence home to the masses around. In this noble scheme of usefulness, Keith-Falconer was associated nearly from the first, as a most devoted ally of Mr. Charrington, and as a most munificent supporter.

The work was one which irresistibly appealed to him. The needs, spiritual and other, of the East End of London were, and are, so great as to force attention from the most casual observer : the attempt proceeded throughout uniformly on what he most justly felt should be the true

principle of civilizing by Christianizing, not with the idea
that the religious life will come more readily when the
material conditions of life are improved.   There will, it is
true, often be great material need.   In such cases the duty
of a teacher of the Gospel is clear.   He will not follow so
suicidal a policy, deserving to fail as it surely will, as to
offer Christian teaching to men and women in bodily need,
without making any effort to meet those needs.   But, on
the other hand, he will not insist on first civilizing in
every possible way, save by religion, the masses of the
lowest class, by art, by general education and the like, and
then, and only then, allow religion, if needs be, to be brought
to bear.

Let the evangelist come forward with the Gospel in one
hand and his material appliances, be they what they may,
in the other ; then will the benefits from each, on soul
and body, act and react on one another, till many a
changed man and woman will by their lives testify to the
noble perfectness of the plan.

Although the growth of the Mission is primarily, under
God's blessing, to be referred to the self-devoted efforts of
Mr. Charrington, still so deep was Keith-Falconer's interest in it, and so weighty and so loyal was the support
which he gave, that it becomes the clear duty of the
present writer to speak in some detail of the scheme.[1]

The Mission whose central rallying point is the Great
Assembly Hall bears the name of the Tower Hamlets
Mission.   This name, Tower Hamlets, seems strangely
suggestive of something very different from the rather
grim reality.   It shews, however, what the district ori-
ginally was, " a cluster of villages, starting from the Tower
of London, and extending along the River Thames for
some miles."   Gradually, as time went on, the intervening

---

[1] The matter of the subsequent pages is largely drawn from
Keith-Falconer's own pamphlet, *A Plea for the Tower Hamlets
Mission*, undated, but published in 1882.

spaces were built over, until fields and country-lanes and
green hedge-rows had given place to interminable streets;
and what were once beautiful rural spots have become the
principal part of the densely peopled East End of London,
now numbering more than one million souls.   In the
centre of this, the largest mass of working people in the
world, the work of the Tower Hamlets Mission is carried
on.

Keith-Falconer had first made the acquaintance of Mr.
Charrington, who was six years his senior, when, in or
about 1871, the latter was on a walking-tour in Aberdeenshire, and was invited to Keith Hall by the late Lord
Kintore.   From that time forward each was to the other
a most valued and trusted friend.   In later years, when
Lord Kintore had passed to his rest (July, 1880), Keith-
Falconer writes to Mr. E. H. Kerwin, the Secretary of the
Mission; " It is pleasant to me to reflect that it was my
father who first introduced me to Charrington and his
work, and that he so cordially supported the Tower Hamlets Mission.   I hope that his sudden departure may be
the means of blessing to the careless, perhaps to some who
heard him speak in the Assembly Hall."

In the pamphlet above referred to, Keith-Falconer tells
the interesting story of the way in which the Mission
was begun.   Mr. Charrington was " the eldest son of the
late Mr. F. Charrington, a partner in the well-known firm
of Charrington, Head and Co.   The large brewery is perhaps the most striking feature in the Mile-End Road.
Its remarkable ladder is seen against the sky for a long
distance, and its many chimneys and handsome frontage
must catch every stranger's eye."

In the year 1869, Mr. Charrington was travelling with
a friend in the South of France.   His friend had pressed
upon him the truth that this life was meant to be something more than one of pleasure and living to oneself
alone, however innocently; and at parting prevailed upon

him to read the third chapter of St. John's Gospel. While
doing this, the light of God broke in upon the reader, and
he determined to devote himself henceforward to the service of God and the teaching of His Gospel.

Shortly after this, a further thought came to Mr. Charrington, which resulted in a very striking act of sacrifice
on his part. He told the story himself in his speech at
the opening of the Great Hall last year.[1] He was in the
habit of going, evening by evening, to a little mission-
hall, and had to pass a certain beer-shop, called the
" Rising Sun," where night after night he saw wretched
women waiting outside for their husbands within. Over
the beer-shop was the name of Charrington, Head and
Co., and it occurred to him that whatever good he was
doing with one hand, he was undoing and more than undoing with the other. He determined therefore resolutely
that he would have nothing further to do with the drink
traffic. On his father's death, a few years after, he had
the alternative allowed him either of taking as eldest son
his due share of the lucrative business, or of being content
simply with a younger brother's portion. Needless to say,
he chose the latter.

The first efforts of the young missionary were in a
night-school, under the direction of the Rev. Joseph
Bardsley, then Rector of Stepney. Till the accommodation proved too small, he, with two or three others, worked
in a hayloft over a stable, lighted by two or three small
paraffin lamps hung up on the rafters, and tried to do his
best with some ragged little boys.

Soon the little hayloft grew too small, and a schoolroom had to be taken; and gradually Mr. Charrington
and his friends were led on to further work among lads
and started a Boys' Home. One of the cases which led to
this was the following :—

[1] Feb. 4, 1886.

" At the close of one of the meetings, a little boy was found sobbing. With some difficulty he was induced to tell his tale. It was simple. His widowed mother, his sisters, and he, all lived in one room. Everything had been sold to buy bread except two white mice, the boy's pets. Through all their poverty, they had kept these white mice ; but at last they too must go ! With the proceeds he bought street songs, which he retailed on the ' waste,' and so obtained the means of getting more bread for his mother and sisters. Now they were completely destitute. The boy was accompanied home. *Home!* It was a wretched attic, in one of the most dilapidated houses. It was a wretchedly cold and dismal day. In the broken-down grate the dead embers of yesterday's handful of firing remained. On the table, in a piece of newspaper, were a few crumbs. The air was close and the smell insupportable. ' My good woman,' said Mr. Charrington, ' why don't you open the window ? ' ' Oh ! ' she replied, ' you would not say that if you had had nothing to eat, and had no fire to warm you.' The family was relieved."

Among the good results of this new effort, it may be mentioned that a gang of juvenile thieves, known to the police as the Mile-End gang, was broken up ; several of its members, including its leader, having been thoroughly influenced for good. Many of the lads were taken out of their evil surrounding and sent to Yarmouth, where they were employed on the fishing smacks.

The next stage was the opening of what was known as the East-End Conference Hall, on November 1, 1872. This was a building in Carlton Square, capable of seating 600 persons, in which the Gospel was preached for some years with remarkable success. The reason why it was left, or rather, was given up to another body of workers, who still are doing good work in it, was, as was so often the case in connexion with this mission, that it was becoming too small for the needs of the work.

Accordingly, a move was made to Mile-End Road, at the

corner of White-Horse Lane. Here there was a large piece of ground which for years had been used by travelling showmen with waxworks, merry-go-rounds, theatres and so forth. Naturally, the respectable inhabitants and the police alike concurred in rejoicing at the demolition of dilapidated buildings which had afforded such facilities to persons of the lowest character. On this land a tent was erected, in which services were held every night for two whole summers. A large number of the speakers were soldiers of the Guards, who came all the way from the West-End barracks, many of them walking the whole way there and back, a distance of ten miles, in order to preach the Gospel.

At last a yet better site was obtained at the broadest part of the Mile-End Road, and that no time might be lost, a large tent was at once set up, and was opened on May 21, 1876. It was the largest tent they could obtain, the great one from Wimbledon Camp. This was replaced in April, 1877, by the first great Assembly Hall, large enough to hold nearly 2,000 persons, yet hardly deserving the name of great when contrasted with its gigantic successor. It should be added that this Hall was from its first inception intended merely to be temporary, being made of corrugated iron, though it might last till something more durable could be obtained.

For nearly nine years this Hall was open every night all the year round, with an average attendance on week-nights of over 600, while on Sunday nights the building was crammed and hundreds were sent away for want of room. The late Lord Shaftesbury, speaking in this Hall in 1879, said :—

"It is a mighty thing to have achieved such results in the wild and remote districts of the East End of London. Would to God we had a hundred halls such as this, where men of God should stand and daily preach the Word of the Lord, and minister consolation to those who come."

Before I come to speak of the erection of the present building, there are one or two other points which are noteworthy. The first of these is what Keith-Falconer called "preaching the Gospel from the walls of the city," that is, by means of placards containing texts of Scripture, direct personal appeals, and short pointed stories with pictures. Keith-Falconer remarks : [1]—

"We have several of these stations in the East of London, around which numbers of people may often be seen eagerly reading the Words of Life. On Sunday mornings, working men out for their weekly stroll, stop to read the parable of the Prodigal Son, or the story of 'The Patchwork Quilt.' In the dead of night, the poor fallen girl, as she passes along, is startled to see the familiar text she learned as a child in the Sunday School; the policeman, who walks along his solitary beat, turns his bull's-eye lantern, and while all is hushed around him, reads the story of a Saviour's love; and the profligate, as he returns from some scene of revelry, is arrested for the moment as he reads the solemn words, 'Prepare to meet thy God.' The result of this work has been that large numbers of people have been brought to hear the Gospel."

The idea was, so far as I am aware, a novel one; it is one which might perhaps provoke a certain amount of adverse comment; but remembering the intense earnestness of these young teachers of the Gospel, their resolution to leave no method untried which might be productive of good, the careful deliberation with which each step was weighed, and above all, the undoubted success which has attended this method, one cannot but echo the sentiment of Clement Marot's remark, "Why should the devil have all the good music?" and ask why to the highest purpose of all, and to that alone, should the walls be denied?

For more reasons than one, both from the insufficiency of space in the Assembly Hall, large as it was, and with

---

[1] *Plea for the Tower Hamlets Mission*, p. 8.

the view of getting hold of a different element of the
population, various music-halls were hired for Evangelistic
work. One of these, called the Foresters' Music-hall,
capable of holding 2,000 persons, was used through three
winters. They were also enabled to take, for two succes-
sive winters, Lusby's Music-hall, the largest building of
the kind in the East End, holding 3,000 persons. In
describing the opening of the latter, Keith-Falconer
says: [1]—

"The opening night in November was very remarkable.
The crowd was so great that it extended beyond the tram-
lines, which are seventy feet from the entrance, and before
the doors were opened a line had to be made for the tram-
cars to pass through, and we were thankful that there was
no accident in so terrible a crush. The hour of service was
seven o'clock, but at half-past six not a seat was vacant in
any part of that vast building, and whatever standing-room
could be found was quickly occupied."

Besides all such works as the above, Keith-Falconer
warmly sympathized with Mr. Charrington's attempts to
draw away people more and more from the music-halls
and public-houses, not merely by the counter-attraction of
something purer and better, but also by direct personal
appeals addressed to persons entering such places. This
naturally excited a great deal of angry opposition and for
some time there were a number of very unpleasant disturbances, which the owners of the property, thus becoming depreciated, sought to lay to the charge of Mr.
Charrington, who on one occasion was actually arrested by
the police in consequence.

"I shall never forget," writes an eye-witness, Mr. E. H.
Kerwin, "the night when Mr. Charrington was taken off
by the police, falsely accused of disturbance outside Lusby's
Music Hall. I was not there, but hearing of the incident

[1] *Plea for the Tower Hamlets Mission*, p. 12.

I went off to the police station, and on nearing it saw a
large crowd. In the dark I could see one tall man, standing in the centre, head and shoulders above everyone else,
and perfectly white: this was Keith-Falconer, who had
been covered with flour by the frequenters of the music-
hall. He gave evidence on this occasion. . . . . He also
gave evidence at Clerkenwell Sessions against the character
of Lusby's Music Hall."

Not only therefore had these messengers of the Gospel
to contend directly with drunkenness and vice, but also
with those who had a strong pecuniary interest in main-
taining the existing state of things, who would say with
their prototype Demetrius, " By these things we have our
wealth." It is often withheld from workers for God to see
with their own eyes the fruit of their labours, but Mr.
Charrington has been blessed in seeing very decided results
during his seventeen years' work. Here is a significant
fact. One public-house in the neighbourhood, that less
than twenty years ago was sold for £15,000, was sold two
years ago for less than £7,000.

Still, however, with all this, much remained to be done;
not only was the existing Assembly Hall, large as it was,
often insufficient to contain the numbers who flocked to
it, but many other useful agencies had either to be somewhat cramped in their usefulness, or had to be postponed
altogether. Thus within a few years of the opening of the
Assembly Hall in 1877, Mr. Charrington and Keith-
Falconer began to discuss a further advance.

Before proceeding to speak of the wonderful development of their foregoing schemes, and the marked blessing
which has been granted to these indefatigable workers, I
may call attention to a somewhat different duty which
befell them in the hard winter of 1879, that of the wholesale feeding of the hungry. I again quote Keith-Falconer's remarks: [1]—

[1] *Plea for the Tower Hamlets Mission*, p. 14.

" During the hard times of the winter of 1879 (due to
the long frost and the depression of trade) a work was
forced on our Mission which we had never contemplated
taking up. The difficulties and dangers of wholesale charity
are very great, and our desire has been to avoid them,
except in extreme circumstances. But the distress of that
winter *was* extreme, and for many weeks we opened our
halls and fed the literally starving multitudes with dry
bread and cocoa. The austere distress began in December.
Hundreds of men were waiting daily at the Docks in the
hope (nearly always a disappointed hope) of a job. Starving
men were found in several instances eating muddy orange
peel picked off the road.

" Our feeding became a very public matter, as there was
much correspondence about it in the *Times*, the *Daily
News*, the *Echo*, and other leading papers, and many people
came from long distances to see for themselves. The public
supported us liberally with funds, and we were enabled to
give no less than twenty thousand meals from January 1st
to February 14th, beside which we assisted over three
hundred families every week in their own homes. We
look back to the time as one of very great blessing."

All who were Keith-Falconer's intimate friends during
the last six years of his life must have heard from him a
great deal as to his hopes respecting the new building, his
careful elaboration of plans for the maximum of usefulness, and his hearty thankfulness at the completion of the
work.

In 1880, however, the undertaking to be achieved must
have seemed simply gigantic. The whole cost of the
present buildings, including the site, has mounted up to
about £40,000. Of this the site had been previously purchased for the former Assembly Hall at a cost of £8,000;
for the remainder, which it was expected would not exceed
£24,000, but which has been found in reality to be nearly
£32,000, appeals were issued.

As the Honorary Secretary of the undertaking, Keith-
Falconer published the pamphlet from which I have

already largely drawn. It consists of a general history of
what had already been done and concludes with a direct
appeal for help. This appeal is so characteristic of the
writer, so thoroughly earnest (entertaining as it does no
doubt but that the money will be forthcoming), and, as
was his way in such things, so quaintly methodical, that I
reproduce it here in full.[1]

" PROPOSED NEW HALL.

" We now appeal for funds in order to erect a new and
larger Hall.

" The *present building* is altogether unsuitable.

a.   It is far *too small*. On Sunday nights hundreds are
     turned away for want of room.   When, during two
     successive winters, the adjacent Lusby's Music Hall
     (one of the largest in London) was opened on
     Sunday nights simultaneously with our own hall,
     the united congregations usually amounted to 5,000
     persons.   These facts tend to shew that if we had
     a building sufficiently large, we could gather as
     many persons as the human voice can reach.

b.   It is a *temporary* structure, which by the Metro-
     politan Buildings Act must come down sooner or
     later.

c.   The corrugated iron is becoming dilapidated and lets
     in the rain, so that rows of umbrellas are often put
     up during service.

d.   The cold in winter is intense.

e.   The acoustic properties are inferior.

" Please add to this that *our site is the very best in all
East London*.   It ought surely to be utilized to the fullest
extent.   The present building only covers half of it.

" *We have got the site, and we have got the people.*   May
we not have a hall to accommodate them ?   The willingness to hear is very remarkable, and it is distressing to see

[1] *Plea for the Tower Hamlets Mission*, pp. 15, 16.

hundreds and thousands turned away for mere want of room.

"*The guarantees which the public have* that the work is a proper one, and that the new Hall will be properly used, are :—

1. The *testimony of trustworthy persons* who are acquainted with the Mission. Mr. Spurgeon has written a warm letter. Lord Shaftesbury is an old friend of and worker in the Mission. He has delivered several addresses in the Hall. The late Lord Kintore was a warm and constant friend of the work. Mr. R. C. L. Bevan has both promised £2,000 and consented to act as Treasurer.

2. A *trust deed* has been drawn up, and signed, transferring the property to Trustees, namely :—F. A. Bevan, Esq. ; Fredk. N. Charrington, Esq. ; Richard Cory, Esq. ; Hon. Ion Keith-Falconer ; James Mathieson, Esq. ; Samuel Morley, Esq., M.P. ; Hon. Hamilton Tollemache ; Joseph Weatherley, Esq. ; and specifying the objects for which it is to be used.

"It may be objected that the East End ought to supply its own wants. This is impossible. The population of the East End consists of the working classes, who, though they furnish the sinews of wealth which resides elsewhere, are poor themselves. Thus the East End has a double right to look outside for help. It is poor and cannot help itself adequately, and the wealthy are responsible for the wellbeing of their servants, the toiling thousands through whose labour they derive their riches.

" The character of our Mission is *evangelistic, unsectarian, and* SOBER. I say sober, because of late years some have despaired of reaching the masses except by using certain unseemly and sensational methods. Our work is an emphatic protest against this practice, and a standing disproof of its necessity.

"Finally, the building for which we plead will cost £20,000, a small sum indeed when we consider what amounts many are willing to spend on their own comforts and pleasures. This sum will not only build a suitable Hall, but a Frontage in addition, embracing a Coffee Palace and a Book Saloon for the sale of pure literature. The site has already been paid for."

The nature of the assistance rendered by Keith-Falconer to the work carried on by Mr. Charrington was manifold, though much of it has been rather implied than expressed in the foregoing pages.

He supported the work with liberal pecuniary aid. His donations from first to last amounted to the large sum of £2,000; and a glance at the names in the subscription list shews that some of the largest donations were due to his friendly influence.

Again, when every wheel in that gigantic machine had to be carefully and anxiously planned, Keith-Falconer was ever at hand as a shrewd and patient adviser. He did not often address the evening meetings, though sometimes he gave an expository address on a portion of Scripture at the gathering on Sunday morning. Mr. Charrington tells me that he was especially struck with one which dwelt with great power on St. Paul's speech on Mars' Hill. Any fear that Mr. Charrington had for a moment that the speaker might be getting over the heads of his audience was quite dispelled when he observed how keenly they entered into his graphic description of the scene from Mars' Hill, of the various elements of the crowd there assembled, of the apostle's recognition of each of these in his speech, and how forcibly the speaker brought the old but ever fresh lesson to the hearts of his audience.

It was, however, with individual cases that he rather preferred to deal. Distress of any kind found in him a ready and generous, but discriminating, helper. Cases of this kind were numerous, they were as a rule known but to few.

To give a mere cursory enumeration of some of these would not be of much use, but the following may serve as a typical case. W. was a painter living in the East End of London, a steady, hard-working, married man. Keith-Falconer had first met him at the Assembly Hall, and had shewn him much kindness, and subsequently told him to apply to him if he should be in trouble. At last trouble came; work being very slack, he was forced to pawn his tools, his best clothes, and, at last, most that he had which was worth pawning. Soon poor W.'s health broke down, and letters now before me shew how timely and how considerate Keith-Falconer's help was. Then when he was just able to keep his head above water through this help, a fresh trouble befell him. Failing to receive payment for some work which he had done, he found himself unable to discharge a debt amounting to about £4, and was sent to prison. To add to the trouble, the poor wife was daily expecting to be confined of her sixth child. Again did Keith-Falconer intervene, and the man was freed from prison, and the wife and children saved from the workhouse.

In a letter written by W. after the sad news from Aden had reached England, the writer dwells with warm gratitude on the change in his own position, and, with deep grief at the news, adds; " He told me if, by reason of the frailty which is in man by his evil heart of unbelief, I should fall into sin, ' Remember sinking Peter ' ; that One who raised him to the surface of the water can give me strength to get up again."

Keith-Falconer's habit was to run down for a week at a time and help. Sometimes he stayed longer, as when once he spent three weeks with Mr. Charrington giving careful tuition to a friend who was preparing for an examination. Often too he accompanied Mr. Charrington on the occasion of the annual excursions in connection with the Assembly Hall; and was exceedingly kind and helpful when 2,500 of the attendants at the Hall visited Southend.

Although it is carrying this part of the history beyond

the period as yet reached in the other divisions of our narrative, still it will be convenient to speak in this place of the ultimate completion of the work in the success of which Keith-Falconer was so intensely interested.

The sum to be raised was, as we have seen, a very considerable one, but those who had thus put their hand to the work held with Napoleon that the word ' impossible ' should have no place in their vocabulary ; and so persevering were their efforts, and so fully did God aid their enterprise, that by the beginning of the year 1886,[1] there were ready for use not only an Assembly Hall of much larger dimensions than the previous one, but numerous other rooms used in connection with various beneficent purposes. Of the whole £40,000 of the cost, more than £25,000 had been already received ; but unfortunately the estimates were exceeded in many points, so that a very considerable debt still remains on the building.

The Hall is capable of holding comfortably 4,300 persons, so that on occasion, with a little pressing, it could be made to accommodate nearly 5,000. On one striking and, I fancy, novel feature of this Hall, Keith-Falconer was very fond of dwelling, both before and after the attainment of his idea. This was that there should be an unbroken view from the street into the Hall, so that the speakers on the platform should be clearly visible through the intervening glass doors. Keith-Falconer held, and doubtless very justly, that many a man or woman of the poorest class is often deterred from entering a place of worship by the closed doors and the fancied obstacles behind them.

To give any detailed description of the Hall would be out of place here ; it will be sufficient to state that the ground-floor area is 130 feet long by 70 feet wide, the height from floor to ceiling being 44 feet. Two large gal-

[1] The building was opened on Feb. 4, 1886 ; on Mr. Charrington's birthday.

leries run round three sides of the building, while on the remaining side are two platforms, one above another, with a large organ behind. Abundance of windows of slightly tinted yellow glass yield a pleasant light by day, while shutting out entirely the outside view. At night, brilliant as is the light given by the continuous row of gas-jets, the ventilation is admirable.

Of the space between the great Hall and the street, the central part is occupied by a large vestibule, where passers in and out may meet and exchange friendly greetings; and the two wings by a book-depôt for the sale of pure literature, and by a spacious coffee-palace. Upstairs, various organisations have their home, a Young Men's Christian Association, a Young Women's Christian Association, an Emigration Depôt, and the like.

In the summer of last year (1886), I accompanied Keith-Falconer to see the building, and we were taken by Mr. Charrington to the central point of the upper gallery of the great Hall to gain the best general view of the room. As we sat there, I could not but be struck with the similar expression on the faces of the two men. It was one in which joy, and keen resolve, and humble thankfulness were strangely blended. One great work for God, which Keith-Falconer had striven hard to further, he was allowed to see in its fullest completeness, carried on by men working there with heartiest and purest zeal.

Not while any of the present generation of workers survive, will the name of Ion Keith-Falconer fade out of loving remembrance in the great building in Mile-End Road.

CHAPTER V.

" High nature amorous of the good,
But touched with no ascetic gloom."
TENNYSON, *In Memoriam.*

OUR chapter on Keith-Falconer's student life at Cambridge
ended, it will be remembered, with his last examination,
the Semitic Languages Tripos, in February, 1880. At the
time of this examination his knowledge of Arabic was but
slight, and simply sufficient for the requirements of the
paper on Comparative Grammar in the examination.

The Tripos over, he turned his attention definitely to the
study of Arabic, the language, which, like Hebrew, had a
wonderful fascination for him from the first, and to which,
as his knowledge widened, he became more and more devoted ; though realizing ever, as he went on, how vast was
the field of work. As he expressed it in a letter written in
March, 1887, " I expect to peg away at the Dictionary till
my last day."

The time until the end of May was mostly spent in quiet
study at Cambridge, broken by short occasional visits to
town ; and during the latter part of this time he worked
assiduously at Arabic with Dr. Wright. On leaving Cambridge early in June, he spent some time at his father's
house in London, and about the middle of the month
started for Royat, in Auvergne, where he purposed remaining for several weeks.

It was while he was here that a very grievous sorrow

befell him in the almost sudden death of his father, whom not long before he had left in perfect health, and between whom and himself the most perfect confidence and love had always existed.

In a letter which I received from Keith-Falconer, dated July 25, he says :—

" . . . . The event was a fearfully sudden one. I received at 6 o'clock on Monday morning a telegram as follows :— ' Your father very ill, come at once.' At 8 I was in the train. Reached Paris at 5 P.M., telegraphed for further information to be sent to Dover. Arrived at Dover at 4 A.M. Tuesday, a telegram was put into my hands, saying, ' Your dear father passed away peacefully on Sunday night at twenty minutes to seven.' I got home at 6.30, and found my father, whom I had left in perfect health five weeks before, in his coffin.

" He was perfectly well on Sunday excepting that a fortnight before he had sprained his ancle. On Friday or Saturday he remarked that he never felt better in all his life. On Sunday afternoon he received two friends, and chatted with them in his usual lively, happy manner. When they had left, he and my mother went out in the carriage. They had not traversed more than two or three streets, when he said, ' I feel so ill, I must go back,' and began to change colour and to tremble violently. The horses were turned instantly, and when home was reached, he put his hand to his side, exclaiming, ' I am dying : carry me in.' The servants carried him to his room in a half-fainting condition. . . . . He said good-bye to my mother, and quietly expired. My sisters were on a visit in the country at the time."

After referring to the cause of death, which lay in the fact that the sprain had resulted in the formation of a clot of blood which had gradually worked up to the heart and interfered with its action, the letter continues :—

" Fancy dying of a sprain ! Life seems to hang by a thread. It is noteworthy that my father always hoped for a sudden death, and dreaded the thought of a lingering illness. He also told Mr. ——, of Aberdeen, when last there, that he would like to die on a *Sunday.*

" It seems like a dream. I do not realize my loss, but must do so in time.

" We laid him in his grave to-day, next Arthur, in the family burial-ground next the parish Church of Keith-Hall, up the hill. About 600 attended. . . . ."

This is not the place to write a detailed account of the numerous good works with which the late Lord Kintore was associated. A man of profound religious convictions, he endeavoured consistently to let his religion be the animating principle of the whole course of his actions. He wore " the white flower of a blameless life," and set a noble example of simple Christian goodness. He was most generous at all times in his support of all good works, and especially of those connected with the Free Church of Scotland.

Of this Church he had long been an elder, and with it his sympathies were very strongly bound up ; though, like his son Ion, he was most tolerant of the views of those who, while agreeing as to essential truth, differed from him in details. Father and son alike, though holding to their own views unflinchingly, preferred to dwell in conversation with their friends on the points which they held in common, rather than to battle about those on which they differed.

Towards the end of the summer a case occurred which shews how ready Keith-Falconer was, while even the shadow of his great sorrow rested upon him, actively to interest himself for anyone who, he felt, had a legitimate claim upon his sympathies.

Dr. Wright had mentioned to him in the course of conversation the difficulty experienced by the well-known German scholar, Dr. Lagarde, in meeting the cost of the publication of his books. Dr. Lagarde had succeeded Ewald as Professor of Oriental Languages at Göttingen, and had published a very large number of works mostly having a direct bearing on the text of the Old Testament. Going as many of these did somewhat off the beaten track of studies, they would appeal to a rather limited public even in Germany, and thus the cost of publication would be but slightly reduced by the sale of the books. The more numerous the publications, the greater the loss, and therefore it seemed inevitable that works of very considerable value, in a part of the field where none too many workers have worked, must cease from lack of funds.

A letter from Keith-Falconer to his mother, dated August 28, 1880, tells her all this, dwells on the fact that all exact work on the elucidation of the text of the Old Testament is a thing to be cordially welcomed, and urges that it is a reproach to those who have the cause at heart, and can afford to help, to allow such work to be hindered from simple want of funds.

He accordingly tells her that having had full assurance from Dr. Wright that the facts were as he had stated them, he wished to raise a fund of £1,000 to help Lagarde to carry on his work. He undertakes to give £100 himself, and begs his mother to contribute £250, adding, " I have not got patience or time to go asking for a pound here and a pound there."

One of the books specially aided by Keith-Falconer's kind interposition was an edition of the Septuagint, for which some fresh MSS. had been examined. In the preface to the first volume, Lagarde warmly and gracefully alludes to the opportune help he had received, the names there given of his supporters being with one exception due to the advocacy of Keith-Falconer.

In this same letter, he alludes to a book on which for some years he spent pains most ungrudgingly, and of which I shall give a detailed description in its due place. This was the *Kalilah*, a book of which Dr. Wright was preparing the Syriac text for publication, and had urged

Keith-Falconer to bring out an English translation with an Introduction, promising to send him the proof-sheets of the original as they appeared.

For some time Keith-Falconer had wished to have an opportunity of studying at a German University, not, it needs not to be said, from any feeling that he could there obtain teaching in Arabic of a higher kind than at Cambridge, for a letter, which will be given presently, shews what his views were as to the Cambridge professor ; but partly from the wish to become yet more thoroughly versed in German while pursuing his Arabic studies, and partly, I fancy, from the wish to see something of a type of university and of students differing in many ways from our own.

Accompanied by a friend, a student of like pursuits, he established himself at Leipzig, which he reached on October 23, and where he remained for nearly five months.

The following letter to a friend, dated October 24, gives an amusing account of his arrival. After speaking of his journey from London, *via* Calais, Brussels and Düsseldorf, it proceeds :—

" We started at 1 P.M. from Düsseldorf, and were due in at 11.42, but did not arrive till 2 in the morning. A. was much tried hereby. *I* sat it out patiently enough, but *he* otherwise. Towards 1 A.M. his face assumed an aspect of resigned despair. He was *very* cold and *very* hungry and *very* tired. When at length we got in, we found no cab, except two which had been taken. So we had to wait about till one could be fetched.

" In the meantime A. found that his book-box had been taken away by mistake by another party. He was indeed in a frenzy. But he got better when our cab finally came, and still better when we found his box at the Hauff Hotel, where we went. But he could not get anything to eat, and so went to bed supperless. Next morning he was up early, thinking that the whole day would be required to fix ourselves ; but I, on the contrary, persisted in laziness, though every half-hour A. came entreating me to make haste and sally out with him in quest of rooms. So I had breakfast in bed, then a hot bath, then dressed and shaved to my satisfaction. It was now 1 o'clock, and at last we went out together; but it struck me at this point (1) that it was time for dinner, (2) that we had better first go and see ——, who would be able to give us good advice about rooms, etc.

" We then separated, I to dinner at the table d'hôte, and A. to make purchases, as he could not eat for fuss and anxiety. They gave us a splendid dinner, and towards the end A. came in and felt inclined to eat, and as they keep the dishes hot for late comers he got his dinner. . . . . After dinner we went in search of rooms, and to make up for my lazy immobility of the morning, and to set him more at rest, I promised him he should have the first good rooms we found. In about an hour we discovered a splendid set, which he took at once. . . . . After getting his rooms, I went to get some for myself. This I soon did, but they are not as good as his."

A later letter (February 18, 1881) to the present writer, graphically describes his course of life and his surroundings :—

As to study, I think I can claim having laid a good foundation in Arabic. Three days in the week we (that is A. and self) go to Professor X. to read Koran. We have read about fifty pages in Fluegel's large edition. Besides this we read in a Chrestomathy book by Arnold—not with X., but in lecture where Professor Y. holds forth. X. is not like some German professors, for he is tidy, without spectacles, nicely dressed, polite and affable, moderate in his views, and does not smoke. . . . . X. lectures in the university in Arabic and Turkish. He can read besides Persian, and has an elementary knowledge of Hebrew and Syriac. His knowledge of the Bible, especially of the Old Testament, is marvellous. It would indeed astonish you. Till a fortnight ago he had never heard that the golden calf is reported to have been broken, ground to powder, mixed with water, and partaken of by the Israelites. He confessed to his ignorance in the most naïve and artless way. The chapter too in Ezekiel about the dry bones—he had never heard of. He certainly knows less of the bare contents of the Bible than most English—and all Scotch—children of nine or ten years old.

"Y. *does* wear spectacles, talks in a loud, rough voice, interlards his every lecture with frequent exclamations of "Du lieber Gott,' 'Ach Gott,' and smokes like a chimney. But still he is tidy, and keeps his hair short. But he and X. are really very kind and goodhearted to a degree.

"Y.'s lectures—twice a week from October to March—cost me the moderate sum of 9*s.* 6*d.* But I have almost entirely ceased to attend them. I first went to them to learn some Arabic, afterwards I continued to attend them to learn some German, and now I cease going at all because I can learn neither. He can't lecture a bit, and carries on a most inelegant, conversational, slipshod, rough and ready, broken conversation. X. on the contrary speaks admirable German, and is in every respect "höchst bescheiden.' Old Dr. Fleischer, the Arabist, I have called on. He is over eighty. Fresh and merry as a cricket. Active as ever.

"I also know Prof. Windisch (Sanscrit and Old Irish, which he learnt from Mr. Standish O'Grady), who is a very pleasant and exhilarating person. . . . . Professor.—— I met a few days ago. He talked Chinese in his youth, his father having been connected with China. Of Scotch ballads he has a large collection, and recited one to me. He is a good stenographer, and can write longhand backwards or upside-down, or backwards and upside-down. Philosophy and art are the pegs on which he manages to hang never-ceasing harangues. Smokes like a chimney. Was formerly a *Judge* in Dresden, and studied Chinese in spare hours. His acquirements you see are varied and peculiar.

"Among German *students* I have no acquaintances at all. . . . . But I must not omit to say that I have made friends with old Dr. Delitzsch. He is highly esteemed and beloved in the town and university. He is by far the greatest theologian here. He is very small of stature; white hair; neck encased in white bandages; his head is broad and flat, and not high and intellectual-looking. He is very poetical and mystical in his conversation; and is

very kind and homely in his manner : he has numerous
acquaintances among the students, and hunts up all the
English-speaking students—especially the Scotch. He
thinks very highly of the Free Church of Scotland. He
does not like —— at all. Thinks him *keck*, and one in whom
the ' Verstand prädominirt,' while the *Geist* and *Gemüth* fail
to occupy their proper place. . . . . All this I gathered from
a long conversation, which I may say I was privileged to
have with him lately. I was drinking coffee in the Re-
stauration situate on the ground floor of the house in which
I used to lodge, and in comes the old gentleman. So I induced him to come up to my room, and kept him for a long
time. F. Klein, mathematical professor, closes my list
of learned acquaintances. They all have a profound respect for our Dr. Wright, and from all I can gather, Scotland can boast of having produced the best all-round
Semitic scholar in the world. . . . .

" Delitzsch, I suppose you know, has just published a
pamphlet called ' Falsche Wage ist nicht gut,' in reply to
Rohling's ' Talmud-Jude.' Rohling is a Roman Catholic
priest, and bigotted to an absurd degree against the unfortunate Jews, who are universally disliked in Germany. I
asked a gentleman the other day, ' Woran erkennen Sie
denn einen Juden ? ' answer, ' An seinem allgemeinen *bru-
talen* Wesen.' This gives the key-note to the general anti-
Jew agitation in Germany. No specific charge against them
as a body ; only a strong antipathy to the Jew.

" I used to lodge in splendid rooms in the centre of the
town, from which I had the best view in Leipzig. But the
waiting was not satisfactory, and the sitting-room was
much too large—a huge salon with polished floor—and
being a corner room, fearfully susceptible to cold winds,
and so big that the *Ofen* could not heat it. So I have
changed and now lodge as above. Here I have *verkehr*
and *umgang* in the family, consisting of a well-to-do business man—formerly in excellent circumstances, but now,
as so many since the war, in reduced position—his amiable
lady, a middle-aged daughter and two younger ones. I
am learning a lot of German from them, as they don't know
any English, though they are supposed to have learnt it at
school.

" I dine at 1.30 at the table d'hôte of Hotel de **Prusse**—
a splendid dinner—7 or 8 courses for 1*s.* 6*d.* (abonnement)
if wine is taken, 2*s.* if not : extraordinarily cheap. Everything is cheap here : ridiculously cheap. I can buy a cigar
for 2½*d.* here which in Cambridge would cost 6*d.* ! You can
get *excellent* light wine for 2*s.* 6*d.* a bottle. I have dined
fairly well for 6½*d.* ! (soup, two courses of meat and vegetables and *compot*). Lodgings also : one can get an excellent pair of rooms at 50*s.* a month. Books, however, are
not much cheaper than in England. I have just purchased
a hardly used copy of Freytag in four vols. for £5. . . . .

" I also want you to look up a Peerage and trace my connection with James Keith, the Field-Marshal of Frederick
the Great. I am going to Berlin before I return home, and
I shall look such an idiot if I do not know how I am connected with him.

" Christmas, you will be surprised to hear, I spent at
Cannes, where my mother and sisters are, I went there
via Paris and Marseilles : returned *via* Genoa, Milan,
Verona, the Brenner and Munich.

" Dresden is the town which most pleases me, of all those
which I have seen. Berlin is very unattractive : so cold,
and angular as a Dutch garden, and prosaic and flat.
Leipzig is delightful, so long as one keeps strictly in the
town, for the suburbs and surroundings are painfully
hideous, compared to which those of Cambridge are charming and gorgeous. (So rest and be thankful.)

" I hope to spend the summer term in dear old Cambridge. A great friend of mine, J. E. K. Studd, has
secured the lower rooms, which is pleasant for me. Kalilah
goes ahead, though slowly. I have done about 100 pages,
but go faster and faster as I progress. . . . ."

This brings before us the picture of a genial and light-
hearted, but diligent student, and of a shrewd observer of
what went on around him. All this Keith-Falconer was,
but it is only half the picture.

There are some natures (and I speak here of natures
altogether sincere), which, being animated with love for
God and Christ, yet will not be content with allowing that

love to permeate the whole nature, letting its light shine before men as our Saviour bids us, but must bring up the innermost feelings to the surface at all times.

To read some of the so-called religious biographies it would seem as though for everything save the actual religious duties, a sort of half apology were needed, as if every form of honest secular work, every form of innocent recreation were rather to be tolerated than approved of.

The bright geniality of many of Keith-Falconer's letters co-existed, as his friends know well, with the deepest thoughtfulness in religious matters. It was not his habit constantly to bring such topics into his ordinary conversation, but the thoughts lay there; and when duty called for it, or in more private talk with intimate friends, he would speak out unreservedly.

Some of the following extracts taken from letters written to a friend at this time, bring out another side of Keith-Falconer's character.

The first extract is from his answer to a letter in which a friend had urged upon him how high the standard of Christian life ought to be.

"You have tried to picture what the Christian life ought to be. You do not, and cannot overdraw the picture. But this hardly touches the important and the practical question, how to attain to it. It does not seem to me sufficient merely to ' own the presence of the Holy Ghost.' I believe in the presence of the Holy Ghost in the Church (ever since the Lord ascended); and I believe that the Holy Ghost will dwell in me, that is *reign* in me, if I will surrender myself to Him. And this surrender is not a thing to be done once for all; it is continuous and lifelong. Like other habits it becomes easier the more it is persisted in, but it is a struggle. The Christian is described as a *warrior* in the New Testament, and not only so, but as a struggling, hard-fighting, agonizing one—see 1 Peter v. 7-10 and elsewhere. If by simply and once for all surrendering ourselves to the Holy Ghost, we could ensure ourselves against sinning, why does the New Testament teem with warnings against particular sins and temptations, instead of simply telling us ' surrender yourselves to the Spirit once for all ; the Spirit will then fight your battles for you.'

" As to the two ways of putting the Gospel, ' Christ for us,' ' We for Christ,' I perfectly agree with both. In fact they seem to me identical

Christ for us	*We for Christ*
Our Lord	His servants
Our Head	His members
Our Brother	His brethren
Our Saviour	His ransomed people
etc.	etc.

and Cant. vi. 3 binds together these two sets of relationship.
. . . . . ' We for Christ ' is strikingly brought out in Ps. ii.
7, 8.   Cf. Prov. viii. 31."

In a subsequent letter he writes :—

" *Nov.*, 1880.

" As to the *wisdom* so often deprecated in the New Testament, it seems to me that Greek philosophies and Rabbinical follies are aimed at.   But *scholarship* in our sense of the word did not exist when the New Testament was written.   Scholarship is a laborious and, to a great extent, mechanical way of getting at the original text. Scholarship assumes no doctrine, and denies none.   It is colourless.   Scholarship can hardly be called wisdom, any more than I can be called wise because I know English. The words chiefly used in the New Testament to denote wisdom, viz. σοφία and γνῶσις, mean something else, namely Rabbinical lore and tradition and Greek (Alexandrian) philosophy, which afterwards made a compromise with Christianity, and produced ' Gnosticism.'   The more of a ' scholar' one becomes, the more one fathoms the depths of one's ignorance, and estimates the measure of one's dependence on God's Spirit.   To take the immense trouble of learning ancient languages in order to ferret out correct readings, is a silent, but most emphatic protest, against the claims of *a priori* reasoning or philosophy. Rationalists are no scholars, because they begin by assuming ideas and theories—which scholars do not—and then adapt the text or the translation so as to suit them. You can refer to any commentary of the Tübingen School, and you will see the force of this remark."

"*Nov.*, 1880.

" People forget that while the sacred writers were inspired penmen, yet they were pen*men*, and that each retained his individuality, yet without sin or error, and that consequently the style, diction, and habits of one writer differ from those of another. It is impertinent and impious to postulate that God *must* have laid aside the individuality and humanity—in itself first created and not sinful—of each writer, and used him as a passive, dead, inanimate, senseless, pen or instrument. God *might* have done this, but he did *not* do so: God may take pure Hebrew and use it; he may take corrupt Hebrew and use it. He may take a writer, who has a gift for splendid and gorgeous descriptions, as Isaiah, and use that gift. He may also take a writer, whose style is more monotonous, and less thrilling, as the author of Ecclesiastes, and use *his* style. Inspiration lies apart from these considerations. All I know about inspiration is that it makes the writing free from all error and untruthfulness, and that every word is to be considered the word of God. Speaking very roughly, I refuse to believe that our English Bible, as we have it, preface to King James and all, fell down from Heaven."

In March, Keith-Falconer had rather a severe illness, which confined him to his bed for about a fortnight. When he began to regain his strength, the time had almost come at which he had purposed to return home. His companion wished to defer his own plan of visiting Switzerland at this time, so as to be able to accompany him, as not yet quite recovered, as far as London. This, however, Keith-Falconer, always one of the most unselfish of men, refused to allow, and insisted that he was strong enough by this time to go quite safely to England alone.

He reached London early in April, and shortly after this had the very great pleasure of being introduced to General Gordon, and having several long conversations with him.

On these conversations Keith-Falconer often dwelt afterwards. There were certain common elements in the two men which must have tended to draw them to one another. In each there was the same deep, simple faith, ingrained and unwavering; the same absorbing realisation of the workings of God's Providence; the same utter abnegation of self when the thought of duty came in; and, to a certain extent, somewhat of the same unconventionality in both speech and action.

In Keith-Falconer's mind there had previously been the highest admiration for Gordon from what he had read of him: now that he had met and spoken to him, he enshrined Gordon in his heart as one of his heroes. He set great store, as may well be imagined, on a little book which Gordon had given him, Clarke's *Scripture Promises,*—promises which both men had come so absolutely to trust.

The following letter is the second of two written by Gordon to Keith-Falconer in April, 1881: it shews that the elder man saw that there was sterling metal in the younger. The invitation was one which Keith-Falconer frequently regretted that circumstances had prevented him from accepting.

"5, ROCKSTONE PLACE, SOUTHAMPTON, 25, 4, 1881.

" MY DEAR MR. KEITH-FALCONER,

"I only wish I could put you into something that would give you the work you need, viz. secular and religious work, running side by side. This is the proper work for man and I think you could find it.

"Would you go to Stamboul as extra unpaid attaché to Lord Dufferin; if so, why not try it, or else as private secretary to Petersburg? If you will not, then come to me in Syria to the Hermitage.

> " Believe me with kind regards,
> " Yours sincerely,
> " C. G. GORDON."

As was the case when any subject lay near his heart, Keith-Falconer talked much at this time to his intimate friends of Gordon and his wonderful career. One incident, I remember, he was very fond of dwelling on. When the " ever-victorious " Chinese army under Gordon's leadership had accomplished its work, the richest gifts were gratefully pressed on him. Pecuniary rewards of every kind he absolutely refused; the only thing he would accept being a gold medal, the sole material result to him of his marvellous successes. Some time after his arrival in England, wishing to contribute to the Cotton-famine Fund, and finding himself somewhat short of money at the time, he deliberately gave up his gold medal for this purpose.

When Gordon was sent out for the relief of Khartoum, Keith-Falconer followed his movements with the keenest interest and eagerly looked for tidings. As the news came of the long, solitary watch in that far-off post, where that noblest of the noble waited, without fear and at last without hope, for the help which England, or rather her rulers, would not send, Keith-Falconer's anxiety became intense. When at last the news came of the treachery at Khartoum and the bloody massacre, he at first hoped against hope that the news was false, and that the sacredness with which Gordon was known to be invested must have sufficed to save him. When all hope was clearly gone, his grief as for a most dear friend was blended with the keenest indignation that one of England's noblest sons should have served as a mere counter in the reckless game of politics.

The May term of this year was spent by Keith-Falconer in quiet study at Cambridge.

Writing to the friend to whom the three foregoing letters were addressed, he says:—

"*May* 4, 1881.

"Pray constantly for me, especially that I may have my path in life more clearly marked out for me, or (which is perhaps a better request) that I may be led along the path intended for me."

On May 28, Keith-Falconer started on a bicycle tour through Oxford, Pangbourne and Harrow. This was, however, intended but as a "preliminary canter" to a much more ambitious effort. Accordingly, on June 4, he went by train to Penzance, fully intending to achieve the ride from the Land's End to John o' Groat's House in the extreme north-east of Scotland. After waiting at Penzance for several days, he was reluctantly forced to give up his scheme, on account of the persistent bad weather; and, returning to town, paid a visit of several weeks' duration to Mr. Charrington. The following letter well indicates his feelings at the time:—

"STEPNEY GREEN, *June* 12, 1881.

"It is overwhelming to think of the vastness of the harvest-field, when compared with the indolence, indifference and unwillingness on the part of most so-called Christians, to become, even in a moderate degree, labourers in the same. I take the rebuke to myself. . . . . To enjoy the blessings and happiness God gives, and never to stretch out a helping hand to the poor and the wicked, is a most horrible thing. When we come to die, it will be awful for us, if we have to look back on a life spent purely on self, but—believe me—if we are to spend our life otherwise, we must make up our minds to be thought 'odd' and 'eccentric' and 'unsocial,' and to be sneered at and avoided.

"For instance, how 'odd' and 'unsocial' of my heroic friend (Mr. Charrington) to live in this dirty, smoky, East-End all the year round, and instead of dining out with his friends and relations, to go night after night to minister to the poor and wretched! . . . . But I like to live with him and to watch the workings of the mighty hand of God and to catch a spark of the fire of zeal which burns within him, in order that I may be moved to greater willingness and earnestness in the noblest cause which can occupy the thoughts of a man. This is immeasurably better than spending my afternoons in calling on people, my evenings in dinners and balls, and my mornings in bed. . . . . The usual centre is SELF, the proper centre is GOD. If therefore one lives for God, one is *out of centre* or *eccentric*, with regard to the people who do not."

After leaving Mr. Charrington, Keith-Falconer rejoined his mother and sisters at Keith-Hall, where he remained till August 20. From a letter written at this period I extract the following exceedingly sensible remarks as to the true function and benefit of vigorous physical exercise :—

"*July*, 1881.

"It is an excellent thing to encourage an innocent sport (such as bicycling) which keeps young fellows out of the public-houses, music-halls, gambling hells and all the other traps that are ready to catch them. I wish I had ridden last year. It is a great advantage to enter for a few races in public, and not merely ride on the road for exercise, because in the former case one has to train one-self and this involves abstinence from beer and wine and tobacco, and early going to bed and early rising, and gets one's body into a really vigorous, healthy state. As to betting, nearly all Clubs forbid it strictly, and anyone found at it is liable to be ejected promptly. A bicycle race-course is as quiet and respectable as a public science lecture by Tyndall. . . . . If we exercised and trained our bodies more than we do, there would be less illness, bad temper, nervousness and self-indulgence, more vigour and simplicity of life. Of course, you can have too much of it, but the tendency in most cases is to indulge the body, and not exercise it enough, and athletic contests are an excellent means of inducing young people to deny themselves in this respect."

On August 20, Keith-Falconer left home for a short visit to Germany, travelling by way of Harwich, Rotterdam, Amsterdam, Cologne, Frankfort and Carlsruhe to Herrenalb in the Black Forest. Here he remained for some weeks, but his letters written at this time dwell entirely on points of purely personal interest.

After a flying visit to Leipzig, he set out for home, passing on his way through Stuttgart and Strasburg, and reaching London at the end of September.

His next journey was a much more distant one, and but for his illness might have proved decidedly adventurous.

CHAPTER VI.

Πολλῶν ἀνθρώπων ἴδεν ἄστεα καὶ νόον ἔγνω.
                                                    HOMER.

ALTHOUGH Keith-Falconer had by this time devoted very considerable attention to classical Arabic, he was anxious to gain, what no study of books alone could give him, a ready colloquial use of the language as spoken at present.

To do this it would be necessary to reside for some time at a place where not only could satisfactory teaching of the kind he needed be obtained, but where to a certain extent he would be forced to use his Arabic and not be tempted on all occasions to have recourse to some more familiar language.

A place fulfilling the necessary conditions was Assiout on the Nile, about 200 miles above Cairo, and the furthest point as yet reached by the Egyptian railway. The place was very little frequented by Europeans, and at the time when Keith-Falconer first went there was not even an hotel. Fortunately, however, a Scotch missionary, Dr. Hogg, resided there, and was an accomplished Arabist.

Accordingly he left England towards the end of October, intending to remain in Egypt for three or four months.

The story of Keith-Falconer's residence at Assiout may best be told by extracts from his own letters. Those here given are addressed either to his mother or to Miss Bevan, his future wife.

(First he describes his journey by way of Calais, Paris and Marseilles):

"At Marseilles I went to the Terminus Hotel. This morning I was very busy making purchases in accordance with Baedeker's directions. I got a strong pocket-knife, two balls of twine, four note-books, steel pens and pencils, ink and inkstand, paper and envelopes, drinking-flask and a bottle of gum. . . . . The steamer is decidedly a fine one, and we do hardly anything but eat all day long. . . . . We reach Naples early on Saturday. Then after a few hours straight to Alexandria, where we are due on Wednesday morning. . . . . I am studying Baedeker, which seems to be quite a compendium of information and learning, and hope even to acquire enough Arabic during the voyage to get on with at first."

"CAIRO, *Nov.* 10, 1881.

"The train got to Cairo at 10.25 last night, and the hotel omnibus met us at the station. After a very jolty ride along one of the main thoroughfares of Cairo, we entered the Muski, or the 'City' of Cairo, where the best shops are and much of the business is done. I was on the box, and with difficulty kept there along the Muski. The hotel was reached at the end of a street, too narrow for carriages to drive along, but when reached, a very pleasant house, arranged in a quadrangle, and a garden in the middle. . . . . After breakfast, I went to the Kutub-Khâneh, or Vice-regal Library, where I saw Dr. Spitta-Bey, the chief librarian, to whom I had a letter of introduction from Dr. Wright. He was very kind and agreeable. Then on to the American Mission, where I presented my letter to Dr. Watson. He will write to Dr. Hogg at Assiout, and on Monday I shall know if I can live there. I mean this afternoon to go to see Miss Whately, and to have a bath in native style. . . . . Cairo has about 400,000 inhabitants, including 20,000 Europeans, principally Italians. The streets are not paved at all—but it would take sheets to describe the town. . . . . There is something very nice about many of the people—many of them have such good faces. They have a good reputation for honesty, especially the Nubians. . . . . Flies are a plague. One sees people lying asleep on the road-side, *covered* with flies, mouth, nostrils, ears, eyes, swarming with them—a disgusting sight.

" I intend to spend a month or five weeks at the vernacular, and then to resume the ancient language, under the guidance of a sheikh.

" I have just visited the mosque of Sultan Hasan, the finest specimen of Arabian architecture to be seen anywhere: it is beautiful. The greater part of it, the Sahn el-Gä'a, where the congregation stand, is uncovered. One has to put on slippers over one's boots to walk about in the mosque."

"CAIRO, *Nov.* 13, 1881.

" Yesterday I visited the Pyramids of Gizeh, and mounted the Great Pyramid. The Arabs spoilt all the fun with their jabbering importunities for money and their clumsy assistance. The begging here is something dreadful. It is a recognised thing among high and low. They seem to imagine that strangers come out here on purpose to shower money round them, and that sight-seeing is only the excuse for so doing. . . . . I have also visited two mosques, and the bazaars of course. A bazaar means a dirty narrow street, where all the shops—wretched holes— sell the same wares. There is the bazaar of the jewellers, the blacksmiths, etc."

"ASSIOUT, *Nov.* 20, 1881.

" I am here at last. The journey from Cairo was very unpleasant. The dust—I shall never forget it. I tried to read (Dozy's *Islamisme*), but in a short time the book and I got so filthy with the dust, that I became irritable and uncomfortable and could not read. After lunching on a dusty chicken, a dusty bit of cheese, dusty apples, dusty ham, dusty bread and some wine, I laid myself on the dusty seats and had a sleep for a couple of hours, and shortly arrived.

" I was met by one of Dr. Hogg's students, who could speak a little English. He had brought donkeys and a lamp; for the town is not lighted at all, and the streets are narrow and winding. After 15 or 20 minutes' ride right through the centre of the town, we arrived. The house is on the extreme edge of Assiout, looking out on the town on one side, and on the other on a green expanse terminated by an imposing range of hills, the commencement of the Great Desert. The Nile is right away on the other side of the town, and a good mile from here. There is an hotel at the station, which will be ready on Dec. 1, and I intend to live there from that date. The proprietor or manager is a Greek. There are numbers of Greeks in Egypt, and they dislike anything like manual labour, preferring to keep shops, and especially restaurants and hotels. Dr. Hogg is a *first-rate* Arabist. He preaches in Arabic perfectly fluently. He teaches his students in Arabic, including the Sol-Fa class. (The Arabs have wretched ears, and Dr. Hogg tells me that it was only by means of the Sol-Fa that he could get anything approaching to music out of them.) Family worship in the morning at 7.15 is conducted in Arabic. . . . . I have taken a teacher. He is to come two hours a day, and to receive £3 a month. So you see learning is wonderfully cheap here. . . . . Dr. Hogg is most accomplished. He knows Italian thoroughly, and can preach in it. He has preached in Turkish, but has dropped it. He is very fond of philosophy, and has translated Calderwood's *Handbook of Moral Philosophy* into Arabic. He has a good voice, and can play, and lead the psalms and hymns. He knows phonography, and used to write it when a student in Edinburgh."

"Assiout, *Nov.* 25, 1881.

"I have had a touch of fever and a heavy cold. . . . . The family are very kind to me. . . . . Dr. Hogg has been running in and out all day long. He is a splendid nurse, being strong, and has no doubt about what ought to be done. . . . . As to my Arabic studies, I have learnt a good deal, and can make myself intelligible to servants and porters. I have a teacher every day for two hours, and translate from a child's reading-book."

Shortly after writing the foregoing letter, Keith-Falconer removed to the hotel. He does not appear to have found any great amount of comfort there. He again writes :—

"ASSIOUT, *Nov.* 30, 1881.

" I am disappointed with Egypt, both as to scenery and climate. It is a *vile* place for catching cold. Buildings seem constructed with a view to as many draughts as possible. The colouring at sunrise and sunset is beautiful —like apricots and peaches. . . . . There are no bells. That is the greatest drawback of all. You have to go outside your door and clap your hands, and when you have repeated this performance five or six times, the Arab servant may begin to have a suspicion that somebody wants someone; and when at last you get him, it will be very wonderful if he does what you want."

"ASSIOUT, *Dec.* 22, 1881.

" A good many travellers pass through here, principally Greek merchants and English : but I am the only person staying here for any length of time. The hotel has been advertised by the owners as a first-class one, but this is hardly true, for there are no carpets or mats on the floors, which are of stone ; no wardrobes or chests of drawers in the bedrooms, no baths of any kind, and no sofas or arm-chairs. The servant, a kind of man of all work, is a Greek, and for stupidity, I think, unrivalled. The cooking is fairly good, I am thankful to say. The hotel is in a line with the station, and the engine draws up exactly under my window. The town is truly and unspeakably disgusting. The streets are all filthy alleys, very crooked and winding, and not lighted at night. . . . . I shall be very glad to get back to civilisation. I cannot call this a civilised place."

"ASSIOUT, *Dec.* 22, 1881.

" I am getting on with Arabic, but it is most appallingly hard. Yesterday I went with my teacher to his house. He introduced me to his wife, child and tea. She was at a college in Beyrout."

"ASSIOUT, *Dec.* 28, 1881.

" There is no ' society ' here at all, of course. I see a missionary now and then, or the Greek doctor and my teacher. Sometimes a traveller or two drops in. There are three Frenchmen here now, awaiting their dahabeah, which is coming from Cairo. They are small, dark, dirty, and of most villanous countenance. My teacher has been styled the 'inspired idiot.' His face is absolutely destitute of expression, and he only speaks when positively necessary. . . . . He is a Syrian, and he invited me to dinner on Saturday the 24th (for Christmas), and I never want to taste Syrian dishes again."

"Assiout, *Jan.* 12, 1882.

" I am meditating a camel ride in the desert. I mean to go from here to Luxor (Thebes) on a donkey, camping out every night, and from Luxor to Kossair on the Red Sea on a dromedary. I must go back first to Cairo to get a tent, bedstead, &c. I have talked it over with a very experienced Egyptian traveller. He says it is perfectly safe, especially in the desert among the Bedouins, who are gentlemen. The Egyptian Arabs are hardly that. I shall learn two things by doing this journey; (1) Arabic, (2) cooking. I expect to take a week getting to Luxor, where I must stay a day or two to arrange about camels. From Luxor to Kossair will take another week. At Kossair there is a missionary station (American Presbyterian). I am advised not to put on native dress, because the European is more awe-inspiring."

"Cairo, *Jan.* 17, 1882.

" I am at Cairo now getting together my necessaries for the journey which I contemplate. I have got vermicelli, rice, chocolate, preserved meats, Liebig's extracts, salt, rope and cord, a measure, soap, sardines, preserved curry, cocoa, two stew-pans, two basins (tin), kettle, knives, forks and spoons, three tin mugs, soup-ladle, fan to blow up the fire, tea, brandy, whisky, &c. . . . . Just bought a mattress and pillow for 10s. I have been racing about bazaars all the afternoon: I have made some capital bargains."

"Assiout, *Jan.* 25, 1882.

" I came away from Cairo on Saturday last, and stay here till Monday week, when I hope to start for my little expedition southwards. I am sending to Cairo for a revolver; I think it is better to take some little precautions. . . . . I am dreadfully lonely here. . . . . It is curious that the French consul invaded me this morning, mistaking me, I suppose, for someone else, and commanded me to return to France immediately."

So far as I can remember, the French consul fancied that he had found in Keith-Falconer a Frenchman who was " wanted " by the police for some misdeed or other, regardless of the fact that Keith-Falconer had come to Assiout two months before with introduction to a well-known resident, and him a Scotchman, and that his appearance and height were certainly not those of a Frenchman. Eager however to manifest his zeal, he actually forced his way into Keith-Falconer's bedroom before he had risen, and was only with some difficulty convinced of his error.

Just at this time, when the journey through the desert had been planned and provided for, Keith-Falconer had a second attack of fever; and though happily it was not severe, still on his recovery he felt it to be wiser to give up the scheme and return to Europe.

He reached Cannes early in February and remained there till the end of March, when he left for Genoa, proceeding thence to Siena. Here he stayed for about a month, largely with the view of increasing his knowledge of Italian, and on his return passed through Milan and visited the Italian lakes.

After his long absence from home, he now turned his steps to England, which he reached on the 12th of May, in remarkably good health and spirits, and bent upon again trying the experiment of a bicycle ride from the Land's End to John o' Groat's House. To get himself into thoroughly good condition for his expedition he essayed first the shorter journey from Cambridge to the Lakes; and then on June 1, travelled down with his " machine " to Penzance, waiting for a favourable day to start.

Of the journey he then undertook he wrote a detailed account at the time, which appeared in an Aberdeen newspaper and in the *London Bicycle Club Gazette.* There is a good deal of racy freshness and vigour about it which induces me to reproduce it here at full length.

" First day.　I left the Land's End point at 4.5 A.M. on Monday, 5th inst., with a S.W. wind blowing me along. Sixty-five minutes' riding brought me over 10½ miles of rough hilly road to Penzance.　Passing through Hayle, Camborne, and Redruth, Truro (36 miles) was reached at 7.40.　The smooth macadam road from Redruth to Truro struck me as being singularly good for an English road, but I have since been informed that it was made by a wily Scot who was awarded a prize for it.　Leaving Truro at 9.0, a very swift ride brought me in sight of Bodmin (60 miles) at 10.45.　Heavy rain was now falling and necessitated an hour's halt.　I had not got 6 miles out of Bodmin when a second and more violent storm of rain and mist gave me a bath all for nothing.　So I pulled up again at a lonely village called Jamaica, owing to its remote situation (70 miles).　Here I sat for five and a half weary hours at a little temperance inn, for there is no public-house in Jamaica.　A copy of Butler's ' Dissertation on Virtue,' which I found here, served, I hope, to reconcile me to the weather.　It was the driest experience I had that day. Starting once more, I rode gingerly over a succession of tremendous hills into Launceston, of beautiful situation (81 miles), where I realised that tea in dripping clothes is unpleasant.　About 10 P.M. the river Tamar, which separates Cornwall from Devon, was crossed, and two miles further on I pulled up for the night at Lifton (85).

" Second day.　The next day was fine, and the ride through Okehampton (100) to Exeter (121), though abounding in difficult hills, and severe collar work, was pleasant enough, the scenery being lovely all the way, and the air most exhilarating.　At Exeter I entered on a plain, and pursuing a fine level road, soon reached Taunton (152), one of the cleanest, pleasantest, and most flourishing of English country towns.　From here a delightful spin in the dark over a smooth country lane brought me to Lang-

port (166) about 11 P.M. A long argument with a commercial traveller kept me up till one o'clock, the consequence
being that next day I was good for nothing (besides having
failed to convince the commercial).

"Third day. During the ride through Somerton (171)
to Glastonbury (183), I became the victim first of stupidity,
then of malice. A waggoner seeing me about to overtake
him pulled very suddenly to the wrong side, and sent me
sprawling over a heap of flints. No harm done. Shortly
after a wilful misdirection given me by a playful Somer-
tonian sent me $2\frac{1}{2}$ miles in the wrong direction, so that I
traversed 12 instead of 7 miles between Somerton and
Glastonbury. Wells Cathedral (188) was one of the few
sights which I lingered to see. It is gorgeous. Then came
the long ascent of the Mendip Hills, and I shall never forget the view of the Somerset Plain obtained from the top.
At the summit of the steepest part the Bicycle Union has
placed one of its boards, inscribed "To cyclists this hill is
dangerous." A beautiful ride took me shortly to the city
of Bath (208), whose glory has departed. Once up the
long hill out of Bath, progress became rapid, and the third
night was spent at Didmarton, a Gloucestershire village
(225). Here a commercial gentleman told me that three
well-known cricketers (who are brothers) learnt all their
cricket from their mother, who, he told me, knows more
about the art than any of her sons!

"Fourth day. A pleasant if uneventful ride led through
Tetbury (231), Cirencester (241), celebrated for its scientific college of agriculture, Burford (258), Chipping Norton
(269), Banbury (282) to Southam (296?). Here my
troubles, which never come singly, began. Rain commenced falling, which soon wetted me through, I lost my
road and went quite a mile and a half out of the way, and
shortly before reaching Rugby (309), the spring broke.
But I felt so well and fit that I could not be glum. So, on
reaching this town, I promptly took the machine to a
mechanic, who had it plated and made stronger than before by next morning, and myself to the Three Horse-
Shoes Hotel, where I received every attention.

"Fifth day. Sunshine and rain alternated rapidly until
the afternoon. My road lay through Lutterworth (316),

Leicester (328), Melton Mowbray (343), Grantham (359), Newark (374), to Retford (394). The last 10 miles were done in the dark, rendered more intense by the rain-clouds. To ride along a stony road on a dark rainy night is a most severe trial of nerve and temper. One cannot see the stones to avoid them, and each time the wheel goes over one, the machine is jerked up, or thrust on one side, and the rider gets a shake that makes his heart jump into his mouth, and brings to mind unparliamentary language. Retford was reached at 11 P.M., and when I asked the landlord of the White Hart whether he often put up bicyclists, he looked at me severely and replied, ' Yes, but not so late as this.'   However, I met with every attention here. I got wet through twice to-day, and hardly slept a wink all night—nerves a little overwrought I suppose.

" Sixth day.   On emerging from the hotel I found to my horror that a furious north-west wind was blowing.   I struggled on as far as Doncaster (412), when I became sick of fighting against that strong man, and threw up the sponge.   After a good dinner at the ' Reindeer,' I went to bed for a couple of hours, expecting that the wind would lull in the evening—it did so, but of course the road got bad then.   A wet greasy oölite road, rendered more delightful by the recent gyrations of a feathery traction-engine, is a treat not soon forgotten by the bicyclist.   I enjoyed it this evening.   Riding was only possible here and there.   I tried to make myself believe that I was on a walking tour, and had taken the machine with me to come in handy now and then.   About 11.30 P.M. I tramped into Wetherby (443).   Two friendly policemen aided me in making sufficient noise to awaken the landlord of the inn here.

" Seventh day.   The wind, still N.W., was blowing gently to-day, and did not impede perceptibly.   The road improved gradually to Borobridge (455).   Instead of running straight from here to Durham, through Northallerton and Darlington, I chose the celebrated Leeming Lane, a smooth flat bit of road full thirty miles long, and often selected for trotting matches.   It is properly the high road to Carlisle, *via* Scotch Corner and Greta Bridge.   The lane has little traffic on it, and steers clear of towns.   High

speed was made through Leeming, Catterick (477), Scotch
Corner (482), where the road to Carlisle bends off, and you
can see the violet hills of the border country in the distance, Pierce Bridge, and over a range of hills to West
Auckland (495), all black and grimy with coal-dust, and
Bishop Auckland (498), hard by, where the Bishop of
Durham resides. Dined here, and met with a young
Japanese who was interesting. Then on to Durham (508)
through Spennymoor, and thence *via* Chester-le-Street to
Newcastle-on-Tyne (523). The county of Durham may
boast of considerable natural beauties, but commercial enterprise has introduced into the landscape so many features
of ugliness that the traveller is glad to leave it behind.
The high-level bridge which unites Gateshead and New-
castle is a grand structure. I had now scored 84 miles
since the morning, and hearing from a policeman that I
could get comfortably lodged at an inn six miles on, I
thought I might complete the 90 miles before halting for
the night. In due time Six Mile Brig hove in sight. It
was a dirty little colliery village. But I was tired, hungry
and wet, and the hour was eleven. So I thundered at the
doors of all the inns I could find. No answer, except at
one place, where a woman looked from a window and told
me that the house was full, which, of course, was quite
true. I shall take care that Dash Mailes, Esq., the landlord of the ' hotel ' which the policeman recommended, re-
ceives a copy of this account. A merry Northumbrian,
prompted by that temporary feeling of generosity inspired
by strong drink, vowed he would not leave me till he saw
me safely housed, and made the locality reverberate with
shouts of ' Tom,' and ' Jack,' and ' Bill,' but T., J., and B.
slept quietly on. At length a tall man came up and offered
me a night's lodging, as well as food. I accepted. The
house to which he took me was a pitman's lodging-house.
He was a pitman. His landlord—also a pitman—and
family lived downstairs, and he upstairs. The landlord
was directed to prepare supper. A vast pot of tea and a
measureless pile of spice-cake, with butter, soon adorned
the festive board. I had ridden 30 miles from Bishop-
Auckland without tasting a morsel of food or drink ; so
I did not count the cups of tea or the planks of cake which

I consumed—I was afraid of getting into double figures. Then half a pipe of twist (for experiment) and upstairs to lie down till it was light enough to go on.

"Eighth day. I was up with the lark, and amused with it too, and shortly found myself in Morpeth (537), eight miles on. Here, as might be expected, I had one of numerous baths and a breakfast worthy the name. Also made the acquaintance of a Presbyterian tailor, full of theology, politics, and good nature. Nineteen miles of fresh open country over a fine macadam road brought me to Alnwick (556). My old enemy the north-west wind got very boisterous now, and I was forced to resume the walking tour, taking the machine along with me, in case it might be of use again in the dim future. The wind was terribly cutting as well as powerful, but a blue jersey, bought at Alnwick, kept me as warm as a toast. Of course I missed my way going out of Alnwick. I always do when other troubles are on hand. They never come singly, and nothing succeeds like success. But the hardest blow was yet to fall. A few miles out of Morpeth my right foot began to hurt at the back; but I thought nothing of it, as I only felt it when walking up a hill. But the walking tour from Alnwick to Belford (572) caused so much pain that resignation and defeat seemed a matter of minutes. However an hour's rest at Belford did good, and on I went. The wind was cruel, and forced me to walk most of the way to Berwick (587). I limped in about 10.30 P.M. and put up at the Red Lion.

"Ninth day. Foot better to-day, and by leaving the boot unbuttoned I seemed to give it the requisite relief. Fortunately I had no walking tour to-day. The wind was still strong, but the road was grand, and 29 miles of hard pushing brought me to Dunbar (616). At this point the road turns in sharply to the west and I felt the wind but little as I rode through Haddington (627), and Traneant (636), into Edinburgh (645). Our city on a beautiful summer's evening presents a spectacle not equalled anywhere else. Quitting Edinburgh shortly after 9 P.M., a ride of an hour and a-half over the finest and smoothest stretch of road I have ever been on in my life brought the traveller to the 'Star and Garter' at Linlithgow (661).

The Town Council had been 'riding the marches' to-day —an arduous proceeding I should suppose, and one requiring substantial refreshment.

"Tenth day. When I awoke the rain was pattering on the window-panes, and a keen N.W. wind was blowing. A shudder, a resolve, a leap, and I was dressing quickly. The road to Falkirk (669) I found hilly, rough, lumpy, and slippery. Add to this wind and rain, and the result is misery. At Falkirk I stopped. Cook let me stand before the kitchen-fire while she prepared breakfast. At 9.30 the rain stopped and I continued. The wind was rising rapidly. More walking tour. Though I tramped most of the way to Stirling (680) and thence to Dunblane (687), my foot gave no trouble. I fondly thought that it had got well. At Bridge of Allan (683½) I dined, and slept an hour. At Dunblane the road turns sharply to the west ; and thence to Crieff (704), by Muthill and Perth (721), the ride was pleasant and prosperous. Dunkeld (736) was reached at 11 P.M.

"Eleventh day. To-day was a failure. After passing Blair-Athole (756), the glen becomes rapidly higher and narrower. The wind came sweeping down as through a funnel. There was a strong draught. Another walking tour. After three miles my foot began to complain. Once past Struan Inn there is no other until you get to Dalwhinnie, twenty miles distant. At Dalnacardoch I was in such pain that I was obliged to invade a farm-house and ask for rest and food, which I got at rather a high figure. Then on past Dalnaspidal Station, over Drumochter Pass to Dalwhinnie at the head of Loch Ericht (780). It was now eight o'clock, and I had only covered 44 miles since morning. At the Loch Ericht Hotel the medical skill of Dr. Peyton, of Broughty-Ferry, worked wonders, and the next day saw me traverse 105 miles with ease and pleasure.

"Twelfth day. Newtonmore (789), Kingussie (793), Aviemore (805), and Carr-Bridge (811) succeeded one another rapidly. The scenery along the road from here, *via* Loch Moy (822) and Daviot (831), to Inverness (837), was glorious. The day too was lovely, and not a breath stirring. Leaving Inverness at six, I rode rapidly through

Beauly (847), Dingwall (859), and Invergordon (872), to
Tain (884), where the last night on the road was spent.
Two miles before Tain the road forks right and left. No
guide-post is there to direct the stranger. It was nearly
midnight. Fortunately I descried a light in a window, and
procured the necessary information. This reminds me that
I did not see a single guide-post in Scotland, except two
close by John o'Groats, put up at the repeated request of
an English tourist, Mr. Blackwell (the first bicyclist who
rode from end to end of our island). Why is this? In
England they abound.

"Thirteenth and last day. I rose to find my foot
horribly stiff and painful. But the day was fine, no wind,
and only 110 miles more to run. Starting at 9.20, I ran
hard to Bonar-Bridge (899), over the Mound to Golspie
(920), where I dined, and slept an hour. Leaving at 4, I
ran rapidly through Brora (926) to Helmsdale (938). I
had limped up the Ord of Caithness by sunset. At Berrie-
dale (948) it was raining hard. At Dunbeath (954) I
stopped to have tea and bathe my foot, which had been
tried severely by the 4-mile limp up the Ord. Wick (975)
I reached about midnight. After refreshing and nursing
myself for an hour and a-half at the Station Hotel, I
started again, to the blank astonishment of landlord, boots,
and waiters. The utter solitude, stillness, and dreariness
of the remaining 19 miles made a most remarkable impression on me. Not one tree, bush, or hedge did I see
the whole way—only dark brown moor and a road straight
as a rule. At twenty minutes past three I stood stiff, sore,
hungry, and happy before John o'Groat's House Hotel.
I had ridden 994 miles in 13 days less 45 minutes. This
gives an average of 76 to 77 miles a day. I had no difficulty in rousing the landlord, and was soon asleep. Thus
ended an interesting and amusing ride.

"I have only to add that the machine which carried me
is a 58-incher, built by Humber and Marriott, of Queen's
Road, Nottingham, and weighing 45 lbs. As an illustration of the perfection of this bicycle, I may mention that
the hind wheel, which revolves 1,000 times a mile, ran
from Dunkeld to John o'Groat's (a distance of 260 miles)
without being oiled on the way. Thus it made over a

quarter-million revolutions on the strength of a single lubrication!"

The summer of this year was spent partly at Keith-Hall and partly in London. It does not, however, present any incident specially worthy of record. His studies and his work for Mr. Charrington fully engrossed Keith-Falconer's time.

CHAPTER VII.

> " I would the great world grew like thee,
> Who grewest not alone in power
> And knowledge, but by year and hour
> In reverence and in charity."
>
> TENNYSON, *In Memoriam.*

FOR the two years preceding October, 1882, Keith-Falconer had, as we have seen, resided but little at Cambridge; most, however, of the ensuing three years, except the vacations, was spent there.

The beginning of term found him in his old quarters on the Market Hill, as keen a student as when of old there was an examination ahead to be worked for.

To so thorough and careful a scholar, the *Kalilah* meant a far larger amount of labour than it might have been supposed would be required by a translation of a fairly easy Syriac book. Still the text existed but in one MS., and that most corrupt, and even with all the emendations of Dr. Wright and Professor Nöldeke, Keith-Falconer found abundant material on which to exercise his critical acumen. We must speak in some detail of the nature of this book, when we come to the time of its publication.

It is not, however, to be supposed that his book, ungrudging as was the labour he devoted to it, absorbed the bulk of his time: his engrossing study was Arabic, in which he was now reading such difficult books as the Mo‘allakat and Al-Hariri.

If he had been asked at this time why he gave so preponderating an amount of time to Arabic, which at no time
he felt to have any *direct* bearing on the exegesis of the
Bible, and whose literature was quite unconnected with his
Biblical studies, he would have said that the language itself
had a wonderful attraction for him ; the labour was its own
reward.

We must now turn to some other aspects of his life.   In
a letter to Miss Bevan, written at the beginning of this term,
he gives an amusing account of the success of one of his
friends, an Irishman, in his examination :—

"CAMBRIDGE, *Oct.* 22, 1882.

"R——— was here yesterday.   He told me how he got a
first class in his Little-Go.   He and another man had
worked for it more or less together.   R——— of course had
hardly looked at the subjects, while his acquaintance, a shy,
nervous man, had conscientiously gone through all the subjects, and worked eight hours a day all the term.

"The nervous man when called upon for viva voce turned
ashy pale, and was so overcome by his feelings'that he was
unable to utter a single syllable and was told to stand down.
Meanwhile Paddy was enjoying it rather than otherwise
from his seat.   Presently the name of R——— was called
out.   Patrick saunters quietly up.   It is needless to say
that this was the first time that he had been introduced to
his subject.   After taking his seat, and arranging himself
very deliberately indeed, he takes stock of the examiner,
who is a red-bearded, pale, stern-looking man.   Patrick is
directed to construe at such and such a place.   He replies
'Certainly, Sir.'   After examining the passage for a few
moments and satisfying himself that an attempt would be
absolutely hopeless, he looks up, bends forward and gazing
steadily into the examiner's face, whispers in tones of impressive earnestness, 'Anywhere but there, Sir.'   The stern
one is taken by storm and shakes with laughter and lets
him go on wherever he likes !   Paddy succeeds in choosing
a particularly easy passage, and not only passes the viva
voce, but gets through the whole exam. with a first-class.
His hard-working, conscientious friend only gets a second."

Early in the following month, Mr. Moody paid a visit to Cambridge. The visit was one which many remember with gratitude, and the tone of more than one College was distinctly raised.

From another letter to the same :—

"CAMBRIDGE, *Nov.* 6, 1882.

"Moody has commenced. I was at the first meeting which took place yesterday (Sunday) in the Corn Exchange. It began at 8 A.M. sharp. There were more than 1,000 people present, chiefly townsfolk. At 8.30 P.M. there was a meeting for University men only. There came fully 1,600 men, nearly all of them undergraduates. I am afraid many of them could not hear, and that was some excuse for the occasional bad behaviour which marred the meeting. Fancy applauding a prayer! A large number remained to the after-meeting. Moody said that he was quite satisfied. Meetings go on all this week. Moody spoke on Daniel. Towards the end I thought he was very impressive."

All this time Keith-Falconer was very much occupied with his work in connection with the mission at Mile-End, of which he was Honorary Secretary, and had published his pamphlet, of which I have already spoken, *A Plea for the Tower Hamlets Mission*. It is true that the great mass of work devolving on Mr. Charrington required that there should be also a secretary living in the midst of the work and devoting his whole time to it; still Keith-Falconer's post was very far from being a nominal one. It must be remembered that at this particular time the special anxiety of the workers was not mainly that of carrying on a gigantic machine, but also of obtaining funds to erect a building commensurate with their needs. The sum requisite for this purpose was believed in 1882 to amount to £24,000; it really has proved to be £32,000. All this entailed a large correspondence on Keith-Falconer. In writing a business letter he was exceedingly business-like: his facts were put in the clearest and most methodical way. A letter from him asking for a subscription was no effusive appeal; it was a quiet, sensible statement of facts, all the more cogent because the writer had shewn himself anxious to take all possible pains to do justice to his case.

Besides all this, frequent flying visits were paid to Mile-End, and in all every opportunity of doing good was caught at. As one who knew him well said, " He never seemed to be able to come anywhere, without trying to do good to somebody." Numbers of men and women received from him in right form, right degree, and in the truest and wisest Christian kindliness, just that help the case needed, bodily or spiritual. Of this, one typical case has already been given in detail. To shew how his kindness was sometimes appreciated, I may note that there lives a certain cabdriver in Whitechapel, who was always most genuinely anxious to be allowed to drive him anywhere about London for nothing.

In Cambridge, besides his interest in the Barnwell Theatre Mission, he had always on hand cases calling for individual aid. These did not assume with him, as a rule, the easy form of taking a piece of money out of his pocket and giving it to some importunate applicant, the truth of the appeal doubtless varying inversely with the importunity. Again and again he spent a great amount of time and pains to adapt the aid exactly to the case which appealed to him. Thus on one occasion he spared no trouble to obtain situations on a railway for a man and boy; he aided a man who had come down in the world to emigrate; he gave a helping hand in more ways than one to a man who was struggling bravely upwards. Of help given to students in Cambridge he was most generous, and I shall speak of it later on.

In the spring of 1883, he was appointed one of the examiners for the Tyrwhitt Hebrew Scholarships, for which he had himself competed successfully in 1879. In this and on other occasions when he acted as examiner, he shewed a thoroughness and carefulness that I have not often seen equalled. He went over the ground on which he was to examine as minutely as if he were one of the keenest competitors himself, so that the paper fairly represented the whole field of work. I remember well his bringing me a copy of a paper he had just set in an examination, and asking, " Now do you call this paper quite fair? I really think no one can say that I have not tried to do justice to each part."

In assigning the marks to the papers sent up by candidates he was also, I hardly need add, exceedingly careful. Of this an illustration may be given. Sometimes, in examinations in Hebrew, it became his duty to set " pointing." [1] To assign the marks properly for a piece of pointing requires exceptional care, otherwise a very false result may be obtained. This Keith-Falconer felt, and accordingly to judge fairly of each man's mistakes he adopted the following plan. For each candidate he took a second copy of the unpointed Hebrew and himself entered in it solely those points which the student had written wrongly. By having them all clearly before him in this form, he was enabled thoroughly to judge of the amount of marks to be deducted in each case.

The summer Keith-Falconer spent quietly at Keith-Hall, in work on the *Kalilah* and at Arabic; and in September he attended the Congress of Orientalists at Leyden. Presumably this, like other similar gatherings, is mainly meant to promote *esprit de corps,* and to give men of like pursuits the opportunity of seeing one another, rather than actually to instruct the visitor. At any rate, Keith-Falconer writes, " The Congress, as far as I can make out, is a failure as regards its ' labours,' and a success as regards its convivial gatherings."

It had long been his wish to obtain a lectureship in

[1] This expression has been explained above, p. 45.

Cambridge, and on his return to the University in October, 1883, he was offered and accepted the post of Hebrew lecturer at Clare College.

He had in a very high degree the gift of teaching. Thoroughly master of his subject, he could also thoroughly realise the standpoint of the beginner. One who knew him well, writes of this time:—

" He took just as much pains in teaching the stupidest man as the cleverest. He often said he did not mind men being ever so stupid, if only they did their best, and did not try to appear clever. He was a born teacher, as I know from experience—he always went to the bottom of a subject, and made it so clear that no one could help understanding. At the same time, he believed in his pupils puzzling out things for themselves, as much as they possibly could, and would only explain when he thought they had done their utmost."

It was not merely that he possessed the gift of lucidity in a remarkable way; he shewed an exceptional amount of kindness in the use of it. If at his lectures, painstaking and clear as he was, a student still failed to grasp the difficulties, again and again would he invite him to his rooms, or after his marriage to his house, and there give his time ungrudgingly.

On some occasions, being thrown into contact with men who had either been badly grounded by previous teachers, or who needed more individual help than lectures would furnish, he gave them all the help which could be rendered by a private tutor, and, having regard to the means of those thus helped, he refused in every case but one to accept the ordinarily recognised University fee. In the one exception, the money was sent as a contribution to Addenbrooke's Hospital, half in his own name, half in the pupil's.

He was appointed in this year one of the examiners for the Theological Tripos, and took part in the examination

of January, 1884, and also in that held under the new
system in the following June.

When the work on the January Tripos was finished and
the list published, he left for Cannes, where he resided
during February, and spent a good deal of time in preparing his papers for the next Tripos.

On February 29 he writes:—

".... A short-sighted lady, sitting next me in church,
told her husband afterwards that next her had sat a very
naughty boy, who drew pictures all through the sermon,
and that she had been on the point of stopping him.....

"On Wednesday I had a most delightful ride on a tri-
cycle across the Esterelles to Fréjus. Once at the top, I
cocked my legs up and went spinning down for *miles* without doing a stroke of work."

On March 4, he was married, at Trinity Church, Cannes,
to Miss Gwendolen Bevan, daughter of Mr. R. C. L. Bevan,
of Trent Park, Hertfordshire. After the wedding, they
spent some time at St. Raphael, near Fréjus, where the
quiet, picturesque neighbourhood greatly delighted him,
and went thence, by way of Marseilles, to the neighbourhood of Naples. Here they duly inspected Pompeii and
Capri, and ascended Vesuvius by the funicular railway.

By the middle of April, Keith-Falconer had brought his
wife to Cambridge, and resided during the May term and
Long Vacation in the house previously occupied by the
late Professor Fawcett, in Brookside.

The term was a busy one. He had spent some time on
his papers for the June Tripos at the beginning of the
year, but a good deal still remained to be done, and the
actual work of examination was itself considerable. His
work as lecturer, interpreted in the generous way in which
he viewed his post, also drew largely on his time; and besides all this, he had his Arabic and the *Kalilah*.

The house he was occupying had been taken only for
six months; but in the course of the summer he found

one that suited him in the Station Road, which had just
been vacated by Lord Rayleigh, on his resignation of the
Professorship of Experimental Physics, and took the
house on lease before leaving Cambridge for September.

The vacation was spent in Scotland, partly at home at
Keith-Hall, and partly on a bicycle tour in West Sutherlandshire, with his friend Mr. R——, already spoken of in
the present chapter.

The following two extracts from letters written to his
wife shew the nature of the tour and bring out the spirit
in which Keith-Falconer entered into a holiday.

"INSCHNADAMPH, *Sept.* 13, 1884.

" I wish you were here to enjoy this wonderful country.
Excepting as to strong air, I think the Braemar district is
distinctly inferior to this. The charm lies principally in
the astonishing variety of lochs. We have seen dozens of
all sizes and shapes. R—— turned up at Inverness as
arranged, appearing on the scene in a wonderful fur-
trimmed ulster! We got to Lairg about 4.30 the same
day. After tea and having put on our riding clothes and
labelled our bags to Lochinver, we rode off at 7.15 to
Altnahara Inn (21 miles). We had to go carefully most
of the way, as the darkness came on at 8. R—— went
off the handles once. Next day we rode across to Tongue,
where we sighted the North Sea. On the way we took a
dip in Loch Loyal. Dinner at Tongue. We had a job to
get across the Kyle. It was very low water and we had
to wade some distance before we got to the boat. We had
a talk with the boatman, who said he had been praying
and searching for many years, but ' couldna find Him.'
We took an age to ride seven miles across the Moine, a
dangerous swamp, to Hope Ferry.

" R—— was nearly run away with down the hill, which
might have killed him. It is the steepest, longest and
most winding hill I have ever seen. Hope River and Ben
Hope looked most grim and black in the dusk. The ferry
is crossed by a chain-bridge. We pushed on three miles
further to Heilim Ferry on Loch Eriboll, which is really
an inlet of the sea. An inn is marked on the map, but on

arriving at the house, we found it was no longer an inn.
A little blarney from R—— worked like an 'open sesame,'
and we got tea and beds; but it was a rough place. Here
we had a dip in the dark just before going to bed.

"Next day across Loch Eriboll by boat and then seven
miles of up and down to Durness. We found the hotel
occupied chiefly by a shooting party. . . . . R—— was
very unwell at Durness, so we staid there all day. Next
day a glorious run to Scourie, through Rhiconich, and
from Scourie to Kyleskee Ferry. The first thing we did
here was to plunge off a rock into deep, clear water. Then
tea. Another bathe next morning. After doing seven
miles to Scaig Bridge, I sent R—— on to Inschnadamph
(where we are now), while I rode to Lochinver, most of
the road skirting Loch Assynt. Coming away from there,
I had a fall over the handles, consequently my right hand
looks rather ghastly. To-morrow to Ullapool or Lairg.
. . . . This place is 36 miles from the rail and we have not
been so near since leaving Tongue."

In another letter to the same he thus gives his general
impressions of the country :—

"We have had the most gorgeous day that mortal man
could enjoy. Balmy air, soft fanning breeze, magnificent
scenery, piles of mountains wrapt in soft, dreamy haze,
profusion of lakes and bays dotted with little rocky islands
and reflecting the scenery so perfectly that one hardly
knows whether one is standing on one's head or one's
heels; a human being only encountered at rare intervals,
charming bathing, salt and fresh, at every turn; a clean,
cheap little inn about every 15 miles. R—— comes off his
machine every quarter of an hour. Happily his cranium
is thick."

On this Mr. R—— remarks, "I only three times nearly
broke my neck."

The beginning of October saw Keith-Falconer settled in
his new house at Cambridge, 5, Salisbury Villas, in the
Station Road. Here he had a large pleasant study look-

ing out on a good-sized garden, in which the sometimes
very audible whistle of the trains no more affected him
than the noises from the Market-Place had done in old
days.

It would seem to have been towards the end of the year
1884 that the idea of work in the foreign mission field first
definitely entered Keith-Falconer's mind.

He had, it is true, often thought, but only in a very
vague way, that he might possibly go abroad some day
as a missionary. Among his heroes for years past had
been Dr. John Wilson, the well-known Scotch missionary.
As far back as 1878, he thus writes to a friend :—

" Mind to get hold of Dr. George Smith's Life of John
Wilson, D.D., F.R.S., the great *Scotch missionary of India.*
He was a Free Church man ; every Indian missionary
must sit at his feet. He was probably the greatest Indian
scholar that has yet appeared. This is most extraordinary,
as he gave most of his time to mission-work. He also
made a name in geology ! His powers of memory were
something incredible. As for his toils for the people of
India, the biographer writes, ' From Central India to
Central Africa, from Cabul to Comorin, there are thousands
who call John Wilson blessed.' . . . . The author too is a
very distinguished writer on Indian subjects."

Nor was this warm admiration for Wilson a mere fleet-
ing fancy, to be forgotten when the next new book brought
a fresh hero forward. On his last visit to England in
1886, he constantly spoke with the same enthusiasm of
this noble worker for Christ.

When, towards the close of 1884, his intimate friend Mr.
C. T. Studd, of Trinity College, had been accepted as one
of the volunteers for the work of the China Inland Mission,
Keith-Falconer's interest was greatly excited, and, with
his wife, he was present at Mr. Studd's farewell meeting
in Cambridge early in 1885, and also attended the Oxford
meeting.

It was not, however, till the February of the following year that the idea of any special place as his sphere of work occurred to him. The whole history, however, of the Aden project and of the immediate causes which led up to it is best reserved for independent treatment in the following chapter.

Early in 1885, was published Keith-Falconer's book, on which an infinity of time and pains had been expended, the *Kalilah and Dimnah*, otherwise known as the *Fables of Bidpai*. This book, as I have already mentioned, when speaking of the beginning of the undertaking in 1881, is a translation from the Syriac, of which the text was published by Dr. Wright in 1884.

It is unfortunately, with one minor exception yet to be spoken of, the only completed literary work Keith-Falconer has left behind him ; unfortunately, not alone from the standpoint of friends who mourn his loss, but also from that of scholars in general, who are taught by the fulness and accuracy of the work how much might have been looked for in years to come from one whose first essay was of so brilliant a promise.

While of course it is not my intention to enter into any long account of the various forms of the text of which Keith-Falconer has spoken in his Introduction, it will at any rate be of interest to speak generally of the stories which make up the book, and of the special form of the text on which he worked.

The book is more familiarly known to general readers under its name of Bidpai's or Pilpay's Fables, from the fact that several English and French translations, ultimately derived from an old Persian version, have been issued under that title.

As Keith-Falconer remarks in his preface, probably no book except the Bible has had so many readers, when regard is had to the array of various languages into which these Fables have been translated.

They were in their origin Indian, and formed a part of Buddhist literature. The Indian original no longer exists in its primary form, but there are extant Sanscrit writings in which it is embodied. The chief of these is the *Pancha-tantra*, of which the late Professor Benfey published a translation with an exhaustive Introduction. This, however, is an elaborate and artificial expansion of the original work, of which we have a fairly faithful reproduction in the *Kalilah and Dimnah*.

The present Fables are of an altogether different type from the Æsopic. In the latter, animals act as animals would; in the former they act as men in the form of animals.

The name Bidpai, which occurs with great variety of different spellings, is that of an Indian philosopher, who tells a number of stories to the King his master, to enforce some particular rule of conduct, each story giving rise to a number of minor parenthetical stories. The first of these tales is that of *Kalilah and Dimnah*, which has thus given its name to the whole collection. Kalilah and Dimnah are simply two jackals, leading characters in the story told to illustrate the maxim, "When a false man comes between two loving brothers, he disturbs their brotherly feeling and destroys their harmony."

The collection of Indian stories passed into Persia not later than A.D. 570; and thence arose a version in Pehlevi, or ancient Persian, in which, it would seem, a Persian element became added. An ancient Tibetan version of part of the book, made directly from the Sanscrit, has recently been brought to light; but the Sanscrit original and the Pehlevi version have unfortunately perished.

From the lost Pehlevi, two surviving versions were derived, an older Syriac version made about A.D. 570, which has remained absolutely childless; and an Arabic version, made about A.D. 750, from which all other known texts are derived. Directly drawn from the Arabic are versions in no less than five distinct languages, Syriac, Greek, Persian, Hebrew and Spanish; each of which, except the first, has been the parent of other versions.

It is this later Syriac version which Keith-Falconer translated. Before proceeding to speak of this, it may be noticed that the Hebrew version, now known only by a unique MS., gave birth to the well-known *Directorium* of John of Capua, and from this again are derived translations into the German, Danish, Dutch, Spanish, Italian, English and French languages.

Like the older Syriac version,[1] so also the later Syriac is known solely by a unique MS. This MS., which was discovered by Dr. Wright in the Library of Trinity College, Dublin, and edited by him, is partly due to the thirteenth and partly to later centuries, and simply teems with errors. In the absence therefore of a second text to act as a corrective, conjectural emendations had frequently to be resorted to. Many of these were furnished by Dr. Wright and Professor Nöldeke, and a large number are due to Keith-Falconer's own critical skill. That he was no feeble novice herein, making a few vague guesses, but resting mainly on the experience of older scholars, follows not only from the fact of his occasionally differing from these distinguished Orientalists, but from the high terms of approval in which they have themselves spoken of his work.

To return, however, to this Syriac version itself. The translator probably lived in the tenth or eleventh century, and was a "Christian priest, living at a time when the Syrian Church lay in an utterly degraded state."[2] Passages often have a different turn given to them, in order to bring in a Christian sentiment.

---

[1] For a very interesting account of the way in which the unique MS. of this was brought to the knowledge of Europe, indirectly through the Vatican Council, see Keith-Falconer's *Introduction*, p. xliv.   [2] *Ibid.* p. lix.

As we have already observed, the fables are of an altogether different kind from the Æsopic. Many of them
are very quaint and striking. The most pleasing of all is
that of the Ringdove,[1] but it is much too long to be quoted
here. A curious interest, however, attaches to the Fable
of *The Ascetic and the Weasel.*[2]

This is the story of a child born to an ascetic by a
beautiful and much-loved wife, after she had long been
childless. Even before the child is born, the wife has to
check her husband from recklessly indulging in plans for
the future of the child, when even its sex is not known.
She bids him, "Commit your affairs to God, and everything that is desirable in His sight and in accordance
with His will shall come to pass." But, adds she, if a
man plans things too soon, there will befall him the fate
of the ascetic when he lost his honey and oil.

Bidden to tell the story, she proceeds,

"It is said that an ascetic derived his nourishment from
a king, that is, the governor of a town, every day so much
oil and so much honey. And whatever he had remaining,
he used to pour into an earthenware vessel which he hung
on a peg above the bedstead on which he slept. One day
while sleeping on the bedstead, with the earthenware
vessel full of oil and honey, he began to say within himself: 'If I sold this honey and oil, I might sell it for a
dinār and with the dinār I might buy ten she-goats, and
after five months they would have young, and after a lapse
of five years these would have young and their number
would become very large, and I should buy two yoke of
oxen and a cow, and I should sow my fields and reap
much corn and amass much oil, and I should buy a certain
number of servants and maid-servants, and when I had
taken to myself a wife of beautiful appearance and she had
borne me a handsome son, I should instruct him and he
would be secretary to the king.' Now in his hand was a
staff, and while he was saying these things, he kept

[1] *Kalilah and Dimnah*, p. 109.   [2] *Ibid.* p. 169.

brandishing the staff with his hand, and struck the earthenware vessel with it and broke it, whereupon the oil and honey ran down on his head as he slept. So all his plans came to naught, and he was confounded."

Here, in somewhat other guise, is the well-known story of Alnaschar and his wares of glass.

In due time the child was born, and on a certain day, the father had to be left in charge of it during the absence of the mother.

" But when the woman had gone, a messenger from one of the chiefs of the town came for him and could not wait. So he left the boy and departed. Now they had in the house a weasel who used to help them in all their affairs, and did not leave a single mouse in the house without killing him. And he left him with the boy and went with the messenger. Whereupon there came forth a powerful snake and sought to kill the boy. And the weasel fought with the snake until he killed him and bit him into several pieces, and the body of the weasel was stained with the snake's blood. When the ascetic returned from the man who had sent for him and saw the weasel with his body stained with blood, he thought that the boy had been killed, and without searching into the matter, sprang on the weasel and killed him. When he had killed him, he looked and saw and lo the boy was alive. And he repented and was ashamed and brought upon himself grief and sighing, and he began to revile himself for mortification, saying to himself: 'Would that this boy had not been born, for then I had not been guilty of this murder.' And the woman returned and upbraided him, saying: 'Did I not tell you not to be hasty and do things too soon before you had tried them, lest you should reap a bad end?'"

Here is a story which, in some form or other, is found in the literature of nearly every civilised nation. It is of course specially familiar to us in the form in which, in the place of the weasel, appears the faithful dog Gelert, the imaginary eponym of Beddgelert, 'Gelert's grave,' in Carnarvonshire.

The Introduction prefixed to the translation, extending over eighty-five large octavo pages, dwells on the literary history of the document, and on the history and bibliography of the versions. It is a piece of work, which, for rich fulness of learning, critical acumen, and clearness of style, might well do credit to an older scholar than the young man of less than eight and twenty at the time of its completion.

To the translation are appended notes, largely, but not wholly critical; there being some very carefully worked out notes on the names of the persons in the story, &c.

The remark was once made to me, half-seriously, half in jest, by one of the most distinguished of living scholars at Cambridge, with reference to the exceedingly long time often requisite for the writing of a short note, which to the general reader may seem to have cost but little trouble:—" I should often like to append a note to this note; 'This note has taken me (so many) hours!'" This thought strikes one forcibly in some of the modest, unpretending notes in Keith-Falconer's Appendix. The work is most thorough, and none but a professed scholar can estimate how long a time some of those notes must have cost their writer.

Of the various reviews of the book, I will refer but to one, that of Professor Nöldeke, one of the foremost of living Oriental scholars, who concludes a very favourable notice with the words, " We will look forward with hope to meet the young Orientalist, who has so early stepped forward as a Master, many a time yet, and not only in the region of Syriac." [1]

Although, as we have already said in the present chapter, Keith-Falconer's thoughts were beginning at this time

---

[1] *Göttingische gelehrte Anzeigen*, no. 19, p. 757 (Sept. 15, 1885).

definitely to turn to Aden, which engrossed his mind more
and more, he yet very cheerfully undertook, soon after the
publication of the *Kalilah*, a somewhat troublesome piece
of literary work, the article on ' Shorthand ' for the new
edition of the *Encyclopædia Britannica*.   I have spoken in
an early chapter of Keith-Falconer's remarkable powers as
a writer of phonography, besides which he had a considerable, though general, knowledge of other systems.   Still
the work for the article involved a large amount of research
and drew somewhat largely on his time.

The article, which, in its printed form, runs to about
thirteen columns in the large quarto of the *Encyclopædia*,
gives a general sketch of the progress of shorthand in
England, since the days of the first pioneers of the art, Dr.
Timothie Bright and John Willis.   The rudimentary forms
of shorthand in use among the ancients were described by a
different writer.

Keith-Falconer states that of *published* English systems
there have been no less than 483, the great majority being
alphabetic, in which each letter has its own symbol.   Thus
of the 201 systems from Willis's time to Mr. Pitman's all
but seven are alphabetic, the remainder being phonetic.

Of Mr. Pitman's system, which, under its name of
Phonography, was first published in 1840, a detailed
account is given.   This system is, it would seem, far more
widely used than any other, and Keith-Falconer considered
it to be the best of existing systems, though he makes
some very just remarks on the wisdom of writers of
different calibres adopting different methods.

After a short account of the systems invented during
the last half century, he gives a clear summary of the
various methods in use in other countries,—Germany,
France, Spain, Portugal, Italy, Denmark.   The article concludes with a concise bibliography on the literature of the
subject.

The essay is characterized both by its lucidity and its

thoroughness. Thus Keith-Falconer paid a special visit
to Oxford for the sole purpose of inspecting in the Bodleian
two books spoken of in the article, the unique copy of
Bright's *Characterie* (1588), and the anonymous work of
Willis, the *Stenographie*, of 1602, of which only one other
copy is known. I speak from direct personal knowledge
when I state that Keith-Falconer used every endeavour to
acquaint himself with everything of worth written on the
subject, and that the very large amount of preliminary
reading can by no means be estimated by the mere length
of the article.

The Easter Vacation was spent at Cannes. Although
Keith-Falconer could always thoroughly enjoy a well-
earned holiday, yet his heart always turned back lovingly
to his books. On April 8 he writes from Cannes :—

"I am weary of idleness and want to get back to my
books. . . . . Old Scotland beats this place hollow in respect to *scenery*, but the climate here is wonderful."

Not long before this time Keith-Falconer had arranged
a matter of much interest, which has already been referred
to in an earlier chapter in the note of the Master of Trinity ;
his foundation of the Kintore Prizes at Harrow. These
prizes, two in number, one open to the whole school and
the other to the younger boys only, were designed to encourage the intelligent reading of Scripture by the boys ;
and to take the place of those which had for some years
been given by Mr. Beaumont. The Kintore Prizes were
first awarded in the summer of 1885, Keith-Falconer acting as Examiner on this occasion.

The May term passed quietly by. The work of study
and of teaching went steadily on, none the less that the
new interest, of which we have to speak in the following
chapter, became more and more engrossing. In the course
of the term, Keith-Falconer was offered and accepted the
post of Examiner for the Semitic Languages Tripos of the

succeeding February.   For this he set his share of the
papers, though he did not return from Aden in sufficient
time to take part in the actual work of examination.   At
the end of the term he resigned his college lectureship,
which he had held since October, 1883.

Ready at all times to do all that in him lay to encourage
a zeal for honest athletic exercise, Keith-Falconer accepted,
on May 2, the post of President of a Cycling Club, that of
the Cambridge Young Men's Christian Association.   In
the previous summer he had acted for them as judge at
their fifth Annual Races, on August 14; but in August,
1885, he was unable to be present and again act as judge,
and wrote a very kindly letter to the secretary regretting
it, offering at the same time a prize for the winner in a
four-miles bicycle race.

August was spent at Trent Park and Keith-Hall, and in
September, Keith-Falconer again went for a bicycle tour
with his friend Mr. R——, over much the same part of
Sutherlandshire which they had visited in the previous
year.

One can hardly conceive a greater contrast than that
which now awaited him.   Fresh from " the hills, and
heather, and lochs, and linns " of the wild north-west, he
was now, after a very short visit to Cambridge, to find
himself a dweller in the grim Arabian settlement of Aden.

CHAPTER VIII

ADEN.

" Um zu überzeugen, sei du überzeugt ;
Um zu rühren, sei du gerührt."

SAILER.

THERE is probably no place on the whole surface of the
habitable globe more utterly arid and dreary to the eye
than Aden. A peninsula of black, volcanic rock, joined
to the mainland by a low, sandy isthmus, a burning
tropical sky, and an almost total absence of vegetation, form
an uninviting picture. "It is not a place," writes a
resident, " to which any one could possibly ever come for
pleasure." Yet from the mission stand-point it is a place
presenting a striking union of exceptional advantages.

Before speaking of these, however, it will be well to
attempt first a very brief general description of the place
itself.[1] Aden is situated on the south coast of the province
of Yemen, in Arabia Felix, about 100 miles east of the
Straits of Bab-el-Mandeb, where the waters of the Red
Sea meet those of the Indian Ocean. The rocky peninsula
of which we have spoken is an irregular oval about five
miles long from east to west, and three from north to
south; and rises at its highest point to an elevation of
over 1,700 feet above the sea-level. It encloses a good-

---

[1] The fullest account of Aden known to me is Captain (now
Major) Hunter's *Account of the British Settlement of Aden in
Arabia*. London, 1877.

sized harbour, where steamers from Europe enter almost daily.

At the western end of the peninsula is the small town known as Steamer Point, whose name sufficiently indicates its character. Here are several streets of stone houses, a church, several public buildings, and the coaling stations of Government and various shipping companies. This is the cooler end of the peninsula, as during the hotter months the breezes here come directly off the sea, whereas at Aden itself, built as it is in the crater of an extinct volcano, hot sandy winds prevail.

From Steamer Point, a road passes through Maala, a village chiefly occupied by the Somalis, of whom mention must be made presently, and enters the Crater through what is known as the Main Pass Gate.

Aden itself, at the eastern end of the peninsula, is a town consisting of about 2,000 houses, and a population of perhaps 20,000, and is divided into two nearly equal parts by the dry bed of a watercourse. The heat, as may well be supposed from the position of the town, is very great, the shade temperature ranging, it is said, from 75° to over 100°.

The question of the water supply of Aden is naturally at all times a matter of great moment. The need is met in various ways; from wells a few miles distant, in or near the village of Shaikh Othman, from which a large quantity is conveyed into Aden in leather-skins on camels and in boats. There is also an aqueduct from the above village, but the water thus conveyed is not fit for drinking purposes. A considerable supply is also obtained from the Tanks, large reservoirs which store up the rain-water. So steep are the hills, and so hard the rocks, and so slight is the coating of soil upon them, that very little of the rain is absorbed; and thus in spite of the small rain-fall, a considerable body of water may altogether be stored. Besides all these sources of the water supply, a fair quantity of good water is yielded by condensers, and it is this which is mainly used by Europeans for drinking purposes.

As regards the history of the place,[1] we find that in 1538 the Turks became possessors of the province of Yemen, having overthrown the native Imams. After about a century of Turkish rule, the Imams regained their power, till in 1735 the Sultan of Lahej broke loose from his allegiance, possessed himself of Aden, and became the founder of a line of independent rulers. In the year 1837, an English vessel was wrecked near Aden, and the passengers and crew suffered ill-treatment at the hands of the Arabs. In consequence of this, it was agreed that, besides other compensation, the peninsula of Aden should be ceded to the English. A lack of good faith, however, was shewn in carrying out this arrangement, and the town was taken by assault on January 19, 1839, and was henceforward reckoned as part of the Bombay Presidency. It was thus the first acquisition of new territory to the Empire in the reign of Queen Victoria.

What now, it may be asked, are the special missionary advantages of this place which can counterbalance its very obvious disadvantages?

First then may be noted its important geographical position. Only 10½ days' journey from England, and nearly equidistant between Suez and Bombay, it may justly be called one of the great central points of the world. It is a coaling station for the steamers of the Peninsular and Oriental and other great lines; so that the traffic of the world, long diverted into the route round the Cape of Good Hope, is now returning on its ancient lines.

But secondly, it is not merely as a depôt for foreign traffic that we must view Aden, great as is the importance which that gives the place, but as the point to which the caravans from the interior converge. These come into

---

[1] Hunter, pp. 163, sqq.

Aden daily. At sunrise, hundreds of camels, laden with coffee, fruit, fodder, grain, wood, water, and other things, are led into the town by their Bedawi drivers. The number of camels that entered Aden in the year 1875-76 amounted to no less than 267,845.[1]

Yet another advantage, and that one of the highest importance, lies in the fact that Aden is British territory, and that British influence extends far into the interior. It is estimated that the independent tribes between Aden and the Turkish frontier number about 120,000 souls, and these are subsidised by our Government, somewhat on the principle of the grants made to the Highland clans before 1745. In return, their good behaviour is secured, caravans can pass in safety, and risks of molestation to Europeans are much lessened. The sheikhs of these tribes come into Aden periodically for their money, and thus possibilities of intercourse are opened up into the interior. This last advantage is obviously exceedingly great, and it is one upon which Keith-Falconer constantly insisted. Striking confirmation of this is afforded by the following remarks which I extract from a paper by Major-General Haig, R.E. :—

"I have recently, while travelling through Yemen and visiting the Somali coast, had occasion to notice again and again what a powerful and far-reaching influence of this kind is exercised by Aden. I had no conception of it before. There are many things there which we regret and would gladly see altered; but these things, though they may detract from, cannot obliterate, the impression made upon the surrounding races and countries by this scene of strong, just and wise government. Aden is visited by thousands from hundreds of miles all round—from Somaliland, from Hadramaut, from Yemen, from the countries along the Red Sea, and all take back with them an ideal of government to which in their own lands they are entire strangers. And often they may be heard contrasting the

[1] Hunter, p. 86.

ADEN

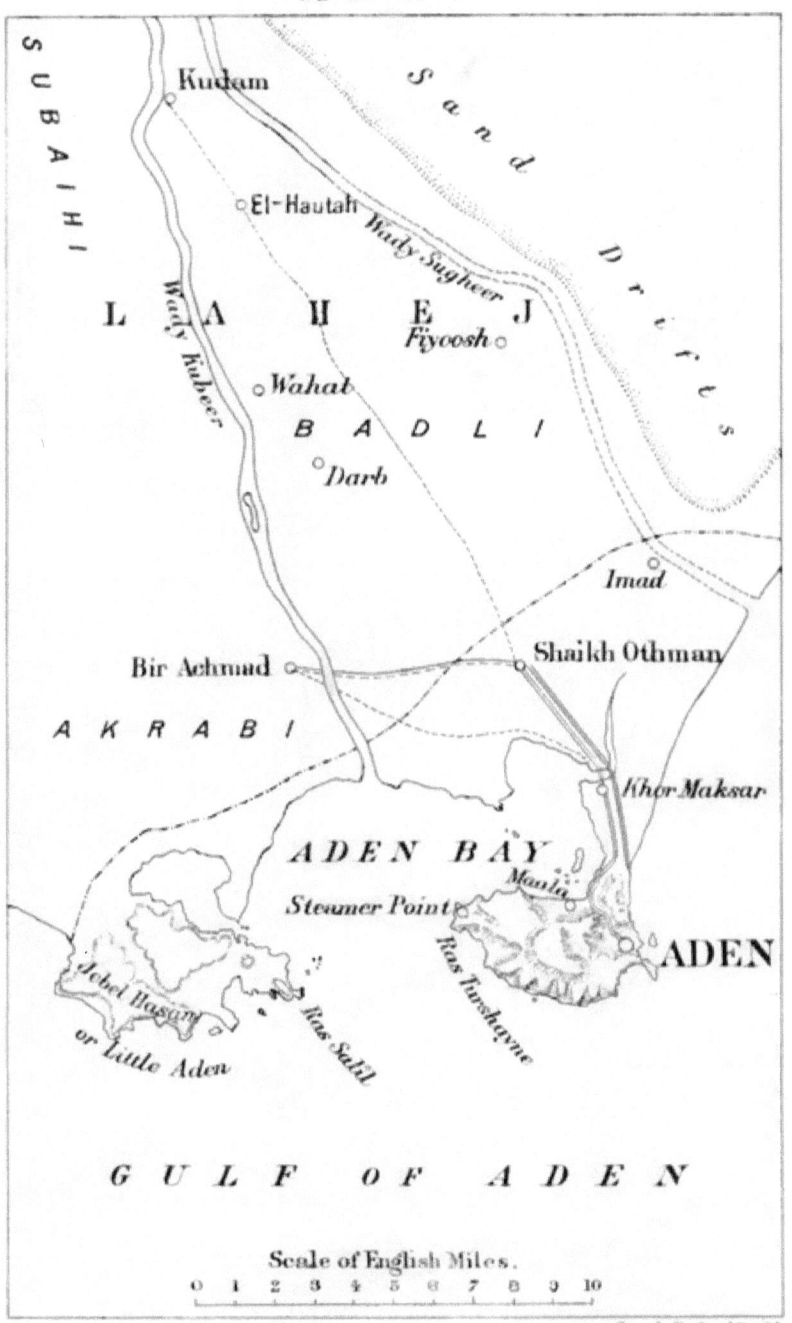

SUBAIHI

Kudam

El-Hautah

Wady Rubeer

L A H E J

Wady Sugheer

Fiyoosh

Wahat

B A D L I

Darb

Imad

Bir Achmad

Shaikh Othman

A K R A B I

Khor Maksar

ADEN BAY

Manla

Steamer Point

ADEN

Jebel Hasan
or Little Aden

Ras Salil

Ras Tarshayne

Sand Drifts

GULF OF ADEN

Scale of English Miles.

0 1 2 3 4 5 6 7 8 9 10

Stanford's Geog.l Estab.t

Cambridge: Deighton Bell & Co.

two conditions—the peace, the order, the liberty, the just administration of the law, the religious toleration (this of the Jews especially) to be found in Aden, with the very reverse of all these things everywhere else. I was constantly reminded of this in Yemen. Aden is known to the remotest corners of that magnificent country, and the people are quietly drawing their own inferences, and sometimes manifesting preferences which are evidently not a little irritating to the Turkish authorities. How much more powerful for good would this influence have been if, instead of the timid policy that would avoid the place because of the evils there, there had been men capable of presenting to its thousands of visitors in their own tongue that Gospel which is the true basis of Christian civilization!" [1]

Weighty and pregnant with grave significance to us, whether as Christians or as Englishmen, is that last sentence.

Finally, two other points may be urged in connection with Aden. The Jews are scattered all over Yemen in considerable numbers,[2] and a good-sized isolated community of them had their settlement near Aden. A very different race, the Somalis, must also be named. Of this people, who belong to the African race on the opposite coast, there are thousands in Aden, and at this point missionary operations might be begun among them before continuous work was attempted on the opposite coast.

Taking all these things into account, it will be seen that a very promising field for missionary enterprise presented itself. Given a missionary possessing the requisite qualifications, indomitable zeal for the spread of the Gospel, a thorough command of Arabic, tact and judgement in plan and in action, and bodily strength which could endure the

---

[1] "On both Sides of the Red Sea," in the *Church Missionary Intelligencer and Record* for May, 1887 (p. 282).

[2] Their numbers are estimated by Gen. Haig to be not less than 60,000. *Ibid.* June, p. 351.

burning heat of Aden—given all these, then under God's blessing, a door might indeed be opened from which Islam might be assailed under the most favourable conditions.

That all these qualifications, except the last, were strikingly united in Keith-Falconer, must be obvious to all who knew him well. He had been a true-hearted servant of Christ throughout his life, and in gradually widening spheres of usefulness he had always sought to teach others how great was the blessing he himself possessed. He had a striking aptitude for the acquisition of languages, and had devoted several years of steady work to Arabic, in whose richness and fulness he took an ever-increasing delight. As we have seen, his patient study of the Arabic of books at Cambridge and at Leipzig had been supplemented by a winter's residence in a rather out of the way part of Egypt, with a view to the colloquial use of the language. After his return to Cambridge in October, 1882, none of his other interests, and there were many, ever dulled his love for his Arabic, and had the *rôle* of the scholar pure and simple been the aim he set before himself, and had his life been prolonged, it is certain that he would in time have ranked high, very high, among the Orientalists of the century.

Such, however, was by no means his ideal. Pleasant and indeed useful as is the life of the scholar, pre-eminently pleasant as he ever felt his own Cambridge life to be, he believed that God had entrusted him with gifts which called for a wider field of exercise. He had, it is true, side by side with his studies engaged in works of evangelization and beneficence here in England; but while to the last his heart was deeply bound up with the work that was being done at Barnwell, and at Mile-End, of which I have spoken in a previous chapter, still it seemed as if some scheme ought to present itself in which Christian zeal and linguistic power might work hand in hand, or rather, shall I say, in which his intellectual attainments and his learning might be to him something more than a mere parallel interest, existing side by side with, but having no connection with, work for Christ.

Viewed in this light, the feeling deepens that in Keith-Falconer was to be found the true type of the champion of the Cross against Islam, the teacher of the Bible against the Koran, the herald proclaiming Jesus against the False Prophet.

In Keith-Falconer's own heart and mind too this feeling had existed in a way for some time before it bore definite fruit; a feeling of which he was only half conscious himself, manifesting its presence by increased zeal in study, increased earnestness in the cause of the Gospel, combined all the time with a feeling of uncertainty, of craving for some line of work not yet apparent. In this state of things, with this impulse working underground, as it were, all that was wanted was the touch which should bring it to the surface, should combine his varied gifts, and make them work as one force to a definite end.

I have said in the preceding chapter that towards the end of the year 1884, Keith-Falconer's thoughts first began to be definitely drawn to the foreign mission field, but as yet without reference to any special sphere of work.

The way in which the idea of choosing Aden as the sphere of his labours first occurred to him was this. A paper had been written by General Haig, from whose interesting articles I have already quoted, strongly urging upon Christians the duty of attempting the evangelization of Arabia. A summary of this was published in the *Christian* newspaper in February, 1885 (no. 785, p. 13), where Keith-Falconer read it, and thenceforward the idea was slowly developed, from an interest in which the mind itself hardly realized how great a hold had been taken on it, to the day when, as though in answer to the question "Who will go for us?" he answered, not with eager but evanescent zeal, not with vague, crude ideas, only half-formed and doomed by their very nature to failure, but with a resolution as calm as it was deep, " Here am I, send me."

The immediate outcome of the perusal of General Haig's article was a request on Keith-Falconer's part for an interview, and he accordingly met the General in London on Feb. 21, 1885, to talk about Aden. In a letter to the present writer, General Haig remarks :—

" My impression of that conversation is that he came not only to get information, but to say that his mind was already made up to go out for six months and see what the place and prospects of work were like. . . . . We joined in prayer that he might be guided and blest in all his thoughts about Arabia."

Besides the advantages presented by Aden from the missionary stand-point, there might further be added the fact that the field was, broadly speaking, well-nigh untrodden. I need not say that this remark is made with the fullest recognition of the important work done at Aden by the resident chaplain, who serves the two churches, at the Camp and Steamer Point respectively. His work, however, moved in altogether different lines to that which Keith-Falconer was beginning now to picture more and more definitely to himself as his own. The chaplain's duty was to Aden viewed as a British possession and to minister to the Christian residents. He was expected *not* to work among the natives. Such work has of course infinite possibilities of usefulness, but is an altogether different work from the missionary's attack on a definite form of error.

There was also, it is true, a Roman Catholic Mission, founded in 1840, and having chapels at the Crater, and at Steamer Point. As to this, Keith-Falconer, writing from Aden in January, 1886, remarks :—

" The two chaplains, besides attending to the Roman

community (Europeans, Goanese, Abyssinians, &c.), work among Somali outcasts and orphans; but I am told that their converts generally lapse into Islam when they quit the Roman Catholic school. There is, besides, a convent at Steamer Point kept by sisters of the 'Good Shepherd,' where friendless girls of all nationalities are received and educated, and brought up in the Roman Catholic faith.[1] The sisters also keep a day-school which is purely secular. From all that I hear, the Roman Catholic missions in Aden have failed. It may fairly be said that nothing effective has yet been done in Aden to lead the people to a living faith in the Son of God."

One of the two great English societies, the Church Missionary Society, had about this time considered the question of an Arabian mission, which had been urged upon them by General Haig. As a result of this, Dr. and Mrs. Harpur were sent out in October, 1885; and after remaining at Cairo for some months to study Arabic, went on to Aden in March, 1886; about the time when Keith-Falconer was leaving it at the end of his first visit.

It may be interesting to add here that on General Haig's return to Aden in December, 1886, he and Dr. Harpur started on a missionary tour in a steamer along the Somali coast, and subsequently to Hodeida, on the Arabian side of the Red Sea.[2] This place seemed to promise an important opening, and I understand that the Church Missionary Society has founded a station there.

All this, however, was, it will be seen, subsequent to Keith-Falconer's first visit in November, 1885; and thus, with the qualifications of the man pre-eminently adapted to meet the special requirements of the place, there was the further satisfactory thought that he was not seeking to build on other men's labours.

One disquieting thought, however, remained, the ques-

---

[1] The Roman Catholic nuns have, since that letter was written, broken up their establishment.

[2] Haig, *u. s.* April, p. 219; June, p. 353.

tion whether the climate was one in which he and his
young wife could live and work. If it should appear that
the constitution of either was really unfitted to live in the
terrible heat of an Aden summer, it would be clear that the
idea must be given up ; it was but a passing impulse, not
the direct call from God.

To settle this question he spared no pains. He read
carefully everything that he could find written about Aden,
he consulted several gentlemen who had had long acquaintance with Aden, and he sought the opinions of the highest
medical authorities as to the personal case of himself and
his wife.

As the outcome of all this, he gradually became fully
convinced that the attempt could be made satisfactorily,
that the heat, though very great, was dry from the absence
of vegetation, and therefore less exhausting, and that by
the exercise of proper precautions it might be sufficiently
borne.

This conclusion afforded him very great satisfaction.
Well do I remember how day by day, as we met, he would
tell with pleasure some piece of fresh favourable evidence.
Thus it appeared that the percentage of sickness among the
soldiers at Aden Camp was distinctly less than among
those at Bombay.   One day with exceeding glee he told me
that an English lady, for some years a resident at Aden,
had said to him, " It is hot certainly, but there were few
days when I could not enjoy a game of tennis during some
part of the day."   This lady however lived, I fancy, at
Steamer Point.

Clear as might be his own belief on this subject, still it
would naturally be with some reluctance that his friends
could be brought to consent to his settling at a place which
bore, justly or unjustly, so bad a name.

To meet these not unreasonable scruples, he resolved
upon the wise course of testing the place for himself by a
temporary residence at Aden, sufficiently long to be con-

vincing, one way or the other, before absolutely taking the final resolve.

Much will have to be said by-and-bye of Keith-Falconer's idea that a prominent part in the work of his mission should be that of the Hospital, where medical and surgical aid should be freely given to Arab and other applicants. He justly felt that the gratitude excited for help thus given might often, by God's blessing, lead men to listen attentively to the message which these helpers in their bodily needs sought to deliver to them.

It was not from any idea that he could himself wisely take a leading part in this element of the work, but, as he humbly expressed it, that he " might be able to help the doctor a little," that for some time before this he had devoted some attention to medicine and surgery ; and had accordingly attended some lectures, and seen a certain amount of operating work at Addenbrooke's Hospital at Cambridge. To know something about drugs, and to have some little familiarity with the practical details of surgery, were wise precautions on the part of a missionary, even though he had as his companion a properly qualified medical man.

One point more remained to be settled, the question as to whether he should go absolutely as a free lance, or should associate himself more or less closely with some existing organization. This did not take long to settle. In spite of some advantages arising from the greater freedom of action in the former case, the advantages on the other side, the sympathy and support from home, the sharing of the responsibility, the help to be had from the experience of others, were obviously preponderating. Nor, this settled, was there any question as to the body with which he should connect himself. His father had always been warmly attached to the Free Church of Scotland, and had been an elder of that Church ; and though educated in England, and having the highest esteem for the Church of England, and counting some of her clergy among his most intimate friends, Keith-Falconer remained throughout a member of the Church in which as a child he had been brought up.

Accordingly, after some preliminary correspondence, he met in conference the Foreign Missions' Committee of the Free Church on September 14, and, after generally describing the nature of his proposed mission, asked to be in some way recognized by the Free Church. The Committee warmly accepted his offer, and commended him and his work " to the Great Head of the Church."

All being at length settled, Keith-Falconer sailed with his wife from England on October 7, on this occasion taking the longer sea route by the Bay of Biscay. They reached Aden on October 28, and remained there till March 6 in the following spring.

It will obviously be best to allow the story of the journey and of the residence at Aden to be told, as far as possible, in Keith-Falconer's own words. The extracts which follow are from a letter to his youngest sister written at sea :—

> "S. S. SURAT,
>   *Oct.* 13, 1885.

" You would enjoy this if you were here. In four hours we shall be at Gibraltar; the Spanish coast is visible. Unfortunately we shall not be allowed to land there, unless the quarantine has been raised, which is not likely. . . . . The sea is dotted with sea-horses, but quite calm, at least the ship does not roll or pitch : the water is a dirty blue colour. You probably imagine we are revelling in warmth and sunshine. This is a great mistake. We are on deck, but with our great-coats on, and would be in the saloon, but for the sake of the salubrious marine atmosphere.

" We had a rough and dangerous time in the Bay of Biscay. . . . Shortly after passing Ushant, the gale predicted by the Yankees swept down on us. Friday night, Saturday, and Saturday night, we were the sport of the waves. 'My interior is so admirably organised that I was not the least inclined to be sick; but poor G. was awfully ill. . . . . The pitching was highly inconvenient. The saloon in the morning was a mass of broken glass and crockery. Every single pitch made all the glass and crockery slide violently as far as they could: and every now and then, a particularly violent lurch would produce effects which would have done credit to a bull in a china shop. Besides the pitching and noise of shivering crockery, we enjoyed *close* proximity to the screw. Every two minutes it would get out of water and buzz round so as to give our end of the ship a perfect ague fit. The doctor—a jolly young paddy—was in constant attendance, and said G. was one of the worst sufferers. Hardly any one—not one quarter of the people—came to meals all through it. The top of the saloon was carefully closed to keep it from the waves, and darkness was added to danger. The engines were stopped for eight hours on one of the nights and every effort was made to prevent the waves filling the ship. The Captain told me that for some hours it was blowing as hard as it could well blow, and that if the storm had gone on longer, the results might have been disastrous. One of the boats was swept by a sea from one of its davits and they cut it away. The crash of that wave nearly killed an old lady with terror, she thought that all was up. By Sunday the gale had abated, and we have had a beautiful run. . . . . The waiters showed great skill during the storm: fancy helping you to soup when the ship is like this [here is given a rough sketch of a ship rolling heavily]. There were a great many falls and bruises; I got a nasty one: I had grasped an iron rail and it gave way. . . . . There are several dogs, including two collies, on board: also a parrot, a cow and goats and sheep, and three pussies, and ducks and chickens. . . . .

"If you are in London when Charrington's hall is opened, I wish you would go with M. and every one you can get, to assist at the ceremony. It will be a magnificent sight. The building, very nearly as large as Spurgeon's, will be crammed. Very likely Spurgeon will be present and give an address. . . . .

"I was so busy at the the last moment writing notes and sending cheques to tradesmen that I had only five minutes

wherein to say goodbye to ——, and must have seemed un-
feeling; but I hate these long, sentimental leave-takings,
and they are better avoided."

The following letter to myself was written a few weeks
after his arrival at Aden, and gives some further details as
to the voyage. It is somewhat later in date than the two
which follow it, but I have placed it first because of the
continuous account which it furnishes. After describing
the storm in the Bay of Biscay, he proceeds :—

"We got one good day at Malta, and enjoyed the trip
ashore very much. We drove some four miles to the
governor's summer residence and roamed in the garden
there. The country was very parched owing to the hot
summer they have had. We also saw the 'dried monks.'
In a certain monastery, it was the custom till quite recently to exhume the dead monks after lying one year
underground, and to stand them in niches in the walls of
the underground passages. The island is utterly priest-
ridden. . . . . In the treaty by which the English acquired
the island it was stipulated that no interference with the
religion of the people should be practised. If you give
a Testament away in the street you are liable to arrest. A
little travelling in Roman Catholic countries makes one
realise that the Papacy is a lover of darkness rather than
light. Mrs. —— last year met with a French student who
spoke Provençal, and persuaded him to translate one of the
Gospels into Provençal, as the *millions* of Provençal-speaking
people are still without the Bible in their own tongue. He
did so from the Greek ; but to this day he has failed to
send more than *parts* of his MS. He now confesses that
the priests have persuaded him to throw difficulties in the
way of publishing the Provençal Gospel. Yet I know that
he was quite competent, and the Bible Society had consented to print his MS.

"We had a few hours at Port Said and a day at Suez.
The passage through the Canal was monotonous. We
moved along at about four to six miles an hour, and had to
stop during the night. The canal is just 100 miles long.
The Red Sea was hot and steamy, but nothing to speak of.

The deck had a double awning above it, and there was generally a breeze blowing. We turned the corner at Perim island (where there is now a rival coal company) very early in the morning. The Arabian coast all the way thence to Aden was very fine. We arrived in the harbour about 2.30 P.M.; and rowed ashore in a long boat pulled by Somalis. These people form nearly half the population, and are far more attractive than the Arabs. They are very quick at picking up a smattering of English, and all speak Arabic. Many of them are tall and well-built, while the Arabs are generally short and stumpy. We found our rooms ready for us at the Hôtel de l'Europe, a square edifice built round a court, in which a café chantant used to be carried on. The establishment belongs to a Jew from Smyrna, by descent a Spaniard: but the real manager is a Somali, who proved of the greatest service to us. He can talk Arabic, Somali, Hindustani, English, and a little French. The cooking was excellent, and would have done credit to a Parisian *chef.* Yet the kitchen was about as big as your old study, and for range had only three or four fire-holes in the stone. *All* our cooking utensils that we bought when we came into our bungalow cost under £2 10s. 0d. The cooks here are either Portuguese from Goa or Hindoos, and never expect better kitchen accommodation than what I have described. We stayed at the hotel six weeks, finding nothing to complain of except the tremendous clouds of dust and sand driven in by the high winds which prevail at this time of year. I certainly felt the heat a good deal at first, but one gets accustomed and it is rather cooler now. We were lucky in finding a bungalow.

" Aden town—not 'Steamer Point' where the hotels are —is situated *in* an extinct crater, surrounded by barren, frowning, and cinder-like rocks (the highest is 1700 feet high) on all sides, except where there is an opening revealing the sea. To get into the crater from Steamer Point the road winds through a pass, and our house is situated close to the point where the road emerges from the pass on the crater side. The whole town lies spread out at our feet: the bazaars being about one mile from us. The house is perched on the side of a steep hill and is built in steps, so that our bedroom is much higher than the dining-room. There is a separate building (connected by a bridge with the house) meant for sleeping in: my wife's maid lives in it. We have two rooms and a spacious verandah covered in by boards and lattice work (to break the force of the wind). In the evening we sit on the top of the house, and should sleep there in the summer. The verandah is our drawing-room and reception room; the drawing-room proper we use as dining-room and study, and the room which is meant for the dining-room we sleep in. We feed pretty much as in England, only our meat is confined to mutton (4 pence a pound) and chicken (8 pence each but very small). . . . . The expensive part of our food is the tinned things. We are now getting a box from the Stores. We are badly off for vegetables: we have potatoes, and spinach and tinned things. The native vegetables are nasty.

" I begin the day by giving my wife an Arabic lesson. She is nearly through Socin's little grammar. Then I read Arabic all the morning. About 4, I go to the town and converse with natives, coming home to dinner at 7.30. I always carry an Arabic Gospel, and make a point of reading it with the natives. Though it is done into good classical Arabic, most understand it fairly well.

" Yesterday I met a young Arab whom I knew. He came with me at my invitation to the *tanks*—(great stone reservoirs which catch the rain)—where there is a little garden, the only one in Aden: we sat among the trees reading at the end of St. Luke. He seemed interested, and going back he asked me to let him come every evening and hear more. I should generally look upon such a request as a move towards a further request for bakshish. But I can't help thinking he is an enquirer. All seem to have great respect for knowledge of *nahwi*, *i.e.* grammatical, literary Arabic. I constantly observe people looking at me in the street and saying, ' That man knows Kurân and *nahwi*.'

" Yesterday a *fikih* (*i.e.* schoolmaster who teaches Kurân to the children, and officiates at a mosque) came up to the house, and conversed with me, and before leaving went through his prostrations and prayers for my benefit. These kind of men seem generally very willing to show off. They are supposed to know the whole Kurân by

heart. Certainly this man can reel it off from any point
you like to pitch upon.

"There is a town 10 miles off, within British limits, and
with a mixed population of about 7000; where I hope to
settle. Here there is water and vegetation, and the climate
is perceptibly cooler than in Aden. My notion is to start
an industrial refuge, day-school and surgery there. There
are two principal doors to Arabia, the children who can be
trained up in the faith of Christ and the medical aid.
Arabs often come from a long distance to Aden to be
treated, and these would stop short at our mission-house—
for the town I speak of is on the road to the interior.
There are plenty of orphans and castaways whom one
could get. I find that travelling within a certain radius is
regarded as quite safe: and all the natives I have asked
declare positively that the road to San'â (a large town
garrisoned by the Turks and 200 miles inland) is perfectly
safe. I am sure there is a great opening for a missionary,
especially if accompanied by a surgeon.

"If I build and get a plot granted (which is an easy
matter at Shaikh Othman, the town ten miles off), I shall
hand them over to the Free Church of Scotland. They
have recognized me as representing them."

To his Mother.

"ADEN, *Nov.* 18, 1885.

"The heat has somewhat abated, and it is quite cool
and pleasant indoors. A breeze is constantly blowing,
which is pleasant, but without invigorating effect. I
doubt whether any one could live here long without a
weakening of all his faculties. I read Arabic for several
hours every day, and a native *fikih* or schoolmaster comes
daily to instruct me. . . . .

"Aden is not without its disadvantages as a mission
station. The climate is very enervating and at the same
time there is no hill-station anywhere near for the missionaries to go and recruit: but possibly after a time such
a hill-station will be opened. The relations between the
English and the neighbouring tribes become more satisfactory as time goes on. . . . .

"Last night, —— dined with us. He went out to India with Chinese Gordon and Lord Ripon. Gordon wore an ordinary black *frock-coat* down the Red Sea, and seeing in the newspaper that slavery had cropped up again in the Khedive's dominions, promptly wrote a letter to that potentate, roundly abusing him for breaking his promises and calling him a double-faced rascal. When they got to Bombay, and a grand dinner was to be held, Gordon refused to go in, in fact was found to have *no* dress-clothes. They persuaded him to let them rig him out in a composition suit, half civil, half military, borrowed from other persons. Directly dinner was over, the Secretary had vanished and was found in his room smoking cigarettes, as was his wont, with his legs on the table and the borrowed plumage strewing the floor. Next day he resigned.

"I never cease to regret that I did not spend some time with him in Palestine, as he himself proposed.

"To-day we are sending a little Abyssinian boy, a rescued slave, to Zanzibar, to be educated by the missionaries. The Political Resident asked us to take him. As we could not, we send him to Zanzibar. . . . . We expect in three weeks to enter a bungalow overlooking Aden proper. . . . . We are both perfectly well, but until about a week ago, when the weather became cooler, I felt the heat rather badly.

"G. is struggling with Arabic. Arabic grammars should be strongly bound, because learners are so often found to dash them frantically on the ground."

To the same.

"ADEN, *Dec.* 1, 1885.

"Our bungalow, overlooking the Camp and main town, is almost ready. We have engaged a Portuguese cook and a Portuguese butler and a Somali servant, and hired some furniture. I engaged a Portuguese cook a few days ago, on the strength of good certificates, but I dismissed him to day for drunkenness. I wish I could get a Moslem, as they are abstainers. Dr. and Mrs. Colson—the port surgeon—dined with us last night, and he assured me that we have nothing to fear on the score of health. . . . .

The dust is fearfully bad now, the winds being so strong. The rooms ought to be swept and dusted three times a day. . . . .

" We sleep to-night at Shaikh Othman. There are two bungalows there. The owner of one, a Parsee gentleman, has given us leave to use it. We take food with us and the Somali waiter and factotum of this establishment. He is very clever and speaks about six languages, as badly as he does fluently. We want to see the place, so as to get a better idea of its suitability for a mission station.

" As living is very cheap here compared to what it is in England, I shall have a lot of spare cash to spend in keeping up a staff: *e.g.* my white suit of American drill costs me about six shillings. . . . . I want to get a qualified surgeon to come out with me next year, and an artisan. My idea is to start an industrial orphanage. There is a great dearth of good carpenters. In fact there is not one. If we could, besides bringing them up in the faith of Christ, teach them a handicraft, they would be able to make a living and the orphanage would be self-supporting. Little can be done with Moslem adults, but young children *can* be trained aright."

The following letter to General Haig (Dec. 16), clearly shews the general character of his aims :—

" . . . . First about my connection with the Free Church of Scotland. I am still, as before, a lay member of that body; only their Foreign Missions' Committee have recognized me as a missionary representing their Church. This does not bind me in the very least, while it may be useful to me in my work. Shortly before leaving England I met their Foreign Missions' Committee, and asked that I might be recognized in some way by the Free Church : and they passed a minute stating that I had made the request, and that they—the Committee—recognize me as representing the Free Church.

" Though I am not paid by them, I have their recognition and sympathy. At present there is no need for me to enter into any closer or more formal connection with them, but when a mission-building and school go up, I shall wish to make them over to the Free Church. I fully see the advantages of having an organisation at home to back one up and to share the responsibility of the work.

"I have made up my mind that the right place for me to settle at is Shaikh Othman, not Aden. This will leave Aden and Steamer Point open to the Church Missionary Society. Though I do not think that a medical missionary would have much scope in Aden, I think that a Bible and tract room, and preaching-hall might be started there.

"Now let me tell you briefly what I have just written to Dr. G. Smith, Secretary of the Free Church Missions' Committee.

"Children are far more hopeful than adults. Then a Christian school should be started, if possible. Also, in gaining the confidence of the people, in pushing inland, and in creating opportunities for introducing the Gospel, a medical man (especially a surgeon) would be a valuable aid. Now Aden and Steamer Point are well provided by Government with free schools and free hospitals. As it would be difficult or impossible to compete with the Government in the matter of schools and hospitals, I look for some other place. Shaikh Othman presents itself. Here there is scope for a medical missionary and for a school, the Government provision being very inadequate. Further, the climate of Shaikh Othman is better and less enervating, there is plenty of water there, and the ground capable of cultivation. Also Shaikh Othman is 10 miles nearer the interior, and removed from the evil example set by so many of the Europeans who live in or pass through Aden. It would further be very difficult to get a good site in Aden.

"These are the principal reasons which decide me in favour of Shaikh Othman. My wish is to build a missionaries' bungalow, and start an industrial orphanage and school there. There are plenty of outcast and orphan children in the place, some of whom might be brought up in the faith of Christ and become native evangelists and teachers. I should also like to see a medical mission in connection with this institution, which when built I should wish to hand over to the Free Church of Scotland.

"I have made an informal application for a grant of

land, and am told that I can have it at a nominal rent whenever I begin to build.

" I hope to spend next summer in England, and if all goes well to begin building in October. . . . . I have asked Dr. Smith to make it known in Scotland that I want a surgeon to work with me at Shaikh Othman.

" As yet I can only walk about the town picking up all the Arabic I can and reading aloud from the Gospels. I have made some acquaintances, and find that whenever I go to see one of them his friends and neighbours collect round the door or come inside, so that I have a congrega- tion at once, though rather a noisy one. The coffee shops as a rule are *too* noisy.

" I hope to visit Lahej soon, but fear I shall be unable to go to San'â. I should not know where to leave my wife. When I have a colleague at Shaikh Othman with a wife, the two ladies can be together, while the husbands go to San'â and elsewhere.

" If the C.M.S. Missionaries come here, I trust we shall find ways and means of co-operating and helping one another."

To his eldest Sister.

"ADEN, *Jan.* 17, 1886.

" This morning I mounted a little brick-coloured donkey (artificially coloured) and galloped down to a certain pier, whence I plunged—without the donkey—into the sea. This is my first sea-bathe. The water is quite tepid. On the way back, the little ' donk' (as the boys call it) col- lapsed under my weight, which made me very angry with it, even to beating. . . . . To-day there is a great ziâra, or festival at Shaikh Othman, and every one who can afford, goes over there. Our hammâl, Yûsuf, saw a huge waggon, for 40 people, going there drawn by a *camel*. The people indulge in a great many holidays here. For instance, no Jew will do a stroke of work from Friday evening till Sun- day morning ; and the Arabs and Somalis are always going to these ziâras. You would enjoy the evenings here after sunset. The air is so balmy and the colours are beautiful. After dinner we often sit on the roof, whence we see all

Aden spread out before us. On these occasions I generally send for my Somali servants and converse Arabic with them. They are very ignorant and superstitious. They tell me that the Arabs believe the English to be nearer to them in race than any other people! They explained to me that the reason why the Jews were expelled from Spain was, that a certain Jew had bewitched the Spanish pigs, so that they all ran into the sea! I have begun to learn Somali. It is rather difficult, and the only grammar in existence is not satisfactory. My teacher, a young Somali, who knows Arabic better than most, has got into difficulties through his improvidence. He amassed some money and then did the pilgrimage to Mecca, and so spent it all, besides giving up his employment. This pilgrimage is one of the curses of Islam. The other day a Somali young lady proposed to him, and according to Somali custom he was obliged under pain of disgrace to accept. But he declares he is very fond of her, only he has not enough money to marry her for some time. We have ascended Shumsân's highest peak (1700 feet), and saw the wild black dogs, and the wild sheep, and the kites and vultures. Part of the way was quite green and flowery. At the top, oh joy! we found tea awaiting us. I am learning to speak Arabic quite nicely, but it will be long before I can deliver real 'discourses.'"

To his Mother.

"ADEN, *Jan.* 27, 1886.

"Many thanks for the *Contemporary.* The Bishop of Peterborough's article is very good as far as the last point. Gladstone's reply to Huxley in the *Nineteenth Century* is exceedingly good. . . . . I am reading Moffat, and after that, will take Carey, and then, if time permits, Vinet. I see that V. will interest me least. . . . . You are rather hasty in coming to a certain conclusion about Aden. You forget the summer heat, which is certainly very enervating, perhaps too much so for me, after some years have elapsed. I want to build at Shaikh Othman and pass over the buildings to the Free Church, so that whatever happens to me, the work may be cared for by them.

"Arabic 'portions' are very well received, and even asked for. On Monday week I hope to go to Lahej and the villages with Dr. Jackson, a Scotch military doctor. We go on camels. . . . . The weather is now quite cool, and we have showers almost daily."

To his eldest Sister.

"ADEN, *Jan.* 31, 1886.

"Yesterday I had been telling a group of men about Jesus Christ. Most Mohammedans know that He was the son of Mary and a great prophet; and when I had proved that I knew a good deal about Him, one man said, ' Well, you Franks seem to know about everything.' He did not know that the Christian religion has to do with Christ.

"Many imagine that Europeans are clever people who get drunk and have no religion to speak of. Roman Catholics, when devout, are considered to be idol-worshippers. The priests here have done immense harm. Their converts always relapse. One man told me he had been to a priest to talk about religion, and that the priest had only told him to keep the Ten Commandments. . . . .

"Moffat's life is exceedingly interesting. I bitterly regret not having known him. I might have, easily. And I cannot understand why we never heard of old Mr. Paton before he was on the point of leaving. And Gordon, too! I might have lived with him in Syria. What things I have missed. Not to mention Duff."

The following letter, written to his mother, tells of his furthest journey inland, and is most suggestive of the possibilities of successful work beyond the British frontier. El-Hautah, it may be remarked, is 25 miles inland from Shaikh Othman.

"ADEN, *Feb.* 14, 1886.

". . . . Last Monday I went with a Scotch military doctor to Lahej. The capital, El-Hautah, is in the middle of an oasis about seven miles across. The oasis is fertilized by a stream which loses itself in the sand. The Sultan, a stupid, cruel wretch, owns every inch and does nothing for the people, who are so many serfs. We distributed Gospels, which were most willingly received, and the doctor treated some cases and shot two bustards. . . . .

"The oasis is all cultivated and the sight of so much green was very refreshing. We spent one day at a place five miles beyond El-Hautah, resting under the mango trees by a cool stream. Camel riding is not very pleasant. Our camels were Government ones and very rough riding. One of the drivers in an unwary moment let his camel, a very fierce and powerful brute, get hold of his wrist, when it just lifted him off the ground and shook him from side to side like a rabbit. Fortunately no bone or artery was severed and the man will not lose his hand. This kind of thing is a common occurrence. Sometimes a camel will bite off a man's *head*. The driver had stupidly forgotten to put on the muzzle. There is a terrible amount of disease at El-Hautah, ulcers predominating, and a medical missionary would be welcomed.

To the same.

"Aden, *Feb.* 23, 1886.

". . . . We find the house is haunted by monkeys at night; Dr. Jackson wants to come up and have a shot at them. Gladstone's reply to Huxley we enjoyed very much. Huxley's second reply in last *Nineteenth Century* does not to my mind at all weaken the arguments. I think Drummond must have done himself harm by his contribution to the controversy. Fancy reducing Genesis to the level of George Macdonald's poetry. But Drummond's whole article is vague and intangible to the last degree.

"The weather is gradually warming up, and I expect we shall not need ulsters passing through the Red Sea."

[Continued on *Feb.* 24.]

"Very glad to hear from M. that Charrington's hall is such a success as a building. I knew it would be. He deserves great credit for pulling this grand scheme through."

He then expresses very warmly his wish that he could do yet more than he had been able to do for the great work at Mile-End, adding, " I shall have to spend about £800 to £1000 at Shaikh Othman in all likelihood in a short time. The Resident has directed that the plot I applied for shall be reserved for me till the year ends."

In a letter of February 24 to Dr. George Smith, we learn further details of the journey to El-Hautah :—

" I have applied for a garden plot, and to-day have received a note from the municipal officer to inform me that the site I asked for will be ' reserved ' for me till the end of the year. The plot measures nearly 510 feet by 510 feet, and lies exactly between the old village of Shaikh Othman and the new settlement. A better situation could not be desired. . . . . Since writing last I have been to El-Hautah, the capital of Lahej. It is in an oasis. In the direction of a line drawn from Shaikh Othman to El-Hautah, this oasis extends for fully seven miles, but beyond this I can give you no idea of its dimensions. . . . .

" Though I had been warned to use the utmost caution in introducing ' religious topics ' with the people of Lahej, on account of their supposed fanaticism, I found no difficulty whatever in circulating Arabic Gospels. They were received with the utmost willingness, and several came to the bungalow to get them. Books are greatly valued in Aden and neighbourhood, and the name of Isa, the Messiah, is held in veneration by all. The Injil—Evangelion—a term applied to the whole New Testament, is acknowledged as God's book, and as having come down from heaven. It would not surprise me in the least if a Christian mission, conducted with prudence and self-denial, were welcomed as a message from God. The Roman Catholic missionaries have, I fear, done great harm to the cause of Christianity. They are looked upon by many natives as worshippers of idols and pictures, and so classed with the Hindus. But to return to El-Hautah. The population is said to be about 5000. The houses are all built of mud. The amount of disease and misery is appalling. My companion, a Scotch army-surgeon, treated several cases, one with magic effect;

and we both agreed in thinking that a medical missionary would have his hands full in this wretched town.

" The Sultan owns every inch of the fertile oasis, and the people are so many serfs. His ' soldiers ' get no pay, only their food. One of the natives who came to us for treatment with an extensive sore behind his foot, told us that the Sultan had given him a year's imprisonment for tearing a water-skin, and that the fetter had produced his sore. The Sultan sent to see us, and consulted the doctor about his ailments. On being told that he must take daily exercise, he exclaimed, ' Impossible ! If I shew my nose outside my palace, twenty men run after me crying for justice.' The Sultan took us to see his chief secretary. On seeing this functionary, I was surprised to recognize a man with whom I had conversed at Aden, and to whom I had given a Gospel. He now asked me for the whole Bible. Thus a book given in Aden may be carried far away.

" I was much struck by the comparative coolness of the climate after getting clear of the rocky peninsula of Aden. We got in to El-Hautah at 10.30 A.M., but without being at all inconvenienced by the heat. We rode camels. The nights at El-Hautah (we stayed three nights) were positively cold. I have no doubt it is the same at Shaikh Othman."

It will have been seen how strongly Keith-Falconer insisted in his letters on the importance of the orphanage and the medical side of his mission. I therefore quote some further remarks, shewing in more detail his ideas on these points, from a letter to Dr. George Smith. The orphanage, it will be remembered, was not merely for orphans, but for castaways. These last were mostly Somalis " whose parents are only too willing that they should be fed and cared for by others."

On these points Keith-Falconer writes :—

" It would be necessary to teach the children to work with their hands, and I think that a carpenter or craftsman

of some kind from home or from India should be on the
Mission staff. But the chief object of the institution
would be to train native evangelists and teachers; and a
part of their training should be *medical*. With a slight,
rough-and-ready knowledge of medicine and surgery, they
would find many doors open to them. In the school, reading by means of the Arabic Bible and Christian books,
writing, and arithmetic, would be taught to all; and
English, historical geography, Euclid, algebra, and natural
science to the cleverer children. A native teacher, procur-
able from Syria or Egypt, would be very valuable, and I
think a necessity at first. If it were known in the interior
that a competent medical man and surgeon resided in
Shaikh Othman, the Arabs who now come to Aden for
advice would stop short at our Mission-house; and the
surgeon would have considerable scope both in Shaikh
Othman, El-Hautah, and the little country villages, not to
speak of the opposite African country. Of course the
treatment of surgical cases would involve the keeping of a
few beds. The medical missionary should be a thoroughly
qualified man, as natives often delay to come for advice
until disease has become serious and complicated. The
port-surgeon has impressed this upon me several times.
It should be mentioned that the native assistant at the
Shaikh Othman dispensary often finds that Arabs come
to Shaikh Othman to be treated, and, deriving no benefit,
refuse to go on to Aden and return home. The institution should stand in a cultivated plot or garden. This
would render it far more attractive, and would greatly
benefit the children. It would be possible to arrange for
this in Shaikh Othman, where there is plenty of water
and the soil is good; but not in Aden, where almost utter
barrenness is everywhere found."

One point in connection with Keith-Falconer's life at
Aden, which is not referred to in any of the foregoing
letters, should not be passed over here, the interest he
took in the English soldiers of the garrison. He caused
it to be made known among them that any who wished
might come to his house in the evening, when he would
give them tea, and then have a little devotional meeting.

The soldiers valued the privilege exceedingly, and a dozen or more would come frequently. Often too when out walking, he would, as his manner was, get into kindly conversation with them. He rather surprised them by urging, as he did, the fact that among the greatest hindrances to the cause of mission-work in India and elsewhere may be placed the inconsistent conduct of many professing Christians. It is needless to say that the Aden soldiers reciprocated most warmly this friendly interest taken in them.

The extracts from Keith-Falconer's letters which have been given in the foregoing chapter will, I trust, have sufficiently shown the nature of the work, its difficulties, its exceptional encouragements ; will have shown too with what resolution the young missionary, valiant for the faith, faced his work. Nor was it valiantly only, with the courage that gladly gives up all for Christ, yet fails to give to the sacrifice its full value by neglecting to consider every possible precaution :—a strong, practical commonsense underlies it all, a quality which that first great missionary St. Paul so markedly brings before us.

Thus with all satisfactorily laid in train, and with heart now fully resolved to return in the following autumn and make as his home the place he had experimentally visited, Keith-Falconer and his wife sailed from Aden on March 6, and, after a fortnight's stay at Cairo, sailed from Suez on the 23rd for Brindisi, en route for Cannes. Here he remained for a fortnight, and on April 11 he reached England in the best of health and the cheeriest of spirits.

CHAPTER IX.

PROFESSORSHIP OF ARABIC.

"Den jungen Orientalisten, der sofort als Meister aufgetreten ist." [1]
NÖLDEKE.

ON his arrival in England, Keith-Falconer spent some time at Wimbledon, where his family were then staying, and at Trent Park. On the morning of Easter Day he visited the Great Hall at Mile-End, where he addressed a very large audience on the subject of 'Temptation,' as dealt with in the first chapter of St. James's Epistle. Those who were present speak of this address as the most striking they had ever heard from him.

He returned to Cambridge towards the end of April. He seemed to be in splendid health and vigour of body; and in referring to the two attacks of Aden fever which he had had, said laughingly, " we thought no more of it than you do of colds in England." He was full of the brightest hopes for the success of his work and could now of course speak with much greater confidence than before his visit to Aden. His residence there had convinced him of what indeed he had fully believed in the preceding autumn, that not only was there a vast work waiting to be done, to bring the light of the Gospel amid the darkness of Islam, and that Aden was pre-eminently a place in which to begin the work, but that the climate, hot and trying as it was, need cause him no apprehensions either for himself or his wife, if only proper precautions were taken.

[1] See above, p. 135.

The soldier of the Cross had counted the cost, had weighed with the utmost care every risk, and had taken his final resolve. The manner in which he told his friends this was very characteristic of the man. The resolve was most real and determined, no capricious fancy of an impulsive youth, but the purpose of a strong man who goes forth to the fight, ready to 'spend and be spent' in the cause of Christ. But deep and real as it was, there was nothing stern or repellent in his earnestness. As with his whole nature, so in this particular; he never seemed more genial and sunny than when he told of the past winter's experiences, his house at Aden, his Somali servants, his visits to the interior, and his hopes that God would bless his future endeavours. With the deepest earnestness the most perfect simplicity was blended; it was as though something of the warmth and openness of the boy had been wrought up with the matured reflectiveness of the man.

At this time his plans were to make all necessary preparations in England during the summer, and to leave for Aden at about the end of October.

One chief point was to receive the formal recognition of the General Assembly of the Free Church of Scotland at their Annual Meeting at Edinburgh in May. Another was to find a surgeon to work with him at Aden. It was necessary that his colleague should be a properly qualified medical man, who had had considerable practice in surgery, as cases of some difficulty were likely to occur. But it was no mere scientific man who was wanted, who might be glad to accept the appointment for a few years mainly with the view of studying tropical diseases in a little worked region. His colleague must be a man who, while fully skilled in the details of his profession, which was indispensable, should also be like-minded with himself, animated by the true missionary spirit, bringing his medical and surgical skill, as Keith-Falconer his knowledge of Arabic and his **other** gifts, as his offering to the cause of Christ.

How fully the colleague he ultimately met with justified by his affection and loyalty the choice that had been made, the record of the time spent at Shaikh Othman, during both the sunshine of the hearty work and the anxious time when illness came, fully testifies.

On the 24th of May, Keith-Falconer left Cambridge for Edinburgh to meet the General Assembly; Wednesday, the 26th, being the day specially devoted to Foreign Missions.

At the afternoon meeting, the Convener, Colonel Young, laid before the Assembly the Report of the Foreign Missions' Committee, and dwelt warmly on Keith-Falconer's proposal of the previous autumn to go out as a missionary to Aden at his own expense, asking only for the countenance, help, and sympathy of the Free Church. He referred also to the somewhat parallel case to be found in the Gordon Mission in South Africa, founded in memory of James Henry Gordon, who, had he lived, would have been Earl of Aberdeen, and had formed the plan of purchasing a huge stretch of land in South Africa and of establishing a Christian Settlement under his own personal supervision.

At the evening meeting, at which it was known that the missionaries present would address the Assembly, the great Hall was crowded from floor to ceiling. Keith-Falconer had been placed by the Secretary in the seat which had always been occupied by his father at the meetings of the Assembly and had been much touched and gratified in consequence. After Dr. Dalzell, a missionary from the Gordon Settlement, had spoken, the Moderator, Dr. Somerville, formally introduced Keith-Falconer to the Assembly. He dwelt on the active part taken by the late Lord Kintore in evangelistic work, and then spoke of the resolution of the son to devote himself to a missionary

life, consecrating himself and his means and his brilliant
Arabic scholarship to the spiritual benefit of the Mohammedans.

The following is a condensation of Keith-Falconer's
address to the Assembly.   He said that he

" was to speak about missions to the Mohammedans, and
that before recounting the items of his own experience during
a four months' stay in Arabia, he ought first to allude to
a few of the leading facts connected with Islam, which,
though probably familiar to some, were perhaps only dimly
known to others.   In doing so, he mentioned that the ad-
herents of the Mohammedan religion numbered from 100
to 150 millions of souls, and said that it should be remembered that no Moslem ruler ever ruled over so vast a
number of Moslem subjects as did our Queen Victoria
at this moment.   Therefore Mohammedanism had a distinct claim on our interest and sympathy.   The wonderful
spread of Islam had led some writers to discern in it a
proof of its divine origin, and although the Lord Jesus
Christ had obtained sway over a vast number of human
beings, it had been asked why Mohammed had had a
success that compared with that of our Lord.   The answer
had been made that it was because Mohammedanism
pandered to the passions and natural desires of mankind,
and he maintained that that was the true statement of
the case.

" He next referred to the beliefs of the Mohammedans,
pointing out that they are not heathens ; that they have a
strong belief in the Lord of heaven and earth, one God,
omnipotent and omniscient,—that 'there is no God but
one, and Mohammed is His prophet,' in angels, in spirits,
and in a devil, in the immortality of the soul, the resurrec-
tion, and the judgement day.   As to their religious practices, he mentioned that they must have five prayers a day,
accompanied with fasting, which at certain times lasts for
a month ; that they have all to give alms ; that murder is
forbidden, though, if one murdered an 'unbeliever,' he
takes a high place in heaven ; and that they are forbidden
to use wine or intoxicating drink, to gamble, or to take
usury ; that they are enjoined to make a pilgrimage to

Mecca ; and that one of the last commandments is to make war against infidels.

" As to their regard for the Lord Jesus Christ, He was called the Word of God, and His miraculous conception and birth were admitted; and although His Divinity was most strenuosly denied, at the same time He stood on a higher level than any of the prophets, including Mohammed. They believed in the Gospel, and said that the Koran was sent in verification of it.

" As to Aden and the vicinity, he said the Gospel might be preached without let or hindrance in the British settlement of Aden. The climate was exceptionally good. He had a letter from the senior surgeon at Aden, who had been there five years without a day's illness, saying that no one need fear the climate. The natives were undoubtedly willing to receive the Gospel. He had been again and again urged to come and set up a school. One day a Mohammedan asked him for a piece of paper, and then wrote in a mysterious way, 'If you want the people to walk in your way, then set up schools.' This was an hajjee, one who had gone the pilgrimage to Mecca, where probably he had been fleeced of all the money he had, as they generally were. He offered the hajjee a copy of St. John; but he said he would not have it. He asked why, and the reply was, that he liked the historical part, but that there were parts that made him tremble. He pointed to the fourth chapter, where there was the conversation between Christ and the woman at the well, to whom Christ said, 'If thou knewest the gift of God, and who it is that saith to thee, Give me to drink ; thou wouldest have asked of Him, and He would have given thee living water.' 'That verse,' he said, 'makes my heart tremble, lest I be made to follow in the way of the Messiah.' He thought that a striking testimony to the power of God's Word.

" He managed with little difficulty to get into the interior, and had the company of a Scottish military surgeon, a true Christian man. They stayed some days there, and although the authorities at Aden had warned him not to broach religious subjects for fear of a rising, he had many opportunities of conversing with the natives. Many came to him most anxious to have the Gospel explained, and to

have their ailments treated by the doctor. Of course they
were taken to see the Sultan of this little town. After
describing his ailments, he took them to see his chief
secretary, whom he, the speaker, had happened to meet
in Aden. He gave him a copy of St. John. He said he
had read it with great interest, and he said, ' I want you
to do one thing—to pray to God that I may get well ; '
and from the tone of his voice he could see he recognized
the sympathy between them as two religious men.

"They might ask what means he proposed for carrying
on missions to these people. First, he proposed to have a
school for the children ; and at the place where he had
decided to recommend the committee to settle him, there
were 1000 children, all ready to receive education. Then
he proposed the careful and discriminate distribution of
the Scriptures. He was decidedly against the broadcast
scattering of copies of God's Word—many of them to be
torn up. What he did in Aden now was to say this:
' Now you ask me for this book ; if you can read it, and
understand it, I will give you one.' He tested that by
asking the man to read ; and if he could not read, he did
not get the book. In that way they valued the book more
than if one distributed it broadcast. It was not always
zeal that was best ; they must have zeal mixed with a little
common sense.

"The third thing he proposed was a medical mission.
What they wanted was a surgeon to go out—to offer himself. He believed the Church was willing at his instance
to appoint a surgeon at the station at Aden. He must be
a man who was specially skilled in surgery, for the Arabs
thought more of surgery than of medicine. They were accustomed to medicine from roots, but they came long distances
to a surgeon ; and what was wanted was a skilful surgeon,
who would come forward and devote himself to this work.
Undoubtedly the difficulties were considerable. The language was a difficult one to learn—it had many sounds we
were unaccustomed to, and the vocabulary was very large
—and the Mohammedan was one of the most stubborn of
all religions. They wanted to rouse the consciences of the
people. By the Mohammedan religion a man was saved
by good works ; and yet for all that there was a feeling

that it was not enough, and that at the last day there would be an intercession."

The great meeting listened with the profoundest interest while the young missionary spoke of the past winter's work, and of his now definite resolve to go forth again in the ensuing winter to resume the work as a permanent undertaking.

At a later period of the evening four young candidates for the Foreign Mission field were introduced to the Assembly by the Moderator, and solemnly committed to the grace of God for their future distant and arduous labours. When these four young men had taken their places and the Moderator had begun to speak, Keith-Falconer said to the Secretary, near whom he sat, " How much I should have liked to have stood up with them. Is it too late even now?" At this point, however, it seemed wiser not to interfere with the settled plan.

Keith-Falconer had deliberately offered himself to his Church; and unanimously and cordially had he been recognized as a missionary fully accredited by them, and earnestly was God implored to bless the work of a mission, which, so far as man might see, had begun with distinct and exceptional promise.

The thanks of the Church, moreover, had been with equal unanimity given to Keith-Falconer for his generous proposals regarding the medical missionary who was to accompany him.

That there should be a second missionary, and he a medical man, had been Keith-Falconer's original idea; and though his colleague had not yet been chosen, the whole summer as yet lay before them. Consequently, the general arrangements as to the appointment might be agreed to beforehand.

Those arrangements testified alike to Keith-Falconer's generosity and his good sense. Not only, as we have seen, did he propose to go out entirely at his own expense as regarded himself and his wife, taking also upon himself the whole cost of the building of the Mission-House and Hospital ; but he further proposed to be responsible for the stipend of the medical missionary. Still, with equal delicacy and good sense, he did not propose to pay this stipend directly to his colleague, who might in that case have come, perhaps, to feel himself too much a mere subordinate. Instead of this, he undertook to pay, for a period of not more than seven years, the sum of £300 annually to the Treasurer of the Free Church, which sum would be devoted by the Church to paying the medical missionary's stipend.

Up to the end of May, Keith-Falconer had not heard of a surgeon such as he needed, who was also physically able to endure a tropical climate. Early in June, being told that he might perhaps find a man suitable to his purpose at a small hospital in the East End of London, and having also been asked by Mr. Charrington to come up to report an address to be given by Mr. Spurgeon at the great Assembly Hall, he arranged to combine the two in a flying visit to town. It was with very hearty pleasure that I accepted his invitation to accompany him, and now look back upon that short two days' visit as bringing out the manysidedness of that noble character. Part of the first day had to be devoted to two German ladies who had arrived that morning on their first visit to England, and for whose comfort and enjoyment Keith-Falconer shewed the most careful and perfect thoughtfulness. The result, however, of a long drive intended to give the visitors some idea of the great size of London was that the train which was to convey the two ladies and Mrs. Keith-Falconer to Cambridge was only caught with literally not a second to spare. As the carriage-door was shut while the train was actually in motion, he laughed delightedly like a boy and said, " I often told them we were a very business-

like people and never wasted time, and now they will
see it."

Mr. Spurgeon was prevented by illness from giving the
address, but another speaker took his place; and both
that evening and the following morning both Keith-
Falconer and Mr. Charrington shewed with what would
have been enthusiasm, if it had not been so methodical,
the numerous striking features of the great building.

After this, a call was made at the hospital previously
mentioned, where Keith-Falconer had been told that there
was a chance of hearing of a possible colleague.[1] Although
nothing resulted from this visit, it made a great impression on Keith-Falconer, and he often referred to it afterwards.

The hospital was one serving as a small outpost, as it
were, of the Mildmay Mission, in a narrow street some little
distance to the north of Bethnal-Green Road, and in the
midst of as low and miserable surroundings as can well be
conceived. The amount of good wrought by the hospital
to such a neighbourhood must be incalculable, but the
people round had hardly yet realised this truth. The
lower windows were broken wholesale with stones again
and again, till the plan was devised of protecting them with
wire guards; when, with cruel ingenuity, the stones were
replaced with mud. The hospital, moreover, which contained about fifty beds, was only just large enough for the
patients; the devoted ladies working there having consequently to take rooms in a house across the narrow street,
involving the traversing of two very steep flights of stairs.
Keith-Falconer took the deepest interest in all the details

[1] It is most interesting to add that the gentleman of whom
Keith-Falconer had heard at this Bethnal-Green Hospital, Dr.
Alexander Paterson, though then from other engagements unable
to accept Keith-Falconer's invitation, has now (March, 1888) gone
to carry on the work at Shaikh Othman. Dr. Paterson is the fifth
medical man who has gone from this little hospital into the foreign
mission field.

told us, and talked for some little time very tenderly to some of the patients in the children's ward.

As we thought of the patient devotion, the utter abnegation of self, the work for Christ shewn within those dingy walls, and the pandemonium of vice and drunkenness and profanity around, we could but thank God that constraining love for Him could fight such a battle.

Early in the summer Keith-Falconer received the gratifying offer of the distinguished post of Lord Almoner's Professor of Arabic in the University of Cambridge, vacant by the resignation of Professor Robertson Smith. The offer was made by the present Bishop of Ely, Lord Alwyne Compton, with whom, as Lord Almoner, rested the appointment to the Professorship.

This Professorship, together with a corresponding post at Oxford, was founded in 1724, by the then Lord Almoner, out of the Almonry Bounty. At first, the post was sometimes held in conjunction with the other Professorship of Arabic, founded by Sir Thomas Adams in 1632, but latterly the existence of the two professorships has resulted in a division of work. Among recent Lord Almoner's Professors may specially be mentioned the late Mr. E. H. Palmer, famous for his colloquial knowledge of Arabic in various dialects, and well-known to general readers by his work on the " Desert of the Exodus."

The offer came to Keith-Falconer at rather a critical time; he was now definitely looking forward to leaving England about the end of October, and to beginning [to build at Shaikh Othman as soon as possible after his arrival at Aden. Thus, to accept a Professorship, necessarily entailing certain duties, would be anyhow to make an inroad on time none too plentiful already.

After very careful consideration, he formally accepted the offer. Two things weighed with him in forming a decision. In the first place, the duties of the post, though not indeed quite nominal, were not such as to be in any sense a tie; the patent of appointment merely binding him to deliver one lecture a year, so that, viewing this as the academical year, nearly a year and three-quarters might, if necessary, intervene between two consecutive courses of lectures.

Again, Keith-Falconer felt that if the Professorship could become to him an additional source of influence, if he could make of it a vantage ground, enabling him, a missionary to Arabia, to speak with greater weight as to the evangelisation of Arabia, because he spoke, not as a missionary only, but also as a professor of Arabic in a great English University—then indeed the offer was one not lightly to be let slip.

The offer once accepted, there was no time to be lost in considering the question of lectures. The subject on which he first fixed was the 'Sects of Islam;' but this seeming on the whole too technical, he ultimately chose one more likely to be of interest to a general audience, though requiring a large amount of careful research. This was the 'Pilgrimage to Mecca,' regard being had to the early political and religious importance of Mecca, to the legends circling round the Pilgrimage, to the manner in which the Pilgrimage is performed, and to the successful attempts made by various adventurous Europeans in disguise to see the ceremonies in and near the sacred city.

At this time, too, the proof-sheets of his article on 'Shorthand' in the new edition of the *Encyclopædia Britannica* had just come to hand; and, written as the article was on a highly technical subject, and condensed as much as possible, even the presence of the proofs meant that a good deal of time and care had yet to be expended.

No surgeon, moreover, had yet been found for the mission, and this fact entailed a considerable correspondence and several journeys, besides being a distinctly disturbing factor.

In addition to all these cares, the cares as to his future mission-work which required his personal attention, the cares as to the literary work for which he had made him-self responsible, and pre-eminently his lectures, there remained plenty of cares of the ordinary business description, none the less imperative because running in a lower groove. The disposal of the lease of his house, the choice of articles of furniture to be taken to Aden, arrangements as to the sale of the rest, the gradual purchase of a multiplicity of articles for the new home, which could be got better in England than on the spot, the division of his books into those to be taken with him, forming of themselves a considerable library, those to be stored away at home, and those to be given away where they would be useful—all these things might of themselves fairly have occupied a man's whole time.

Yet here was a scholar, not only attending carefully to these, but also engaged in laborious scholarly work, involving the reading of all books on the subject on which he could lay his hand, both in various European languages and in Arabic. To shew his exceeding thoroughness in this respect, it is worth noting that on finding that one of the most valuable books on the subject of the Pilgrimage was written in Dutch,[1] a language of which he knew next to nothing, he forthwith spent three weeks in thoroughly working up the Dutch grammar and so was enabled to read the book with comparative ease.

But with all this, his mood was always the same, always bright and kindly and genial; ready to think at the busiest time, if needs were, of the wants of another; to discuss a difficulty; to advise, where advice was needed; to be of practical use, where such help was required; and then to return, steadily and patiently, to his work.

In August, he again acted as judge at the bicycle races of the Cycling Club of the Young Men's Christian Association at Cambridge, of which I have previously spoken. In

---

[1] Snouck-Hurgronje, *Het Mekkaansche Feest* (Leyden, 1880).

this he had for some years taken a friendly interest, and held at this time, as in the previous year, the office of President of the Club. He had occasionally given special addresses to the young men of the Association on Sunday afternoons, and now, as his departure from Cambridge drew near, he shewed the warmth of his good feeling by a very generous contribution to the library.

On August 26 was held the annual supper of the combined athletic clubs of the association, and Keith-Falconer was present and took the chair. The toast of his health was drunk with great enthusiasm, and he replied in a kindly little speech in which he gave a humourous account of his early attempts at bicycling, and wound up with some very wise remarks as to the true function of bodily exercise and amusements :—" It was to be better fitted for serious work. He did not like to see a man, long after he had come to years of maturity, simply absorbed in sports, cricket, or whatever it might be."

The preparation for the lectures on the Pilgrimage involved a very great deal of work. Any clever man, with a ready pen, can, by merely going rapidly over one or two good modern authorities, present facts in a clear convenient form, regardless as to how far he has surveyed the whole field. Not so Keith-Falconer, not so any true scholar in like case. Nothing on which he could lay his hand relevant to the subject was passed over by him. He read steadily on, making, as his friends so well remember, brief notes in shorthand on the margin of the books, and fuller notes, also in shorthand, in the note-book by his side.

How carefully and methodically, when all this was done, were his facts marshalled into shape, like a well-disciplined army swayed by one mind. In Mr. Bowen's note of Keith-Falconer's Harrow days, he dwells upon his exceeding clearness of exposition.[1] This clearness, this

---

[1] See above, p. 18.

recognition of the standpoint of the reader or hearer as well as his own, was shewn in everything of the kind Keith-Falconer put his hand to. The same beautiful lucidity and the same orderly arrangement characterize alike the Introduction to *Kalilah*, already spoken of, the Lectures on the Pilgrimage, and the article on ' Shorthand.'

About the middle of August, Keith-Falconer heard that a young surgeon, on the staff of the Western Infirmary at Glasgow, wished much to join his expedition. With this gentleman, Dr. Stewart Cowen, an appointment for meeting in Glasgow was agreed upon, and on August 16, Keith-Falconer and his future colleague met; and each speedily saw that he had found a man to be absolutely trusted, and from whom complete sympathy and support could be looked for. With growing acquaintance, Keith-Falconer came to see that no more loyal, no more zealous companion could have been found. After events shewed clearly how well-grounded the choice had been.

His family were staying for the summer and autumn at Darn Hall, a large house a few miles north of Peebles, situated on the edge of a deep glen, and surrounded by hills, one of which, Dundreich, rises to a considerable height. A neighbouring house, Portmore, had been the home from which Mackenzie had gone forth, the first missionary bishop of Central Africa.

Keith-Falconer remained at Darn Hall during September and the early part of October; his lectures and the correspondence about the Mission fully occupied him.

On the evening of the last Sunday in September, advantage was taken of his residence so near Peebles to hold a Missionary meeting in the Free Church there, so as to hear from the young missionary an account of the nature of the work to be done at Aden, and of the hopes with which they would be faced. All this, drawing not merely from books, but from his own experience of the foregoing winter, Keith-Falconer put forth with exceeding clearness and simplicity. His speech was not that of a brilliant rhetorician, but it was eloquent in the truest sense, from the perfect sincerity which animated him, and his complete mastery of his facts; all this enhanced by the tall, handsome figure of the speaker, and his clear, musical voice.

This speech was not reported, but it was in substance much the same as those delivered by him at Edinburgh and Glasgow in November, which were his last public utterances on the subject of his mission before he left England. As such, I have reproduced it later nearly in full.

The large gathering of people listened with keen, quiet attention, as Scotch audiences do, and by the mouth of their minister wished the speaker God's blessing for himself, his companions and his work, with its infinite possibilities.

Keith-Falconer himself throughout this time was as industrious, as earnest and as bright as ever. A long morning's work at a German, a Dutch, or an Arabic chronicle of the Meccan pilgrimage would find him blithe and buoyant at the end of it, ready to amuse or be amused. Walking over one day into the pretty little town of Peebles, he recounted very merrily, and with the inimitable Scotch accent which he could reproduce when he pleased, the story of an enthusiastic native who, having seen the world and found no place like home, embodied his idea in the remark, " I've seen London, and I've seen Paris, but for pure pleasure, give me Peebles ! "

He paid several visits to a young Scotch ' probationer,' staying for his health for a short time at Peebles, who had had somewhat of a hard struggle with circumstances in his determination to get a University degree, the ultimate aim being the foreign mission-field. Him, I have reason to believe, Keith-Falconer had aided in more ways than one, and took at all times the liveliest interest in his progress.

About the middle of October, Keith-Falconer returned to Cambridge, having now fixed his lectures for the second week of November, leaving for Aden immediately afterwards. Up to the very last the work went briskly on. He took an infinity of pains to secure the highest amount of clearness and accuracy; the matter which represented the first lecture being written out at least four times.

A slight digression ensued on October 29. On the evening of this day, the annual dinner of the London Bicycle Club was held at the Holborn Restaurant, having been put earlier than its usual date to enable Keith-Falconer to be present. As I have mentioned in a previous chapter, he had been uninterruptedly President of the Club since May 1, 1877, and he had very rarely missed the annual dinner.

Naturally, after so long an association, the relations between the Club and its President were exceedingly cordial, and the various speeches testified to much warmth of feeling. There was a large gathering, and the President took the chair, and made several pleasant genial speeches in the course of the evening.[1]

First he proposed the Queen's health "since whose accession some fifty years have circled, or rather may I say more appropriately have cycled, round." Later in the evening he proposed the health of 'the visitors,' and told the following anecdote of one of his own guests:—

"Then we have my very old friend, Mr. —— ; he comes from the sister isle. He is the hero of a hundred bicycling exploits, and perhaps I might recount a small incident. We were riding in the north of Scotland—it only shews you what a daring cyclist he is—far away from railways and civilization; I said, 'Ride carefully, don't go fast down these hills.' It was no use, speed was everything; presently I came gingerly round the corner. I saw a bicycle lying in the road, and a foot peeping up through

---

[1] *London Bicycle Club Gazette*, Nov. 4, 1886.

the hedge. It turned out he had dislocated his elbow, but he jumped on again and rode with me 20 miles. That evening we saw a first-rate London doctor, who was visiting in the neighbourhood. He said, 'You must give up your tour; fomentations, cold-water taps, etc.; you must go home.' He was not satisfied with that prescription, for he thought it might be remedied then and there. We got to a local surgeon's, who looked at the limb, and said, 'Oh, that's just dislocated; I will put it straight in three minutes,' and went for the chloroform. My friend laughed at the idea of chloroform. He got him on the sofa, I sat on his legs. The surgeon came, and said, 'Now, if I hurt you, what will you do?' 'I will hit you in the eye.' 'Then I'll hit you back.' However, in ten seconds the arm was right, and in twenty-four hours we were in the saddle, and completed our tour. I think that will shew you that he is an admirable representative of the pluck of the British race."

In combining with this toast that of 'the Press' Keith-Falconer said:

"I have always a fellow-feeling with gentlemen of the press, especially those who are experienced in the art of shorthand. That is an art to which I have been a devotee for many years, and I always think of it as the literary bicycle; it clears the ground so quickly. I think, you know, that cycling and shorthand somehow go together."

Before leaving England, Keith-Falconer's thoughts were, as might be supposed, warmly turned to the various schemes for good, with which he had been associated, for which he had worked and written and spoken and prayed. For Mr. Charrington's great institution at Mile-End, now working like a huge machine, whose wheels are the hearts and brains of men, he took measures to insure his life for a considerable sum shortly before leaving England.[1] The

---

[1] It is right to say that while the Insurance Office declared Keith-Falconer's life to be a 'First-Class' one, they refused to grant the policy, save at a prohibitive premium, on hearing of his proposed place of residence.

Barnwell Mission had pursued its quiet career of usefulness for some years past, and throughout that time Keith-
Falconer's general help had been steadily given, both in
money and personal effort. No very long time before
leaving England, he started the idea, taking the hint from
Mr. Charrington's book depot, of having a lending library
of wholesome books in the Theatre, and helped not only
by contributing money, but by choosing the books in the
first instance.

It was he also who originated the idea of a Barnwell
Missionary, promising to contribute £50 a year for two
years towards the cost of maintenance. This was in no
sense intended in any spirit of rivalry to the work done
most devotedly for the last four years, by the present
Vicar, the Rev. A. H. Delmé-Radcliffe; but was an attempt
to reach some of a class whom, even yet, though happily
in an increasingly less degree, the existing organisation
was unable adequately to touch. Keith-Falconer writes
on this subject to the Vicar of Barnwell as follows:—

"ADEN, ARABIA,
Dec. 9, 1886.

"MY DEAR MR. RADCLIFFE,

"On arriving here yesterday, I found your kind
letter at the post-office. (I left Cambridge on Nov. 13.)

"I have *no* objection to a churchman being our missionary, and have written to Mr. —— to tell him so. As
we are undenominational (what a word!), the man's particular form of worship is not of any moment to us. And
as we believe you to be doing a genuine Christian work in
the place, we should be very glad to work with you and
for you. I am much obliged for the offer of a donation
annually, it will be thankfully accepted.

"The idea of a town missionary working in the way I
described did not occur to me till just after leaving Cambridge, else I would have discussed the matter with you.
I must leave it with you and Mr. —— to decide the
details. But I would suggest that those streets and houses
whose inmates are known to be habitual neglecters of

Sunday worship, should be considered the proper sphere for the missionary, and you and your curates might note some special cases which they might consider peculiarly suited to a plain town missionary.

" If the people he reaches all go straight to your church and not to the theatre, I shall not grieve. So long as they come under the power of the Gospel, I am satisfied. (Never call me a bigoted dissenter after this!) With very kind regards to Mrs. Radcliffe,

" I am yours ever."

At the beginning of November, Mrs. Keith-Falconer left Cambridge for Cannes, where her parents were then staying; and on Saturday, the 6th, Keith-Falconer started for Scotland, to deliver his final public addresses in connection with his mission, and to say farewell to his family at Darn Hall.

The Sunday was spent quietly at home, and in the deepening dusk of the November evening he left for Edinburgh, where he gave an address to a very large and highly-interested gathering, which was repeated substantially the following evening at Glasgow. This address, the last of his public appeals in England or Scotland, so unmistakeably spoken from the depth of his heart, so touching in the way self is set aside, so strong and emphatic in its statement of the needs of the case, and the means of meeting them, is here reproduced nearly in full.[1] Though he who then spake the words lies in his lonely grave by the Indian Ocean, yet shall the living ardent faith of that utterance endure while the Church Militant lasts.

" Since the Muhammedan religion is professed by the people of South Arabia, the consideration of missionary prospects there involves the question, Whether Islam is, or is not, the impregnable fortress which it is commonly supposed to be?

---

[1] I have merely omitted the paragraph describing Aden itself, which has been virtually given already in another form.

" I wish to show (1) That there are weak points in Islam, which, if persistently attacked, must lead to its eventual overthrow, while Christianity has forces which make it more than a match for Muhammedanism (or any other religion), provided always that it has free play and a fair field ; (2) That the efforts already made to christianize Muhammedan countries have produced commensurate results ; (3) What practical encouragements we had during our four months' residence at Aden. In conclusion I wish to make an appeal.

" (1) The great truth which the Arabian prophet preached was the truth of the one God, the Creator of the worlds, who brought us into being, who does as He pleases, is merciful and pitiful, the requiter of good and evil, the all-wise and all-powerful. But while he taught rightly that there is one God, he did not show the way to Him. The Gospel does this, and therefore has an infinite advantage over Islam. The Kuran is intensely legal, and all defects in the true believer will be pardoned, that is, overlooked, by the Merciful One. As the law to the Jews, so Islam to the Arabs, is a schoolmaster to bring them to Christ. Again, the Kuran is in a sense founded on our Christian Scriptures. The prophet did not profess to come as a destroyer, but as a renovator and a completer. He posed as the restorer of the true religion of Abraham, which had become grossly corrupted, and the building of the Kaaba, the Meccan temple, he ascribed to that patriarch and Ishmael. Of Christ he ever spoke in terms of the greatest reverence, and even admitted His miraculous birth. ' The Word of God,' ' the Spirit of God,' are among the epithets applied to Him in the Kuran. Muhammed himself was the last, the seal, the greatest of the prophets ; and the Kuran, he said, was sent down from heaven to men as a confirmation, or verification of what they already had in the Gospel and the law. As the Messiah and the Gospel had superseded (not overthrown) the law and the prophets, so Muhammed and the Kuran had superseded all that had gone before. What a handle has he thus given to us ! for a Muslim cannot logically refuse to receive the Gospel, since it was to confirm its truth that the Kuran was given.

"When a Muhammedan realizes that the Kuran and the Gospel are inconsistent, he must either renounce his faith or pronounce our New Testament a forgery. I remember that on one occasion an intelligent hajjee (pilgrim to Mecca), after reading a few chapters of St. John, in which the Lord makes claims and promises infinitely transcending those of Muhammed, returned me the book, refusing to read it any more, because 'it made his heart tremble lest it should be seduced to follow after the Messiah.' He had realised that to follow Christ meant to forsake Muhammed, but, lacking courage, he shut his eyes to truth. Muhammed while professing to acknowledge Christ, ignored or was ignorant of His claims, and has succeeded for more than twelve centuries in standing between men and the Light. Give the Gospel to the Muhammedans, and they must at any rate be *logically* convinced that their prophet has fearfully misled his followers, for their prophet and his Kuran fall infinitely short of our Prophet and His Gospel. How should they then supersede these? Further, it is well known that the natural inclinations and passions of mankind find full provision made for them in the prophet's religion. It is quite sufficient to point to the well-known position of women in Islam, Islam's recognition of slavery, and the combination of religion with political power, which has always formed a pillar of the Muhammedan state, to see that the lust of the flesh, the lust of the eyes, and the pride of life, which Christ taught men to repress and deny, were simply legalised and regulated by Muhammed. It is no wonder that so many millions of human beings are content to embrace a religion, which, while professing to satisfy the inborn cravings of mankind after God, at the same time offers him such carnal attractions. But this is no more than saying that Islam is as strong as human nature. Any-one who takes the trouble to read the Epistles of Paul (and not all of the writers on Islam will take so much pains) can convince himself that Christianity has proved herself more than a match for the worst, the most inveterate, vices which enslave mankind. Can a religion like that of Islam be described as a powerful one, *quâ* religion, which has owed its propagation and continuance so largely to such base and carnal means? From its birth, Islam has been

steeped in blood and lust, blood spilt and lust sated by
the sanctions of religion. Certainly there was a time in
the prophet's career, when he had in him something of the
spirit of the old prophets ; but when driven out of Mecca
at the flight to Medina, he left his prophetic mantle behind
him, and thenceforth became little more than an earthly
ruler aiming at absolute power. From that time he employed all the arts of an unscrupulous policy. The force
of arms, threats, concessions and compromises (which sometimes shocked his friends), the promise of rich booty,—all
these he did not scruple to employ. By preaching the
truth of the one God, he raised himself to a certain platform of power and influence ; the sword and the spear,
diplomacy and statecraft, raised him much higher.

" But Islam not only owed much to its own power and
attractions, it was indebted also to the weak and divided
condition of the Christian community in Arabia at the
prophet's time. Christianity was well known in various
parts of Arabia when Muhammed appeared. Shortly
before his birth, a Christian army from Yemen stood
before the gates of Mecca, with the intention of demolish-
ing the Kaaba, when a sudden epidemic of smallpox wrought
such frightful havoc among them that a miserable remnant
returned disheartened to their own country. There were
Christian kingdoms, too, in Lakhm and Ghassan ; but the
Church was split by dissensions as to the nature and person of Christ, and the worship of the Virgin. The sight
of the bitter quarrels of the Nestorians and Eutychians
must have contributed not a little to prejudice the Arabian
prophet's ignorant mind against Christianity ; and Islam
was destined soon to sweep it completely out of the peninsula. Nor can the crusades in later times have failed to
embitter the Muslims, and mislead their minds as to the
true nature of the religion of Christ ; and speaking generally, it may be said that the Church is itself to blame for
the very rise of Islam. The Arabs were sunk in idolatry.
The Church, instead of holding out to them the lamp of
truth, was engaged in internal warfare. The gross ignorance of the prophet with regard to the Scriptures and the
true nature of Christianity, proves how remiss had been
the Church in Hijas in obeying the command to preach

the Gospel to every creature, while his general acceptance
and recognition of those Scriptures goes far to shew that
had he known and understood their contents, he would
never have entered on the career he did. But these considerations ought not to cause the slightest misgivings as
to the imperative duty to take the Gospel to the Muhammedans, or as to the success which must follow. For,
where the Gospel in its simplicity has been faithfully,
patiently, and honestly preached to them, the desired results have ensued.

" (2) Raymundus Lullius, a Spanish noble of Majorca
in the 13th century, after vainly endeavouring to persuade
the Romish Church to institute a Mission to the Muslims,
became himself a missionary to the Arabs of North Africa.
Nine years he spent in the study of the Arabic language,
the Kuran, and the Muhammedan traditions. After this
preparation he preached boldly, carrying his life in his
hand. You will find the story told in Dr. G. Smith's
Short History of Christian Missions.[1] He suffered many
hardships and imprisonments, but ere he died had raised
a small Christian Church, now long since dispersed. But
it was not until this century that the Church could be said
to awake to her duty in the matter. Notably the American
Presbyterians have done much to shake Islam, although
they work mainly among the degraded Christian Churches
of Egypt and Syria. In the American and other Mission
Schools, thousands of Muslim boys and girls are daily
taught the truths of the Gospel. Within quite recent
years some fifty Muslim converts have been baptized in
Egypt by the Americans, but there are many more unbap-
tized converts. In Peshawur, where the Church Missionary Society have long been represented, a Christian church
is filled by Muslim converts, and a large school for Muslim
children flourishes there. Are not these startling and en-
couraging facts? The success in Egypt and Syria would
have been far greater had not a Muhammedan government
done its best to check and thwart the missionaries; but a
new day is dawning, European and especially English influence is rapidly gaining ground in Egypt and the East.

[1] Pp. 102-108, ed. 2.

Not many years ago, a Muslim convert to Christ had to fear for his life, and baptism would have ensured his speedy death, yet a few months ago the government of Egypt did not dare even to degrade a sergeant of police who had received Christian baptism. Western education is rapidly gaining favour in the East, and widening the cramped boundaries of Eastern thought. The Kuran is doomed.

"(3) Many a time was I asked by natives in the street and the market, when was I going to set up my school, as they wished to send their children to it. A man once handed me a slip of paper on which he had written, 'If you want the people to walk in your way, then set up a school.' Our Arabic Gospels are constantly clamoured for, and received with the greatest readiness. To my question, 'Why do you want the Injil?' I several times received the answer, 'Because it is God's book, sent down from heaven.' In the town of El-Hautah, where lives the sultan of the neighbouring Abdali tribe, our books were welcomed. The amount of sickness is frightful. The road through the Abdali tribe is perfectly safe, and the sultan is extremely civil to the English governor.

"In conclusion, I wish to make an appeal. There must be some who will read these words, or who, having the cause of Christ at heart, have ample independent means, and are not fettered by genuine home ties. Perhaps you are content with giving annual subscriptions and occasional donations, and taking a weekly class? Why not give yourselves, money, time and all, to the foreign field? Our own country is bad enough, but comparatively many must, and do, remain to work at home, while very few are in a position to go abroad. Yet how vast is the Foreign Mission field! 'The field is the world.' Ought you not to consider seriously what your duty is? The heathen are in darkness, and we are asleep. Perhaps you try to think that you are meant to remain at home, and induce others to go. By subscribing money, sitting on committees, speaking at meetings, and praying for missions, you will be doing the most you can to spread the Gospel abroad. Not so. By going yourself, you will produce a tenfold more powerful effect. You can give and pray for missions wherever you are, you can send descriptive letters to the missionary meetings, which will be much more effective than second-hand anecdotes gathered by you from others, and you will help the committees finely by sending them the results of your experience. Then, in addition, you will have added your own personal example, and taken your share of the real work. We have a great and imposing war-office, but a very small army. You have wealth snugly vested in the funds, you are strong and healthy, you are at liberty to live where you like, and occupy yourself as you like. While vast continents are shrouded in almost utter darkness, and hundreds of millions suffer the horrors of heathenism or of Islam, the burden of proof lies upon you to shew that the circumstances in which God has placed you were meant by Him to keep you out of the foreign mission-field."

On the Tuesday evening, Keith-Falconer returned to Cambridge, the lectures on the Pilgrimage being announced for the following Thursday, Friday and Saturday afternoons.

The lectures were delivered in one of the rooms of the Divinity Schools of the University before an attentive audience. The MS. from which the lecturer read, was, save for an actual Arabic word here and there, written entirely in shorthand; although no one who had not previously been aware of the fact could possibly have guessed it, so completely at home was the reader with his hieroglyphics.

The first lecture dwelt mainly on Mecca itself, the importance of its position as a commercial centre, to which large numbers of caravans converged, and its religious importance, as being a place possessed of special sacred associations before the time of Mohammed. It was pointed out that the Meccan pilgrimage was no creation of Mohammed, but an ancient institution he sought to utilize for his own advantage.

The second lecture was occcupied with an account of

the pilgrimage itself, and of the various **rites and customs** attending it; **and in the last, the** lecturer gave **a very interesting** résumé **of** all the recorded visits **to Mecca made** by Europeans, who, disguised as Moslems, **had** made the journey safely, but **at very** considerable risk. **All who were present at the lectures will** testify **to their clearness and fulness, and to the skill which gave point and interest to the more** technical **details.**

The last lecture over, Professor Keith-Falconer, for once to name him by his official title, left the lecture-room for Mr. Turner's house in St. Andrew's Street, where he was then staying, passing the great Gate of Trinity College, through which for years he had gone in and out almost daily, and across the Market Place, on which in old days he had so often gazed from the windows of his lodgings in the intervals of work. Once arrived, and having laid aside the University cap and gown, never again to be worn by him, it was necessary to give undivided attention to much that yet remained to be done. The lecture had not been finished till 3 o'clock and the train by which he proposed to go to London left at 7.

Two men were engaged in packing a large quantity of books, many of which he had wished to be able to use to the last. Giving directions to these men, carefully sorting various papers, constantly interrupted even in the midst of a hasty dinner by persons to whom orders had to be given, Keith-Falconer, in the midst of a chaos of packing and a multiplicity of details of business, and on the eve of a journey half across the world, was as calm and undisturbed as if he were simply leaving home for a few days.

He was very bright and cheery, but not with the exuberance of hopefulness sometimes seen in one about to essay new work far away. It was an unruffled composure; and no excitement, no hurry, no thought of the personal side of the enterprise, seemed to mar the bright, perfect calm.

So too was it to the last. As he stood on the platform of the railway station, accompanied by his little dog ‘ Jip,’ which was to go with him to Aden, and has since returned in safety, it seemed inconceivable that a man starting on so long a journey, with work so anxious awaiting him at the end of it, should have shewn himself not merely happy, but absolutely calm and undisturbed.

A few short minutes while the train stopped, and then, one of the most gifted, many-sided of the sons whom our dear mother Cambridge ever reared had left her walls for ever.

CHAPTER X.

"He, being made perfect in a short time, fulfilled a long time."
WISDOM OF SOLOMON.

WE have seen in the preceding chapter that various causes had somewhat delayed Keith-Falconer's course of lectures, rendering it necessary for him to leave Cambridge on the evening of the day on which he had delivered his third and concluding lecture.

Encumbered with a vast amount of luggage, huge boxes of books, one very large box containing a deck chair of special construction for his wife's use on the voyage on the Mediterranean, and other things, he found it was so late before these had all been safely deposited at the London terminus, which he purposed leaving the following night, that, instead of going to his sister's house as he had intended, he went, accompanied by his little dog 'Jip,' to Mr. Charrington's house in Stepney Green.

The following afternoon he devoted to his sister, and, various farewell visits paid, and with many hearts keenly and prayerfully dwelling on his movements, he left Victoria by the evening Continental express for Paris, in order to get the day there for some purchases, including some Oriental books he had failed to procure in England. Leaving Paris that night, he rejoined his wife at Cannes on the following afternoon, and sailed from Marseilles in the French steamer *Alphée*, on Thursday, Nov. 18. They reached Alexandria on the following Tuesday evening, and landed the next morning.

A letter written during the voyage shews him as being in very good spirits. He dwells with much humour on an account of a rather tempestuous meeting which had been held at the Mansion House, when Mr. Charrington had felt it his duty to protest against a ruling of the chairman. Then he tells of his flying visit to Cannes, and then reverts to his plans for the future. Dr. Cowen had sailed from London on November 16 for Aden, and it had been Keith-Falconer's intention to join him on his arrival at Suez, leaving his wife with friends at Cairo till some provision for her comfort could be made at Aden. This plan enabled Keith-Falconer to spend six days at Cairo, after which he left his wife under the friendly roof of Dr. and Mrs. Watson, of the American Mission House. Here she spent her time in taking long Arabic lessons and visiting in the native houses.

On the arrival of the English steamer it was found that there was no room on board, and consequently Keith-Falconer took passage from Suez in an Austrian steamer, which was passed so closely by the other in the Red Sea that the two missionaries could distinguish each other plainly. Dr. Cowen arrived at Aden on December 7, and Keith-Falconer himself on the following day putting up at his old quarters, the Hotel de l'Europe, at Steamer Point.

On December 12 he writes to me as follows:

"Arrived here—Jip and I—all right early on Wednesday morning last, December 8, in the Austrian Lloyd boat *Berenice*, from Suez. There was no room for me in Cowen's steamer, which passed us quite close in the Red Sea, so that we signalled one another. His boat was crammed, while I was the only 1st class passenger in mine, which was bound for Hong Kong, and every bit as good as any P. and O. boat I ever was in, excepting in speed. We stopped at Jidda, but to my great disappointment, quarantine prevented me from going ashore. I gazed long at the hills which hid Mecca from us. At Jidda, the only other 1st class passenger got off, an Indian Musalman going to Mecca. His card runs thus:—H. M. Ismail Khan, of Datauli, Aligarh [North-west provinces]. . . . . As he was going to relations at Mecca, I asked him whether it was true—as Keane states in his ' Six Months at Mecca '— that an Englishwoman had lived there as a Muslima for many years. He said, ' Yes, she now lives in my house at Aligarh.' I then asked him some questions, and his answers tallied exactly with Keane's account. She is known as *Zuhra Begum*, which might very well be rendered Lady Venus, as Keane does. Was not that a curious coincidence?

" We spent a pleasant six days in Cairo : I left my wife at the American Mission House with Dr. and Mrs. Watson. I travelled to Suez with D. A. Cameron, just appointed consul at Sawakin. He said, ' I swear by the American missionaries. Half of these Bulgarian deputies were educated by them at their schools at Constantinople and elsewhere.' And curiously, Cowen heard exactly the same thing from an Armenian merchant who spoke English. The Americans are certainly doing a fine work in Cairo with their schools.

"Our plans are maturing nicely. . . . . Dr. Harpur is now with General Haig on a cruise to the Somali coast, to see whether there is an opening there. I expect to see him at the end of next week.

" We have met with cordiality itself here. The General, Major Seely, the two surgeons, Jackson and Colson, the chaplain, Streeten, and my old Somali servants, Jusuf and Ahmad, welcomed us with great kindness.

" The General's account of Maharaja Dhuleep Sing was highly diverting. D. S. insisted on being made a Sikh. The ceremony was performed at the Residency. The General refused to be present. D. S. had to strip and put on a very scanty and simple attire ; and in the middle of the ceremony ran out thus dressed into the General's study. . . . .

" We are having what in England you would call the most delicious summer weather, warm and breezy. If the voyage were not so long, I could send you plenty of beautiful flowers from the gardens at Shaikh Othman.

"My old friend Isma'il, the schoolmaster, is back from Zabeed, restored to sanity. He says that he shewed the New Testament I gave him to the mufti and to his own family and others at Zabeed, and that some of these are now copying it out in writing. This shews how rare and how valued is the New Testament in Arabia. . . . .

"My furniture, books, &c., I expect shortly. My wife comes on here in P. and O. ship *Thames* in about fourteen days.

"Shaikh Othman is growing fast : 50 native infantry men will go there, as soon as the lines are built. . . . ."

For five or six days after their arrival, Keith-Falconer and his companion stayed at the Hotel, going out two or three times to Shaikh Othman. Subsequently, they accepted the hospitality of General Hogg at the Residency and of Dr. Colson respectively. It was thought that Dr. Cowen, who had not been in Aden before, might learn much from an experienced surgeon who had resided there for some years.

On the 28th Mrs. Keith-Falconer arrived; Keith-Falconer, writing on the following day, says :—

"My wife came yesterday in P. and O. ship *Thames*. The General sent out his launch and cutter to land her. Lord and Lady Aberdeen also came ashore for tea at the Residency, as well as Lady Brassey and daughters. My wife is very well and enjoyed herself immensely at Cairo. Dr. Watson travelled with her to Benha, an hour from Cairo, where she joined the Indian mail, and so got to Aden in perfect safety and comfort."

It is now necessary to speak of a somewhat unpleasant incident which occurred soon after Keith-Falconer's arrival at Aden ; which of itself would only call for a passing remark, but, in the light of subsequent events, acquires a very grave significance.

There can be no reasonable doubt that the external conditions under which Keith-Falconer was living during the time he spent at Shaikh Othman were not in themselves such as to be conducive to good health : a structure of wood and iron and matting is not the kind of house which a native of a country like England should choose to live in, in a specially hot part of the Tropics.

It might not unnaturally be asked, why so questionable a step had been taken, why a missionary should fail to use the fullest precautions for the physical well-being of himself and his companions ; and were the facts not definitely set forth, there might seem to be in the present instance a lack of necessary forethought most foreign to Keith-Falconer's character.

I feel it will be well therefore to give the facts in some detail. It will be remembered that Keith-Falconer, on leaving for England in the spring of 1886, did so with the full intention of settling at Shaikh Othman, and there building his house and the Mission-Hospital and School. A grant of land had been 'reserved' for him to the end of the year. Thus even though the work should be commenced immediately on his return to Aden, some months must necessarily elapse before the house could be ready for occupation.

Evidently, it would be a pity to live during those months at Aden, or at Steamer Point, involving, even in the former case, a ten miles' journey to and fro. Not only would this be a great drag on the direct work of the Mission, but it would also leave the workmen engaged on the building almost entirely without supervision.

The obvious plan was to hire a suitable building at Shaikh Othman, while the Mission House was being built, all care being taken that the temporary home was such as was suitable for European residents.

There was at Shaikh Othman, as it happened, only one good stone bungalow, besides the one belonging to Government. This belonged to a wealthy old Arab, named Hassan Ali, who is said to be more or less a tool in the hands of expectant relatives. At Keith-Falconer's request Dr. Colson had seen this man in the foregoing summer and had found him professedly wishing to let or sell the house. As Dr. Colson's letter (Aug. 1, 1886) bears striking independent testimony to the climate of Shaikh Othman, another matter of the highest importance, I subjoin the following extracts :—

" I have seen Hassan Ali, and he is not only willing to let you his bungalow, but also to sell it. Whether it would suit your purpose, I do not know. I have not said anything about the rent, as you will doubtless prefer to make your own bargain. Shaikh Othman is certainly far superior in climate to Aden proper. On two occasions I have been there lately. On one, when we left the Camp and on returning to it, it was insufferably hot, but Shaikh Othman was comparatively pleasant. On August 12, we went in a howling, hot and dusty wind ; Shaikh Othman was quite a haven after it. On returning, the wind, as we got near Aden, increased in violence, and the pony could hardly get along. The place, for a hot climate, may be considered very fair. I am glad to say we have all enjoyed excellent health in spite of the heat, which was unusually great in June and July. It is much better now. . . . . .

" Your doctor should be provided with lithotomy instruments. A successful operation for stone among the Arabs will be a great missionary success; and if your doctor makes a name, he will get plenty of work to do, and a proportionate amount of influence."

Naturally, therefore, Keith-Falconer expected that on his arrival at Aden this stone bungalow would be available for his use ; and accordingly he went over it, inspecting it carefully, to see what alterations, if any, might be required. After this, accompanied by Dr. Cowen, he called on Hassan Ali, who at first offered it to them for a few weeks for nothing. Clearly such a course was quite out of the question, if for no other reason than this, that

Keith-Falconer and his party would have no *right* to
remain if the owner wished to put them out. Presumably,
however, Hassan Ali no more thought of his offer being
accepted, than Ephron the Hittite supposed that Abraham
would take him at his word.

An offer was then made to Hassan Ali of a rent, which
Englishmen and Arabs agreed in declaring to be ample,
which same rent indeed a few months afterwards he accepted from the American Consul, on a five years' lease;
but, scenting a possible victim, the old Arab haggled and
demanded what was simply an exorbitant sum. On this
Dr. Cowen writes:—

"To have acceded to this demand would simply have
been ruinous in all subsequent dealings with these men
and those around; as they would have thought he could
be 'done' on every occasion in which money was concerned.

"Accordingly, on another visit to Shaikh Othman, he
found a small hut (40 feet square), which the owner said
he would let and alter for us. The next day, General
Haig and I saw the hut again with him, and he decided to
take it.

"When Hassan Ali's relatives found this, they sent
urgent messages, begging him to renew negotiations. This
he simply refused to do, feeling that he was much better
free from such men. Besides, in any case, they would only
have let the upper half of the house, and to have had drinking and smoking parties occupying the other half, and singing bacchanalian songs in the verandah outside, would
never have done, as the natives would naturally have associated us with them."

I have dwelt on this point at some length, because it
seemed my clear duty to vindicate the memory of the noble
dead from any possible charge of haste or carelessness, of
mere hurry to get to work before looking fully to every
precaution.

Once settled in the temporary home everything looked

very pleasant and hopeful. Writing a postcard on business on December 22, he adds the postcript ' All well and jolly.' In a letter of December 26 to his old friend Mrs. Emmerson, he says :—

" I have got on hire a little house in a garden to live in at the native village where we are going to settle. . . . . We are having beautiful weather, not too hot, and no dust. I have engaged three servants ; one is an Arab cook, the others a Somali butler, and a Somali coolie. All servants here are men, except Indian nurses and women who come in to sweep. Kitchenmaids and housemaids are *men*. . . . . All servants are barefooted, but must wear white turbans on their heads. The natives never touch beer or wine. . . . ."

The letter concludes :—

" I hope that you will get through the winter nicely. But you are an old lady, and God may call you at any time. So make sure that you are trusting in Jesus' blood alone. Not the best person living can be saved except through Him."

That lesson had long sunk deep into his own heart.

In a letter dated December 29, after speaking of the information which Dr. Cowen had gleaned from Dr. Colson, he thus refers to the temporary house :—

" After considerable difficulty I managed to get a temporary dwelling-place in Shaikh Othman. It is a roof on four pillars with walls of iron lattice, the roof extending beyond the pillars on all sides. By putting in three wooden partitions, a dwelling-house, with verandah, two bed-rooms, and sitting-room (used also for eating and studying) is created. The house stands in a garden, and both belong to an Indian merchant. The servants will live in offices made of mud bricks, with roofs of bamboo and matting."

On December 31 he writes :—

" Yesterday Cowen and we went to Shaikh Othman and found the house nearly ready for habitation. The cook, a

Madrasee, had gone over in the morning; and fifty pack-
ages had arrived from the wharf, and fourteen from various
parts of Steamer Point (all despatched by me in the morning). To-day my wife and I go to the Colsons, where she
remains until everything necessary has been unpacked, or
about three days. Then at last we shall be settled for some
months. I am putting up a shed near our house for receiving patients.

"Charlie Studd [1] has written me a delightful letter. He
is at Chungking, Szechuen, living with Bourne, the English
Resident. They are not allowed by the magistrate to go
outside the house, on account of the late riots. He thinks
the Chinese language was invented by the devil to prevent
the Chinese from ever hearing the Gospel properly ! . . . .
He is pleased to notice that the first thing recorded of
Sarai after she was made a princess (Sarah) was, ' she set
to work to cook and make cakes' (Genesis xvii. 15—27).
. . . . You will be sorry to hear that I am *not* going to
publish those lectures. I have turned over the matter well,
and the more I meditate, the less I feel inclined to print
them." [2]

A sad accident happened shortly after the missionaries
had settled in their new abode. On January 5, while a
large well was being dug in the garden by two Jewish
workmen, the earth fell in upon them. Keith-Falconer
and Dr. Cowen were able to aid considerably in extricating
one, the other was killed instantaneously.

The news of the accident drew together a large crowd
from the village, which was about half a mile away, and
served as the first introduction of the missionaries to their
new neighbours. The workman who was killed, a youth,
was buried the same evening; dead and buried within four
hours.

[1] This is Mr. C. T. Studd, of Trinity College, Cambridge, a
member of the China Inland Mission.

[2] This refers to the three lectures on the "Meccan Pilgrimage,"
which he had delivered as Professor at Cambridge in the previous
term.

A few days after this came the first patient, an Arab, the head gardener of the large garden adjoining. Grateful for the help afforded him, and clearly perceiving in what way he might best shew his gratitude to his new friends, he did his best to induce large numbers of his acquaintance to profit by the same help, and in this and other ways proved of great assistance to the missionaries.

On December 31, Keith-Falconer had spoken of putting up a shed near his house for patients. This, when built, was simply a rude hut, some 15 feet by 12, built against the garden wall, with mud walls and planked roof ; and to this a simple verandah of mats was afterwards added. The number of applicants for help very soon shewed that the natives fully appreciated the benefits offered them. During the last week of January twenty new cases presented themselves, besides an equal number attended to elsewhere; and by the end of about six weeks nearly 300 visits had been paid to the dispensary.

The hospital accommodation was necessarily very insufficient. Still, the "shed," besides serving as a dispensary and consulting-room for out-patients, contained also beds for three in-patients, two of whom had come, at a comparatively early period, no less than eight miles to be treated.

In about a fortnight after the date of the last letter the house was ready for occupation. On January 11 he writes, "Our temporary quarters are very comfortable and the books look very nice." Things were now fairly settled, and Mrs. Keith-Falconer was to join him the following day.

Here for a time all went well. Every care had been taken to make the hut, the "shanty" as he was in the habit of calling it, as little inconvenient or unhealthy as might be. A thatch roof was even put on over the ordinary one, at Dr. Colson's suggestion, as an extra precaution against the heat.

I again quote from Dr. Cowen's letter :—

"Once in our little hut, we were very well and comfortable for about six weeks, but of course it was not a place for continued sickness, such as we had (though this again could not have been anticipated), and which indeed delayed the building of our new stone bungalow—in which we might reasonably expect to be well—quite two months altogether. . . . . All this, I think, shews that every precaution that care and thoughtfulness could suggest was taken, and that our living in that little hut was not due to any carelessness or indifference to health on his part. Also his firm stand against Eastern cupidity at the outset made him more respected even by those who tried to swindle him; and his contentment and happiness in such humble quarters were also characteristic."

Now that the party was settled in its temporary quarters, proceedings were at once set on foot for beginning the erection of a permanent home. On January 11, he thus writes to his mother :—

"We have arranged a contract for the wall round our land, and operations have begun. We are to pay about 7s. 2d. per 10 feet of wall. You would have laughed at our meeting with the Arab contractors. The business lasted an hour and a half. First I explained the thing with black board and chalk. Then they began bidding. We started at 12 rupees (= 18s.). There was great excitement at the end.

"Some days ago I engaged a Madrasee cook, and thought I had got a treasure: excellent character, and he sent us beautiful dishes. But he was a drunkard, and I caught him whacking our Somali coolie. So I packed him off then and there. The last thing he did was to kneel before me, and make a + in the sand—perfectly drunk. We have now a Goanese cook, and a Goanese butler."

To the same.

"SHAIKH OTHMAN,
Jan. 23, 1887.

"You will be glad to hear that the medical work has made a start. When the dispensary was finished, we let

it be known that we were in a position to treat patients,
and soon they began to come. Last week we had eighteen
patients : one or two were very satisfactory cases. Most
of the people who came are Arabs, one an Indian Muham-
medam, one a half-Arab, half-African (and a runaway
slave), four are Somalis. They all seem to repose the
most absolute confidence in us.

" To-morrow at 6 A.M. we mount camels for Bir-Achmad,
a village outside British territory, and the seat of a local,
petty Sultan : at 5 A.M. another camel starts with the
medicine-chest, which must be conveyed at walking-pace,
for fear of breaking the bottles. We take with us a man
who has an interest in the garden next to ours, and who
seems to have done a good deal in the way of puffing our
establishment ; he was our first patient. Curiously, after
we had resolved to visit Bir-Achmad, we heard that one of
the Sultan's nephews is very ill : so we shall easily get an
introduction to the Sultan. Bir-Achmad is said to be
eight miles off : we expect to get back by dark. We hope
to make a weekly excursion in future. My own part of
the work at present consists in interpreting for Cowen
and telling the people why we have come. Incidentally
I learn medicine and surgery. I am improving quickly
in speaking and understanding Arabic, but I constantly
need an Arab interpreter to explain what the Bedouin
means.

" As Shaikh Othman has 6000 people, Lahej 5000, and
Bir-Achmad and other villages in the neighbourhood about
1500 between them, we shall have plenty of work without
going far away. We have one interesting case from Lahej,
a man with an enormously enlarged spleen, the effect of
repeated fevers from malaria. We hope to reduce it by
local application of biniodide of mercury. . . . .

" We have at last got our temporary abode in order. The
rooms are really very comfortable, and no one need pity us
in the least. We hope in another ten days to have completed the arrangements for building the bungalow. . . . .

" Here is our day as a rule :—

" 6.30. Get up. I take my bath at the well-side. It
is very deep and big, and a camel walks round and round,
working the wheel which moves a chain of little buckets

descending into the water. I just sit down under the water as it flows out. It feels like warm milk. Then, after dressing, a cup of tea and toast.

"7 to 8.30 is the appointed time for patients : but they often come later, and it will be some time before we succeed in making them observe the right time.

"8.30 to 9.   Bible reading in company.

"9.   Breakfast.

"9.30 to 1.30.   Arabic reading and patients, if any come.

"1.30.   Lunch or 'tiffin.'

"2 to 4.30.   Anything.

"4.30.   Tea.

"5 to 7.   Walk out with Jip.

"7.   Dinner.

"8.   Prayers, after which each goes to bed when he pleases.

"This afternoon we visited three patients in their homes. G. remained outside, and the native women inspected her closely, feeling her dress, etc."

[Continued on *Jan.* 25].

"Yesterday we accomplished the visit to Bir-Achmad. We started about 7 on camels, and the ride took an hour and a half. The ambling trot of the camel is not half bad, and the native saddle is far preferable to the European leather saddle with stirrups which are made for camels.

"We might have stopped for three days and been hard at work all the time. The cases treated amounted to twenty. At first the people were afraid, and we could only hear of two cases. One was that of an old woman with dropsy. She was enormously distended. . . . . She was intensely grateful to us. This at once established Cowen's credit, the news spread like magic, and we were taken to a number of houses to see sick people. All the rooms we went into were beautifully clean and tidy. I left a few gospels with some boys who could read, and wrote their names on the title-pages, which seemed to please them very much. . . . . Several gave us the Muslim salutation, 'Peace upon you,' though they are forbidden to do so to Christians. Our next excursion will be to El-Hautah."[1]

[1] This excursion they were prevented from taking in consequence of the long illness.

The visit to Bir-Achmad is also described in a letter of
February 1 from Dr. Cowen to Dr. George Smith, from
which I make the following extract :—

" We arrived at our destination shortly before nine
o'clock, and were shewn into the upper room in the small
mud gateway of the sheikh's palace. At a distance the
palatial building itself presents a most imposing effect,
which a nearer inspection proves to be a delusion and a
snare. In this mud room we rested, cooked our breakfast,
and had our audience with the sheikh's nephew, a good
specimen of the Bedouin Arab—quiet, hospitable and
courteous in manner; ignorant and superstitious about
religion; with a wholesome belief in the powers (real and
imaginary) of European medicine, and decidedly grateful
for kindness and benefits received. They *thought* there
were 'one or two' sick people in the village; so after reading extracts from the 'Injîl'[1] to the young people, we set
off to visit them. Happily I had brought my instruments
with me; and we were able to relieve a poor woman who
had suffered for three years from ascites, the cause of
which I could not ascertain. So unmistakeable were the
results and the relief to the poor sufferer, whose demon-
strations of gratitude were eloquent beyond all power of
language, that the effect on the Arab mind was striking
and instantaneous. Suspicion was at once disarmed, and
the news of the event spread like wildfire through the
village, and we were literally dragged from house to house
to see sick people of whose existence they seemed previously
to have been strangely ignorant."

At this time everything seemed exceedingly bright and
hopeful. The letters thus far cited shew not merely cheerfulness, for that indeed characterizes the letters written
during the period of sickness, but an evident and resolute
hopefulness. From a letter of Dr. Cowen's to myself I
select one or two incidents illustrating the nature of their
life at this time. He mentions that the verandah of mats
which had been added to the dispensary was a place to

---

[1] See above, p. 163.

which Keith-Falconer was fond of coming, as long as he was able, "to sit and talk or read to the natives who came. His kind and sympathetic manner readily opened the way to their hearts, and 'the English Sahib who spoke Arabic like a book' was everywhere welcome. His knowledge of the language was still mainly that of the written or classical Arabic : he was, however, rapidly acquiring the colloquial tongue when laid aside by fever."

Dr. Cowen further refers to a point I have already dwelt on in an earlier chapter. Underlying Keith-Falconer's kindness of demeanour and of heart, there was a large amount of decision of character and strong common sense. He won respect all the more from those around him when it became clearly seen that with all his generosity he had a decided objection to being imposed upon; and while I very much doubt whether any of his friends ever saw him angry, in the ordinary sense of the word, he could, if the occasion called for it, manifest a genuine righteous indignation at what was cruel or base. An illustration of this may be given. A man in his employ had, when intoxicated, cruelly beaten his wife and cut her head while in Keith-Falconer's garden, and was summarily dismissed. Keith-Falconer in sending the man away addressed him in terms of the severest reproach for his cruelty, "but without a trace of anger." The poor wife, pathetically anxious to mend matters, tried to explain the injuries by saying that she was subject to epileptic fits, and had fallen against a box! He was much touched with the poor woman's behaviour, and hired a camel to carry her and her things away.

The following incident has considerable suggestiveness in its bearing on the question of the view of Christianity likely to be taken by the Arabs of the interior. Dr. Cowen writes :—

"During our first visit to Bir-Achmad we were taken to see a sick man, whose complaint required surgical aid,

and whom he promised to take into our dispensary. He
was to have come in the next day, but fully six weeks
elapsed ere he arrived. The poor wife explained the long
delay by saying she could not get a camel. When he
asked her if no Muslim would lend her one to bring a sick
man in, she replied with an impatient gesture, 'There are
no Muslims now.' He paid for her camel both ways, and
kept her for some weeks, as she wished to attend to her
sick husband. She was very grateful for the kindness
she had received, and, though wretchedly poor, twice
brought us a native basket with twenty eggs. This was
but one of the many instances in which the people shewed
their gratitude by sending presents of flowers, fruit, vegetables, etc."

The Sultan of Lahej, the most influential native potentate in the neighbourhood, of whom, it may be remembered, Keith-Falconer had spoken in his first visit in no
very complimentary terms, called twice at the bungalow,
and was one of Dr. Cowen's patients. During Keith-
Falconer's last illness, he sent in a considerable quantity
of water-melons, bananas and honey, and had previously
asked to be allowed to stock the new garden with fruit
trees. This was the more pleasing, because, as I have
already mentioned in a note, Keith-Falconer's illness prevented him from repeating the visit he made to El-Hautah
in the preceding year.

One day a Turk, passing through Shaikh Othman on
his way to Aden, where he had some official business,
called at Keith-Falconer's house. Here he was very kindly
received, and had a long conversation with his host respecting some extracts from the Gospel which were read
to him. He also received some benefit from a slight surgical operation, and evidently the kindness with which he
was treated left a deep impression on his mind. "On his
return from Aden," writes Dr. Cowen, "he presented us
with three large gourds, filled with honey,—for which he
had sent home, a distance of a hundred miles—besides a

P

pair of tame rabbits : he wished us also to take money. He also promised us letters of introduction, if we travelled inland as we hoped to do."

Keith-Falconer was fond of occasionally dropping into the coffee shops of the village and talking to the natives there assembled. One day, as he passed a certain shop, he found an old man lying in great pain on a rude bed by the way-side. What followed may best be told in Dr. Cowen's words :—

" He asked some of the crowd of men and boys to carry the poor man to our dispensary, where we would take care of him. At once several of them called out for hammâls, or inferior persons, to do so, while they themselves shewed no signs of moving in the matter. He said, 'In our country, if a man were ill in the street, plenty of people would gladly carry him ; but you Muslims don't seem willing to lift a finger.' To this one of the crowd significantly replied by putting his finger to his mouth and saying, 'Lip-Muslims here.' Thereupon he nodded to me, and taking each an end of the bed, we began to carry the poor fellow ourselves. This was too much for them, and immediately any number of volunteers were forthcoming. This method of shaming them into action he practised on other occasions with like success."

I have spoken of this period of the residence at Shaikh Othman as bright and cheerful, and so in one sense it certainly was, most cheerful, most hopeful. Still at times there was much to depress in the surrounding circumstances ; yet not only at this time, but later when attack after attack of illness would have crushed the spirit out of many men, Keith-Falconer retained both his exceeding thoughtfulness for others, and a genial humour and keen sense of the ridiculous. One very hot day, seeing his Somali servant perspiring freely over an ice machine which demanded a great deal of exertion and provided very little ice, he laughingly suggested that the heat was abstracted from the water and passed up the handle into the boy's body, which the boy himself thought fully accounted both for the ice and the perspiration!

All through the time of residence at Shaikh Othman, he was very fond of talking of his old school and college friends and teachers with much affection. Dr. Cowen remarks, " what struck me most was the warmth and duration of these friendships, some of them dating back ten or fifteen years or more." A characteristic piece of thoughtfulness for an old friend may be mentioned. He had a box of carefully selected books packed up and sent to Mr. C. T. Studd, when he heard of his isolation from friends and books in China. Among the books so sent was one which Keith-Falconer read for the first time shortly after landing at Aden, and with which he was much charmed, Blaikie's *Personal Life of David Livingstone.*

The present will be a suitable place for the insertion of the following note. It was found among Keith-Falconer's papers, and tells its story plainly: it embraces the whole range of his employment, other than the direct teaching of the Gospel, and testifies alike to the thoroughness of his missionary purpose, to his zeal for acquiring knowledge, more especially such as bore on his missionary work, and to his methodical grouping of his details.

" Handwriting.
Grammar.
Arithmetic.

Reading practice.
Help G. and Cowen.
Ja'cūbi.

Geography of Yemen, etc.
Bedawi language.
Medicine.
Somali.
Hindustanee.

Learn texts by heart,—(1) Bible, (2) Koran.

Supervise building and garden.

Correspondence.

Light literature.

Catalogue my Arabic books."

In the references to grammar, reading practice, and the learning of texts, we must of course understand Arabic. The *Ja'cūbī*, mentioned in the second group, is an Arabic work, which Keith-Falconer had begun to translate before leaving England, and of which about half had been finished at his death. The work is a geographical description of the countries which had embraced Islam, and though the Arabic text has been several times printed, there is not, I understand, a translation into any modern European language. The part which Keith-Falconer had finished was mainly occupied with the description of Persia.[1]

The mention of Somali and Hindustanee in the third group refers to Keith-Falconer's intention of acquiring at any rate a reasonable working knowledge of these two languages, both of which were largely spoken in Aden. References to both of these will be found in some of the letters yet to be cited.

I spoke in passing, in a preceding chapter, of General Haig's remarkable journey through Yemen. In all the details of this Keith-Falconer took a very keen interest, and it cannot be doubted that, had his life been prolonged, he would have tried in due time to make his way into the interior.

In the early part of February, General Haig met Keith-

---

[1] The book derives its name from its author, Achmad ibn Abi Ja'cub, commonly called Al-Ja'cūbī. The actual title of the book is Kitābū-l-Buldān, or 'the Book of the Countries.' It was written in the year 891 A.D.

Falconer three or four times. The following extract is from a letter from General Haig to myself :—

" Dr. Harpur and I were just starting one day just after my arrival [at Aden] to call on him and Mrs. Keith-Falconer at Shaikh Othman, when he walked in with Dr. Cowen. They spent the afternoon with us, and we had much prayer and talk about the work.

" I saw him last on February 7, when I drove out to Shaikh Othman and spent the evening with them. It was a very interesting time. We walked out through the newly rising town, looked at the half-built enclosure wall round the piece of land he had taken for mission buildings, and talked over various plans. He was then greatly encouraged by a visit which he and Dr. Cowen had just paid to one of the nearer villages, where they were kindly received, and the doctor's medical aid was gladly welcomed in many cases.[1] He looked well and strong, and little we thought how nearly his short course was run. We all knelt together before I left, and commended him and his work to the Lord. . . . . I anticipated for him years of usefulness. But it was not so to be, and it is best as it is. He who doeth all things well has ordered it otherwise, and doubtless Keith-Falconer's early death was more for His glory and the extension of His kingdom in Arabia than many years of life would have been."

On the day of General Haig's visit, Keith-Falconer thus writes to his eldest sister :—

"SHAIKH OTHMAN,
Feb, 7, 1887.

". . . . We are more out of the world here than we should be at Aden, for we see no daily telegrams, and seldom a white face ; but the life here is of a much more interesting nature than it could be at Aden. Here we are in closer contact with the people, and have constant opportunities of meeting with them. We have already three in-patients in the infirmary behind the house. This is a little mud building with planks for a roof, and with a door and

---

[1] This is of course the visit to Bir-Achmad of January 24.

two windows. One patient is nearly blind and very weak : we shall not be able to do much more than improve the general *tone*. One has scurvy and is getting steadily better. The third is a very bad case of heart-disease, liver-disease and dropsy. He is a Bedouin from a town called Ibh, about 100 miles inland. I am afraid he will die soon. Last night I left him crying aloud to Allah, and the Messiah. He is very ignorant, and I had told him that God loves every person who believes in the Messiah.

"General Haig came to-day and stayed to dinner. He has just returned from a journey. Starting from Hodeida, a Red Sea port, and accompanied by the Syrian colporteur, Ibrahim (who sells Bibles for the British and Foreign Bible Society in Aden), and a Somali servant, he went up to San'â, the capital of Yemen, where he was entertained by some Italian merchants. Thence he came down to Aden. He speaks of plenty of cultivation in some districts. The climate in the highlands of Yemen is quite temperate, and he always slept in a house. The roads seem to be quite safe. He found quantities of Jews, all marvellously ignorant. At one place he had a semi-public discussion with them, or rather with the chief rabbi in the presence of the rest.

"Our wall of mud, eight feet high, which is to surround our house and garden, is about half-finished, and we have arranged a contract for the procural and conveyance of 7,200 cubic feet of stone from Aden. There is no stone here. In a few days we hope to have arranged a third contract for building the walls. When the house is built, or a little earlier, we must get the dispensary and hospital erected. The estimate for the house amounts to 5,400, 6,500, or 7,400 rupees, according to the kind of wood we use for it. 7,400 rupees equal £570. The dispensary will come to about £100 or £150 more. . . . . The school and a house for the Cowens will come later. These are all initial expenses, and when defrayed will not occur again."

It was very soon after General Haig's visit that things began for the first time to be clouded over. On February 9, Keith-Falconer and Dr. Cowen paid their second visit to Bir-Achmad, riding on camels as before. On the evening

of the next day the former was slightly feverish, but felt
sufficiently well to rise and speak to a number of Somali
women in the verandah with Mrs. Keith-Falconer. On the
next day, however, he had high fever, and on the 13th Dr.
Colson was called out from Aden to see him. The fever
continued for three days, and then began to abate, so that
by the 19th he was able to rise for dinner, and on the 21st
walked round to the next garden with Colonel and Mrs.
Raper. To aggravate matters, Mrs. Keith-Falconer also
had fever very badly at the same time; though, most
providentially, Dr. Cowen was entirely unaffected by it at
present.

At this time Keith-Falconer writes to his mother,

"SHAIKH OTHMAN,
Feb. 22, 1887.

"Both G. and I are now convalescing after a bout of
Aden fever. I never felt so utterly miserable in all my
life, but Colson declares that there is no danger in it, and
that it leaves no after effects. . . . . One of our Somali
servants has had it too, but coupled with a great deal of
shivering, which we did not have. This morning the butler
says he has fever. There is a great deal of it about now,
owing to the strong winds which have been prevalent
lately. . . . .

"Quinine is quite useless in this fever, one must simply
grin and bear it. When we get into a proper house,
affording proper protection from the wind, we shall not
be so liable to it.

"The Queen's Jubilee was celebrated at Aden a few days
ago. The Parsees, who are hand in glove with the English,
made a great display of loyalty."

Towards the end of the month he had a slight return of
the attack, but on March 2 he was able, with Mrs. Keith-
Falconer, to remove to Khor Maksar. This place is
situated on the Isthmus, about two miles to the north of
the defensive works, and here is stationed a troop of native

cavalry. Khor Maksar formed until recently the limit of British territory at Aden. Here they enjoyed the hospitality of Lieutenant **Gordon, the officer in command** of the troop, whose friendship and kindliness **they** greatly valued. After about a week's stay here they moved, **Mrs.** Keith-Falconer to Colonel Raper's in Aden Camp, and Keith-Falconer himself to Steamer Point, **to the house of Dr. Jackson, then and afterwards a true friend and adviser.** From here he thus writes to his youngest sister:—

>   "Steamer Point, Aden,
>   *March* 9, 1887.

" . . . . When that miserable fever left us, we came away for change of air. First we went to the Isthmus, to Lieut. Louis Gordon's house. He commands the Aden Troop (100 Indian cavalry men, stationed there for duty when necessary), and is a son of Sir H. W. Gordon, brother of Chinese Gordon. He has the 'magic wand,' which the Chinese thought ensured victory to the 'ever victorious army.' We became great friends. His room contains three pictures of his uncle, and he looks on his journals, &c., as a kind of Bible. . . . .

" Yesterday I came here, Dr. Jackson's house. We are both well again, but are not going back till Monday next.

"Our mud wall is finished, and we have got the stone for the house, and arranged the contract for the stone work; 27 rupees (about £2) per 100 cubic feet. The house will cost just about £500. Try and get some fat donations for the hospital. I believe that three of Mrs. ——'s dresses would build it. But I believe that we *can* do it without more help, as we are spending very little on ourselves now. Still a few little cheques would expedite matters. Our cow is a success. It only cost £3. . . . .

" —— treated us to tunes on the *orguinette.* You put in rolls of paper, with slits in them, thus [here follows a rough diagram], and turn a handle. It requires no skill, and gives great pleasure. He treated us to a varied selection. He played the 'Old Hundredth,' then 'Pinafore.' . . . .

"I am acquiring quite a stock of medical knowledge.

Ulcers are my forte at present. We get 100 new patients a month. Some come from far inland. G. is improving in the Arab tongue. I have just written to Dr. G. Smith about the pink leaflet.[1] We have no out-station at Lahej. There is no such thing as 'ripe scholarship:' I expect to peg away at the Dictionary till my last day. Cowen will certainly not travel among the Bedawin till Mrs. C. arrives to keep G. company.

"We have had our roof *thatched*, and the house will be cooler for it. The weather at present is cool and breezy."

After a total absence of three weeks, Keith-Falconer returned to Shaikh Othman, much improved in health, free from fever, eating and sleeping well. It would seem, however, as though a strange susceptibility to a return of fever still remained, and during the next five weeks he had several fresh attacks, partially regaining his strength in the intervals and going about, but never thoroughly strong.

To his Mother.

"Dr. Jackson's, Steamer Point,
March 17, 1887.

"You will be glad to hear that we are both nearly well. . . . . One of the peculiarities of Aden fever is that you think you are quit of it, and for a time you convalesce nicely: then it comes back in a milder form for a day at a time, remitting. We expect to be back at Shaikh Othman on Saturday.

"I am learning Hindustanee. It is a mongrel jargon of Sanscrit, Hindee, Persian, Arabic and English: but I find it is very awkward not to know it.

"The Surgeon-General of Bombay has been making enquiries about our dispensary. I think that eventually the Government dispensary will be discontinued, and we shall get a grant; by which we shall be enabled to keep a hospital assistant. . . . .

---

[1] This is the *Sabbath School Missionary Leaflet* of the Free Church of Scotland (No. 36), "Our Medical Mission in South Arabia."

"If the Turks would clear out of Yemen, a wonderful
field for commerce would be thrown open: for the Turkish
government is vile, and all cultivators are taxed to an
iniquitous extent."

On March 26, he wrote thus to myself :—

"I have not been able to write owing to the long spell
of fever which both my wife and I have been through. I
am now at Steamer Point with Dr. Jackson trying to get
back strength, but it is slow work, and the fever may come
back any day. Cowen has also sickened. My wife is
recruiting at Mrs. Raper's in Aden.

"Did you ever think of reading קדֹשִׁים instead of קרנים
in Hab.[1] Comp. parallel passage in Deuteronomy. Have
just read Scott's *Antiquary*. First class. Now I am in
Heart of Midlothian. I am afraid I don't feel up to writing
a long letter yet."

On or about April 1, Dr. Colson went over to Shaikh
Othman, "and found him looking much better and in good
spirits."

To his Mother.

"Shaikh Othman,
April 4, 1887.

". . . . After lying on my back for nearly seven weeks,
I find that I have little news. . . . . It is now five days
since I had fever, and I am getting rapidly stronger.

"Our house is at length rising from the ground. We are
going carefully to work, and bargaining like Jews. The
weather is very pleasant: the early mornings and evenings
are fresh and the nights quite cold. The white ants are
very troublesome; they have destroyed several of our nice
pictures. The floor beneath our matting is just earth, and
harbours all sorts of creatures. The rats also are very
bold. The mice have nibbled a good bit off my professorial
patent, but I keep it in its box now.

---

[1] This refers to the Psalm of Habakkuk (iii. 4), in which we both
at this time were especially interested.

"We have got all our German books. I am reading 'Die verlorene Handschrift.' . . . . I am trying to learn enough Hindustanee to talk with natives. . . . .

"Official correspondence has been going on about our medical work. We do more business than the Government dispensary. When Cowen has got a native assistant, we shall no doubt be able to make an arrangement with Government, by which they withdraw and give us a grant."

Again, in a letter of the same date to myself, he says :—

"Our illness has thrown us back in every way. In particular, I have been unable to write to you at any length, or to think over Habakkuk's Psalm. My wife has been quite well for more than a week, but I am still weak and not fit for much. This fever is evidently of a remittent nature. I have had five attacks in eight weeks. There is nothing for it but patience.

"Our house is at last rising above the ground. Here is a plan of it. . . . . The verandah is 12 feet broad, and the dining room will form part of it, shut in by wooden partitions, or reeds and mats. The doors have glass in them, and serve also as windows. In this climate one is obliged to have a great many of them. The walls are of stone, the roof of wood and plaster. The floor will be plaster throughout. The verandah will be thatched. The rooms will be about 12 feet high. . . . .

"We get a great many patients, and Cowen has not been thrown out of his work by his fever nearly so much as I. His attack was fortunately a mild one. He will require an assistant when he comes back from England. By that time we hope to have built our hospital. . . . ."

To his Mother.

"SHAIKH OTHMAN,
April 19, 1887.

"We are all pretty well, but neither I nor G. are as strong as we should like to be. We are having nice weather. We never think of going out in the day. The

nights are quite cool, dangerously so.   Next month is said
to be about the worst in the year.

"We have engaged a gardener from Lahej to lay out
our plot.   We must stock it well with palm-trees, because
they thrive here so well, and give such good shade when
grown. . . . . We expect to be home next year for three
months."

A letter dated April 20 was the last I was ever to receive from him.   Considering the nature of the letter, I
felt some hesitation in reproducing it here, but those
whose judgement I value have urged me to do so, and I
accordingly give it almost in full.   The letter was written
in answer to one of mine telling of my mother's grave
illness, at a time when I had all but given up hope and
only a few days before she passed to her rest.   The letter
in reply is thoroughly characteristic of the writer.   Its
deep Christian trust and tender sympathy are what Ion
Keith-Falconer's friends could ever count on finding in
him.   Nor should the lighter touches of the letter be overlooked.   The remarks on points of Hebrew I have allowed
to stand; not as specimens of the deliberate judgement of
the scholar giving forth a carefully thought out theory,
and yet not to be thrown aside because they are only
sparks from an anvil on which good weapons could be and
had been forged.   The letter runs:—

> "Shaikh Othman,
> *April* 20, 1887.

"Your letter of April 3 received yesterday evening.
I am most truly sorry to hear of the dangerous illness of
Mrs. Sinker.   You will know the worst by now.   Thank
God, we sorrow not as those who have no hope: and we
know that death for a Christian is the beginning of life.
I am very glad that H. C. G. Moule has been to see you
so often: and sincerely sorry that I cannot do the same.
I pray that you may not give way to excessive grief, but
on the contrary may be glad for her sake and may dwell

with thankfulness on the thought that God has spared her
to you for so long. . . . .

"Certainly they are to be envied who are just thankful
for all that God gives them, and do not grieve for what
He holds from them. A man was stricken with blind-
ness; when asked if he did not repine, he said, 'On the
contrary, I am filled with thankfulness for all the years of
sight which I have enjoyed.' It is hard to get to this
state, but it can be done. If I am a Christian, I can say—
'Whatever happens to me is the very best thing which can
be devised.' And yet, on the other hand, it is only natural
that one should be sad (without complaining) when a
loved one is taken. I argue hence that grief is *intended*
for us, and must turn to blessing. And so I conclude that
God, by this special grief, has some special blessing in
store for you.

"I have been looking at Hab.[1] again. וְשָׁם חֶבְיוֹן strikes
me as very suspicious. חֶבְיוֹן seems to give the wrong
meaning, besides being ἅπ. λεγ.; I would suggest חִזָּיוֹן,
revelation or unveiling, but the usage of חִזָּיוֹן does not
quite favour this sense. Perhaps we might point חָזָיוֹן?
Is this form used in poetry out of pause? Then again
I should like to point וְנָנַה *vice* וְנֹגַה, and construe תִּהְיֶה
with קְרָנִים. In ver. 16 I think there must be a clerical
error, and would like to read לַעֲלוֹת עַם. Do not shew
these hasty remarks to ——. It would terminate my
friendship with him, if he did not die on the spot of a fit.

"Can you tell me which is the best dictionary of
Scotch? Such a book is needful in reading Scott.

"Yours ever affectionately,
And with deep sympathy."

To his Mother.

"SHAIKH OTHMAN,
May 1, 1887.

"You will be sorry to hear that I have been down with
yet another attack. I am now getting strong again. This
makes my seventh attack. . . . . This rather miserable

---

[1] Habakkuk iii.

shanty in which we are compelled to live is largely the cause of our fevers. It is all draughts. Our address should be ' The Draughts, Shaikh Othman.' I sincerely trust that when we get into our house, which is now six feet above the ground, we shall be exempt from this nuisance. We are going in a few days to Gordon's bungalow on the isthmus to enjoy his fresh sea-air. He is four miles from here, but his climate is quite different from ours, and is more bracing. You need not have the slightest anxiety about us. At the present moment we are distinctly better than we were after the first attack. We are not being gradually worn out.

" Our gardener, newly engaged, is busy levelling, ploughing and laying out the plot, and directly the well is complete, planting and sowing will begin. We expect to begin living in the new house about June 1, though it will not be finished then. . . . .

" I have had plenty of time for reading. I have got through Scott's ' Heart of Midlothian,' ' Antiquary ' and ' Guy Mannering : ' ' Sir Percival : ' enough of ' She ' to shew that it was just a remodelling of ' King Solomon : ' ' Children of Gibeon ' by Besant, capital : Pressensé's ' Early Years of Christian Church,' vol. i. : ' Life of Livingstone ' by Blaikie, splendid : parts of Carus's ' Life of Charles Simeon : ' Forbes's ' Hindustani Grammar,' most : Bonar's ' Life of Dr. Judson,' very interesting : half of ' Dorothy Forster,' which I got tired of : parts of ' Horae Subsecivae ' by Dr. J. Brown : and the first hundred pages of ' Die verlorene Handschrift,' which is very well written, though the story is not intensely interesting so far. . . . .

(Continued) *May* 2.

" To-day is very pleasant. Sun very hot, with a gentle breeze blowing. I am also better and stronger. . . . . Read Bonar's ' Life of Judson,' and you will see that our troubles are nought."

On May 3, Dr. Colson again went over to Shaikh Othman to see him ; " he was looking pale and seemed a good deal knocked-up." Still, it was thought, he was stronger and brighter than he had been for some little time past ; and he wrote an unusually large number of letters for the mail which left on May 4. He had arranged to go with Mrs. Keith-Falconer on May 5 to spend a few days at Khor Maksar with Lieutenant Gordon, as the change to his house on a former occasion had done them both much good. At the last moment, however, Mr. Gordon was compelled to put them off for a day or two.

On May 3 he wrote to his brother-in-law, Mr. Ashley Bevan :—

" . . . . Cowen has nursed us splendidly. He is just the kind of man I wanted. The people like him very much and flock to the dispensary : but he knows too little Arabic to communicate freely with them. He is picking it up rapidly, and is evidently a clever man. We have accommodation for six in-patients, so that as soon as I am strong enough I shall have all the opportunities I want. Islam has no very strong hold on the people. They say themselves, ' There are no Muslims here.' English influence is very great, and extends far inland. The Sultan of Lahej is among our patients : he sends us presents of fruit, and offers to stock our garden. . . . .

" I used to offer patients a choice between our medicine and Zemzem [1] water. They always chose the former."

He writes on the same day to Mr. J. H. Turner, of Cambridge :—

" Since Feb. 10 until a day or two ago, I have been suffering from remitting fever ; for twelve weary weeks, with a few short breaks, on my back a useless invalid. I hope and trust that I have shaken it off now. . . . . We shall soon be in a good stone house which is building, and the hot weather has begun—and the hot months are healthier than the cool—so we look forward to a spell of health now.

" My wife has been about as bad as I have : but, thank God, we are in excellent spirits. . . . . One good point about this fever is that it leaves no bad effects behind it.

[1] The sacred well at Mecca.

The doctors know of no remedy for it.   Quinine is useless.
. . . . Just received a kind note of greeting from G. E.
Moule, Bishop of Mid-China, dated from steamship *Hy-daspes*, written *en voyage* for China. . . . .

"The weather is now warming up.   Yesterday it was
94° in the shade : but we have a double roof and a delicious
breeze.

"The people are flocking to our dispensary, and we keep
a few in-patients ; but Dr. Cowen knows too little Arabic to
preach to them.   I long for health to get at them.   D.V.,
I shall be in Cambridge in May Term, 1888."

Alas, Deo aliter visum.

The two foregoing letters did not reach the hands of
those to whom they were addressed until after the tele-graph had told the news that God had called His servant
to Himself.

For the period which remains I have been permitted to
draw upon a brief diary kept by Dr. Cowen, and Mrs.
Keith-Falconer has put into my hands certain notes taken
by herself.

On the morning of Thursday, May 5, Keith-Falconer
received a visit from Ibrahim,—the Bible Society's agent
at Aden who had accompanied General Haig in his journey
through Yemen,—and was much interested in the conver-sation.   In the afternoon, accompanied by his wife and
Dr. Cowen, he drove to the garden-plot of the Mission-House.   Here they spent more than half-an-hour, while
he examined the work done and gave directions to the
workmen.   In the evening, he did not seem to be at all
over-fatigued.

On the Friday morning (May 6) he felt too tired to rise
for breakfast, and by noon it was clear that the fever had
returned.   It was in the course of this morning, Mrs.
Keith-Falconer believes, that he said to her, "Isn't it very
strange ?   I get generally so depressed when I am unwell,
but now I don't feel in the least cast down.   After all

these weeks of illness, I feel in perfectly good spirits." He
had his books on his bed,—his Bible, Hebrew Old Testament and Hindustani Grammar,—as had been the case all
through his illness, and read a good deal.

On Saturday the fever was present all day. In the
evening Colonel Raper came to see him, and was much
struck with his patient cheerfulness.

For the following extract I am indebted to Dr. Cowen's
diary :—

"May 8. *Sunday.* He took early tea and milk with
usual relish. . . . . Caught a fresh chill, teeth chattered.
Did not get warm for half an hour. Then very hot, followed about 11 or 12 o'clock by heavy perspiration. Feeling of oppression increased, relieved somewhat by sickness.
. . . . Asked me to read to him, chose last chapter of St.
Mark, 'it is disputed, but that doesn't matter.' . . . .
2.30 P.M. At this time and during remainder of afternoon,
pulse imperceptible at wrist or barely present. . . . . Asked
if his wife had been as ill as this. . . . . Stayed with him
that night: very restless, but had one sleep of about three
hours.

"May 9. *Monday.* Still restless. . . . . Objected more
than once to Achmad sitting beside him, while I visited a
sick woman, &c., as A. was not well, and he said it would
tire him. Same when his wife sat with him. Wrote for
nurse. . . . . That evening I talked with him about a
change, which I said was necessary, and said I would stay
after June 7 if necessary.[1] He said he hoped it would not
be necessary, and that I should not get fever. 'Suppose
you caught it three or four days before you were to sail. I
am going to pray that nothing may prevent your getting
away on the 7th of June.' He had been wandering at
times during the day, but seemed to brace himself up for
this, and was perfectly clear; very simply and fervently he
thanked God for my nursing, and prayed for restoration to
health to carry on the work begun; that nothing might

---

[1] It had been planned that Dr. Cowen should have taken the
steamer of this date for England, to complete the medical and
surgical outfit of the Mission.

prevent my sailing as arranged, and that He would 'graciously dispose the hearts of friends at home towards the cause of missions, in the name of our Lord and Saviour Jesus Christ.' I stayed by his side all night : he slept about four hours altogether."

In the course of the morning of this day he had said to his wife, " I want you to thank God that I am so much better ; I feel like a new man ; do pray now." Afterwards he talked of the seeming mysteriousness of the fever being allowed to interrupt the work for so long, but added that God allowed it all and so it must be right. Then he said, " How I wish that each attack of fever had brought me nearer to Christ—nearer, nearer, nearer ; " adding shortly afterwards, " I can most truly say that I am not afraid to die, in spite of my many shortcomings, but I do pray God that I may be spared pain." Then he spoke of his brother Dudley, how much he suffered, and how joyful he was at the thought of death.

The following extract is from Dr. Cowen's diary :—

" May 10. *Tuesday.* Condition much the same as yesterday. About 5 p.m. Mr. Streeten, the chaplain, called, bringing the nurse to help us. He did not feel well enough to see Mr. Streeten, and asked to be excused. I walked to the garden plot with Mr. Streeten, and talked over possible trips : he promised to make all enquiries from P. and O. agent the same evening. I said we could not arrange anything definitely, as it would depend on when he was well enough to move, and when that would be really no one could say at present. In evening was very weak and restless. . . . . Asked me if I thought there was danger : I said ' I hope not,' and tried to cheer him.

" Told the nurse to knock me up at once if anything happened, and shewed her where I slept. Shortly before 9, he took two eggs in brandy and milk, and about 9.30 fell asleep. I stayed with Mrs. Keith-Falconer till 10 o'clock, and had prayer for her husband with her. We talked over his condition and treatment, and could think of nothing else which could be done. Left the nurse in charge with brandy and milk and ice by bedside. Was sleeping quietly and regularly when I left about 10 o'clock, and being very tired I slept soundly till hastily called by Mrs. Keith-Falconer about a quarter to six next morning. The nurse reported that he slept quietly most of the night, and she was thinking how refreshed he would be next day, as he had been rather restless for two nights. About 4 A.M. he was still sleeping quietly and regularly. She then lay down by the side of the bed, and was not awake when Mrs. Keith-Falconer called to her in the morning. . . . . One glance told all. He was lying on his back, with eyes half-open, and hands resting on the bed by his sides. . . . . The whole attitude and expression indicated a sudden and painless end, as if it had taken place during sleep, there being no indication whatever of his having tried to move or speak."

It was indeed the end: quietly he had passed away. "God's finger touched him and he slept." Slept! Nay, rather awakened. Not in the close heated room, where he had so long lain half-helpless,—the weary nurse, overcome with heat and watching, slumbering near,—the young wife, widowed ere yet she knew her loss, lying in the adjoining room, herself broken down with illness as well as anxiety,—the loyal doctor, resting after his two nights' vigil—not on these do Ion Keith-Falconer's eyes reopen. He is in the presence of his Lord: the life which is the Life Indeed has begun.

On the evening of the 11th he was reverently laid to rest at the Aden cemetery, several of the officers of the garrison (H.M.'s 98th Regiment) attending the funeral. The spot is a wild and dreary one, in no sense recalling the peaceful beauty of many an English churchyard. He is far from home and loved ones, yet he rests amid those for whom he laboured with so perfect a love, and for whom he counted no loss too great, if only he might win them for Christ. He died at just Henry Martyn's age. Like him he has " fulfilled a long time in a short time," and precious shall be the fruit that shall spring, in God's good time, out of his blessed devotion to the Lord.

CHAPTER XI.

CONCLUSION.

"'My sword I give to him that shall succeed me in my pilgrimage, and my courage and skill to him that can get it. My marks and scars I carry with me, to be a witness for me, that I have fought His battles, Who now will be my rewarder' . . . . So he passed over, and all the trumpets sounded for him on the other side."

PILGRIM'S PROGRESS. *Death of Valiant-for-Truth.*

IT was almost exactly six months after the young missionary, full of keen hopes and joyous anticipations, had left England for the East, that the telegram told the unlooked-for news of his death and his burial amid the scene of his labours. The cheerful tone of the letters he had written during his illness made it all the harder to realise the fact that one who had been seen so short a time before in the fullest vigour of young manhood had indeed passed away. That warm, loving heart, that keen, active brain, were, for this world, at rest. All the zeal and self-sacrificing earnestness, all the carefully planned and patiently worked-out schemes, all the efforts, all the prayers, seemingly in vain. Yet, God be thanked, it is indeed but in seeming. Who will venture to think, as he looks back on the fair, noble record of Ion Keith-Falconer's life and on his sacrifice of what the world holds dear, that such love and faith can remain permanently effectless? In that noble young Christian hero's life and death a seed has assuredly been sown, the ultimate harvest of which no man may foresee.

The news of his death excited a deep feeling of sorrow
amid a far wider circle than that of his immediate friends
and acquaintances. Few men have died at so early an
age who have elicited from such widely different quarters
such expressions of warm regret.

It so chanced that the sad news from Aden reached
home only a few days before the Annual Meeting of the
General Assembly of the Free Church of Scotland, that
Assembly which in the preceding May had sent its missionary forth with so hopeful a God-speed.

Both the outgoing Moderator, Dr. Somerville, who had
been the mouthpiece of the Assembly on that occasion,
and his successor, Dr. Rainy, paid warm tribute to the
work and the memory of this soldier fallen at his post.

The former, in his sermon at the opening of the Assembly, after referring to the unlooked-for nature of the
news and to the sorrow which would be universally felt,
proceeded :—

"It is a peculiar providence that on the very eve of the
opening of the General Assembly, tidings should have
reached us of the unexpected death of one of the most
chivalrous, distinguished, and beloved of our young missionaries, who, amid the burning heats of Aden, at the
early age of thirty-one, has fallen under the power of that
mysterious malady which has borne from the Church on
earth so many of her noblest and most devoted sons. The
blow that has descended is one which will be keenly felt
throughout every district—I may say, throughout the
country at large. The young Christian hero was present
with us at the last Assembly. His noble parentage, high
intellectual qualities, brilliant attainments, but above all
his self-sacrificing devotion to the highest of all causes,
invest his death with a power which will influence our
minds during all the proceedings of this Assembly.

"What may be the beneficent result which God may
educe from this calamity, we know not. This, however, we
may venture to hope for, that the death of this noble young
man may prove the means of awakening attention, greater

than has ever been directed, to all Arabia's provinces, and
tend to give a lasting wound to that fatal system of Mohammedanism which has so long blighted the souls of millions.
What Christian Scotchman, with qualities in any way re-
sembling those of him who has passed away, will stand
forth to raise the banner of the Gospel in the place of the
gallant warrior who has fallen?"

The new Moderator, Dr. Rainy, in his opening address,
dwelt pointedly on the same thought:—the first volunteer
has fallen in the Lord's battle; who comes next? He
said :—

" Whatever becomes of the mission, of Ion Keith-Falconer we have now the memory only. But it is a very
profitable and admonitory memory. Very visibly he gave
to the cause and kingdom of our Lord Jesus all he had.
His university distinction, his oriental learning, his position in society, his means, the bright morning of his married life, I may add his physical vigour—for he had trained
body as well as mind—he brought them all to the service.
He did so the more impressively because he did it with no
fuss about it. We need not doubt that his free and complete gift was accepted. It was well that it was in his
heart. Suddenly, to our thinking, the Lord has been
pleased to take him up higher. We might think that, had
he been spared, his life might have been fruitful, not only
as a force abroad, but as an example at home; for he was
the first in our Church's experience who was at once able
and willing to inaugurate this special type of dedication to
mission work, and his life might have been a standing
appeal to others. But shall his death have no force as an
appeal? Who comes next? Who will come with youth
and trained mental faculties, and proved success in study
and acquirements, and with position and means that make
him independent, and give them all to the service? Or if
all these cannot be so equally combined, as in our lamented
friend, who will come with the measure of those gifts they
have, giving all they have? It is sad that he is gone. But
it will be a great deal sadder if it should turn out that his
example fails to raise up a successor from among the young
men and young women of our Church."

The Free Church, in its official "deliverance," made
solemn mention of those of its missionaries who had passed
to their rest in the preceding year, concluding with two
whose work was ended in the very spring-time of their
lives :—

" The falling asleep, in the first months of their fervent
service, of Mrs. Cross at Chirenji, the farthest African outpost in East Central Africa ; and of the Hon. Ion G. N.
Keith-Falconer in the extreme Asian outpost of Shaikh
Othman, in South Arabia, gives solemn urgency to the
latest appeal of the latter to the cultured, the wealthy and
the unselfish, whom that devoted volunteer for Christ represented : ' While vast continents are shrouded in almost
utter darkness, and hundreds of millions suffer the horrors
of heathenism or of Islam, the burden of proof lies upon
you to shew that the circumstances in which God placed
you were meant by Him to keep you out of the foreign
mission-field.' "

In Cambridge, it needs not to be said, after the first
shock of startled surprise, there was a very general and
keen feeling of sorrow.   To all came the thought that one
of the most distinguished graduates of our University had
passed away in his prime, under circumstances which
added an exceptional interest to his name ; many had the
further sad recollection that never again in this life should
they see the face of one of the most loveable of men.

In the sermon preached before the University on the
Sunday after Ascension-day (May 22), the preacher, the
Rev. H. C. G. Moule, Principal of Ridley Hall, who had
taken as his subject "our union by the Holy Spirit with
our exalted Lord," dwelt at the close of the sermon on the
loss which the University and Church had sustained, and
on the lesson to which it clearly pointed :—

" I will say no more upon the text.   Bear with me a few
moments longer if I pay my poor tribute as we close to the
blessed memory of him who is but just lost to our Univer-

sity, and to the Church Militant on earth, and whose name
I venture to enrol on the lengthening register of my friends
in Christ gone home. I spoke here of Ion Keith-Falconer
on Thursday, but the comparative privacy of our assembly
then leaves it surely my duty to lay one more wreath of
love and honour now upon his Arabian grave. He was
gifted, as men well knew, in many ways; with the gifts of
birth, which are worse than nothing without goodness, but
a true talent with it; with the physical vigour and address
which Scripture itself calls the glory of young men; with
a mental constitution in which facility and rapidity of
acquisition and accuracy of result were combined as few
men are permitted to combine them. He took his seat at
nine-and-twenty in the conclave of our Professors. And
then, quite unobtrusively and as in the day's work of life,
he went forth, for the Name's sake of his beloved Lord, to
be the evangelist of the Arabians. And then, ten days
ago, before his thirty-first birthday, he lay down and slept
in Christ. . . . . Not many years ago died, in the very
noon of youth, Ion Keith-Falconer's elder brother. It is
on record that for three whole days his dissolution was,
from the medical point of view, retarded by the overflowing joy which filled and vivified his being as the prospect
shone before him of entrance into the presence of the King.
God deals not so with all His dying saints. It may or may
not have been thus with this true brother of the same
blood and the same precious faith, as he also went over
Jordan. But it is sure as the foundations of all truth that
he is exceeding glad now, in great joy and felicity now, in
the everlasting life; welcomed with open embraces into
the eternal tabernacles, into the bliss of the sight of Christ.
And why? The ultimate answer is—because of the blood
of the Lamb, because of the indwelling and the leading of
the Holy Spirit.

"And what to us, what to the Christian Church, says
the silence of his grave? When, forty years ago, the
apostolic Krapf buried his wife at Zanzibar and stood
alone beside the tomb, 'Now,' said he, 'is the time come
for the evangelization of Africa from the eastern shore;
for the Church is ever wont to advance over the graves of
her members.' That omen is fulfilling now. So shall it be

in Christ's name for old Arabia, shut so long against the
Cross, but claimed now for her true Lord by our scholar-
missionary's dust."

It may well be imagined that to the workers in Mile-
End the news of Keith-Falconer's death would come with
peculiar poignancy. He had been one of the mainstays of
that work almost from its beginning, his voice had been
heard in the Great Hall only a few months before, and in
no place had the news from the distant mission-field been
more eagerly dwelt on than here. At the memorial service
held in the great Assembly Hall on the Sunday evening
after the tidings became generally known, the building
was thronged with an immense congregation. Still but the
same lesson:—for him, " the souls of the righteous are in
the hand of God;" for them that remain, let his example
speak forth trumpet-tongued to fight the Lord's battle.

Warm expressions of sympathy were elicited in many
quarters ; other missionary societies than that with which
Keith-Falconer was specially associated, put on formal record their sense of the loss which the Church had sustained.
The Committee of the Church Missionary Society sent a
minute expressing their regret at the death "at an early
age and almost at the very commencement of a missionary
career of singular promise, of the Hon. Ion Keith-Falconer."
They add

" The Committee feel that there is an ample sphere for
both Societies in the Arabian field, and trust that God
will raise up for their sister Society a suitable successor to
carry on the important work which Mr. Keith-Falconer
commenced ; and desire to express their very sincere sympathy with the Free Church of Scotland in the loss which
in Mr. Keith-Falconer's removal they have sustained."

To shew what I believe testifies to the increasing soli-
darity among those interested in the cause of Christian
Missions throughout the world, it may be added that not

a few missionary journals in Canada and the United States contained touching notices of Keith-Falconer's work and death.[1]

Among the various simpler marks of recognition paid to his memory, I cannot refrain from noticing the following mentioned to me by Mr. Charrington. In the East of London there exists a very large benefit Society, conducted on total abstinence principles, known as the 'Sons of the Phœnix.' The members of this are drawn entirely from the working classes, and number, I am told, not less than 30,000. Of this society, a new Lodge for younger members has been formed this summer, under the name of "the Hon. Ion Keith-Falconer Lodge." God grant that the reminder involved in the name under which these youths are enrolled may ever be a help to something higher, towards a fuller realization of truest Christian manhood.

It is not, however, in lament, deep and sincere though it be, or in simply dwelling lovingly on the thought of the departed, that honour may most truly be shewn, but rather in carrying on his work as he would have had it done. If of Keith-Falconer it may be said

> "So brave, so strong,
> Fired with such burning hate of powerful ill,"

it is no true honour, no mark of true affection to the much loved dead, if, among his works manifold, that with which his heart had been pre-eminently bound up, that for the attainment of which he counted not dear anything but the love of the Master, were to be allowed to die out in oblivion. As in the parallel case referred to in his last public utter-

---

[1] From quite another quarter of the world comes a singularly interesting piece of intelligence. The Presbytery of the Free Church of Scotland in Kafraria resolved (Oct. 8, 1887) that "steps should be taken to prepare a Memoir of the late Hon. Ion Keith-Falconer, to be printed in Kafir, as a tract for circulation among the Native Congregations, with a view to impress them with an example of self-sacrifice."

ance in Great Britain, that of Raymund Lully, lying in death amid the Moors whom he sought to bring back to faith in the Saviour, a protest for all time if ever supineness surrenders that region without protest to the false prophet—so do Ion Keith-Falconer's sacred remains lie, in witness and appeal, on that shore where in recent generations he has been the pioneer proclaiming the unchanging message of the Gospel.

My story might justly be charged with incompleteness, if I passed over without mention that which is the truest conceivable way of honouring Keith-Falconer's memory, the maintenance of the work begun at Shaikh Othman.

The news from Aden had reached this country between the outgoing of the old and the election of the new Committee of Foreign Missions in the Free Church; and thus not till their meeting in June could the Committee take official cognisance of the loss. They recorded in eloquent and touching words what Keith-Falconer had done, the causes which had brought his work to an untimely end, and their own expression of deep and sincere regret. " After five months' work, enthusiastic, untiring and hopeful, there remain for us on earth only his memory and the undying power and persuasiveness of his personal life and example."

But this was not all. At the same meeting, the Secretary announced that under God's blessing, Keith-Falconer's work should not be stayed by his death; for by the generosity of his mother and widow, stipends would be guaranteed for two missionaries, one of whom at least should be a medical man, to carry on the work at Shaikh Othman. Dr. Cowen undertook to return to Aden at any rate until the buildings were completed.

An appeal was thereupon issued. asking for a sufficient sum to complete and furnish the buildings. The estimated amount was £1,200, which was raised in a few months, and we may now hope that a few months more will see

the whole set of buildings in complete working order.
The whole of the money already spent on them, amount-
ing to upwards of £300, had been entirely defrayed by
Keith-Falconer himself.

It was of course no light thing to aim at carrying on a
mission the founder of which had fallen so early in the
midst of the work of which he was, humanly speaking, the
all in all. There was indeed no fear as to the zeal and
devotion of men who would volunteer for such a mission-
field; but it was an imperative duty to utilize to the full
the lessons of the past, that the new workers might enter
upon their task under the most favourable conditions.
The well-known Indian Missionary, Dr. Mackichan, who
had succeeded Dr. John Wilson at Bombay, was now on
the point of returning to India, and was therefore re-
quested to visit Aden and Shaikh Othman on his way and
to report generally on it and anything relevant to the
success of the mission.

At a meeting in August of the Foreign Missions' Committee, a second missionary, also a medical man, volun-
teered to go out to Shaikh Othman, and was accepted.
This gentleman, Dr. Alexander Paterson, is the son of the
Committee's first medical missionary to Madras, and
grandson of Dr. Chalmers's parishioner and friend, the
'Missionary of Kilmany.' This successor to Keith-
Falconer's work had never interchanged a word with him,
or indeed seen him, save at a distance; yet, strangely
enough, as I have already mentioned, it was to see him as
a possible colleague that Keith-Falconer paid his visit to
the hospital in Bethnal-Green in June, 1886. Dr. Paterson, after devoting himself at Cairo during the winter to
the study of Arabic and of special Oriental diseases, proceeded to Shaikh Othman at the beginning of the March
of the present year.[1] There yet another volunteer is

---

[1] Dr. Paterson has already an average of twenty cases a day,
Arabs and Somalis, both men and women.

working, who sailed from England in November last. This is Mr. Matthew Lochhead, who speaks Arabic fluently, and who for three years held the post of 'Lay Evangelist and Medical Assistant' in a mission among the Kabyles in Morocco.

When the present chapter was ready to be sent to the press, fresh tidings reached me which call for feelings of deep thankfulness, and cannot fitly be passed over here.

The death of the young missionary and his appeal for men has had so powerful an effect on the Divinity students of the New College, Edinburgh (one of the three Colleges of the Free Church of Scotland), that out of the forty who will complete their seven or eight years' course of study in April next, eleven, besides two of the previous year, have offered themselves for missionary work abroad. Several of these, to whom South Arabia was provisionally offered, were ultimately found ineligible for that post on grounds of health. One of the most distinguished, however, a very promising Semitic scholar, Mr. William R. W. Gardner, M.A., has been chosen by the Foreign Missions' Committee and will be ordained for the work.

Mr. Gardner's father was a missionary in Poona, his sister is a missionary in Bombay, and his elder brother is about to go out as ordained Professor to the Wilson College in Bombay. Mr. Gardner will continue his study of Arabic for the present and will join the Mission in October.

The mention of the Edinburgh New College suggests one point more, the disposal of Keith-Falconer's Arabic books. The choicest of these, upwards of 400 in number, have been made over by his family to the Library of this College, where they will be kept as a special collection under the title of the "Keith-Falconer Arabic Library." Professor A. B. Davidson and Sir William Muir consider it to be the most valuable Arabic library in Scotland.

All that now remains to be told is to speak briefly of the results of Dr. Mackichan's visit to Aden. Having landed on Oct. 1, the first necessary piece of business to be transacted was to take steps for transferring the grant of land at Shaikh Othman to the trustees of the Free Church of Scotland, as Keith-Falconer would himself have done on the completion of the buildings.

It is strangely touching to read of Dr. Mackichan's meeting with Colonel Raper, Dr. Colson, Dr. Jackson, Lieutenant Gordon, and others whose names are familiar as those of cordial friends to the mission party. On Sunday evening, October 2, Dr. Mackichan was taken by Colonel Raper to see the spot where the departed worker for Christ was laid.

" He accompanied us to the place where Keith-Falconer lies buried—a spot that shall ever remain sacred to all who shall read the records of the planting of Christ's Church in Arab lands, and which now and in coming years should call forth the highest manifestations of the missionary devotion and heroism of our Church. Behind it and around it, stand the black mountain rocks—the gloomy hills of darkness to which the departed labourer came with the message of the Gospel's glorious light ; in front of it lies the white, sandy Arabian shore, with the ocean stretching away into limitless distance. As we looked upon it in the quiet of the peaceful sunset hour, it was a scene in which labour and rest, suffering and joy, seemed strangely mingled. The black frowning rocks seemed to speak of toil and suffering, but the still unending expanse before us lifted our thoughts away from the scene of sorrow, to that of the unending and unspeakable joy, in which that labour and sorrow have ended. As we stood by the grave we thought of the mysteriousness of the bereavement which had deprived the land of one so devoted to the cause of its evangelisation, and so eminently fitted for the work to which he had consecrated himself. Colonel Raper interpreted our thoughts and his own, when he spoke of it as the dying of the seed which should yet bring forth much fruit. It was touching to see how carefully the grave was tended. The Colonel had enclosed the space temporarily in a tasteful border of wood, while the loving hands of his two little children had covered it with the shells which they themselves had gathered from the adjoining beach."

On the following day a visit was paid to Shaikh Othman, under the guidance of Dr. Jackson. Dr. Mackichan was agreeably surprised by the comparative coolness of the temperature of Aden after that of the Red Sea, and still more by that of Shaikh Othman. Here he found the old village gradually disappearing, and being replaced by one built by Government with wide, open streets. After a visit to the Government office, a careful inspection was made of the unfinished mission buildings. These, as has been already stated, lie between the old village and the new, and the site was chosen by Keith-Falconer that the mission and its workers should be in the very midst of the people. The plot, which was 510 feet each way, was enclosed by a wall of sun-dried bricks seven feet high, with a gate in the centre of each side of the square. In the eastern corner was the unfinished house, the walls of which had risen to the height of the first story. It had been intended to add an upper story, containing at least one room.

The next visit was to the house where the mission party had lived. Of this Dr. Mackichan says,

"As we went over the little unoccupied dwelling in which Mr. Keith-Falconer's last moments were spent, we realised something of the trials with which our missionaries had to contend in the beginning of their labours. The house is not only small but low-roofed, while the high wall which surrounds the enclosure must exclude much of the breeze which is so essential to healthful life in that region. There can be little doubt that the illnesses from which all the members of the Mission suffered were in great measure due to the peculiar position in which they were placed, rather than to any general climatic cause."

On their way back to Aden, visits were paid to Hassan Ali's bungalow and to Khor Maksar, the residence of Lieutenant Gordon.

Those who have followed with interest Keith-Falconer's heroic missionary career will be glad to read of the impressions left on the mind of an acute observer, written immediately after careful investigation on the spot. Dr. Mackichan had strong grounds for believing from all he saw and heard while in Aden that Keith-Falconer's work while in Arabia, short though it was, had by its intense earnestness left a deep impression on the hearts of the people, and that the influence had spread far into the interior. "We have," he adds, "not merely the assurance that the seed of corn which has died will bear much fruit, but can behold already the up-springing of the tender blades of promise."

Dr. Mackichan informs us that a railway is already projected from Aden to Shaikh Othman, and is expected to be an accomplished fact in six months. This will doubtless largely increase the population of Shaikh Othman, and will in many ways bring great benefits to the missionaries, but not without certain drawbacks.

One important point had to be settled, the question whether the original scheme of the mission should be retained unchanged in all its details as planned by Keith-Falconer. After careful consideration, Dr. Mackichan proposed one important modification, in which he was supported by the "unanimous, almost urgent representation" of those gentlemen on the spot who took a warm interest in the welfare of the mission. This was to provide a residence for the missionaries on a fresh site, reserving the existing buildings and the enclosure for the various purposes of the Mission,—Hospital, Dispensary, Mission School; the present unfinished building being on its completion used as the School, the Hospital being erected on another part of the same enclosure.

There is obviously much to recommend this change, and the proposal has been approved of by the Foreign Missions' Committee of the Free Church. Thus, as Le-

R

fore, the work will still be carried on in the heart of the village, but the missionaries will live rather less than half a mile away, on a spot thoroughly open to the freshest breezes. Here they will not require the high enclosing wall necessary in the village, and thus will be able to obtain after a hard day's toil the rest and fresh air which are absolutely essential to their health and fitness for labour.

Again then does the mission begin, and with bright prospects of success. Humanly speaking, we may well believe that the workers at Shaikh Othman have now a great field opening out before them. In the success of their work all servants of Christ, of every branch of the Church, cannot but feel the warmest interest.

A great price has been paid, a noble life laid down; but by God's will that death may have wrought as much for His cause as a long life spent in missionary service: and, in any case, it is not for us to define the conditions under which God's servants, here or beyond the grave, shall work for Him. The Master had need of him, and has called him.

In those words from the greatest of English allegories, which stand at the head of the present chapter, we have the dying utterance of Valiant-for-Truth. Fittingly may those words be applied to the closing of the short life of Ion Keith-Falconer, short if measured by length of years, and yet

> " One crowded hour of glorious life
> Is worth an age without a name."

Devoted missionary, true Christian hero, he has left a mark on many fields of work, an undying memory in many hearts. " He has fought His battles, Who now is his rewarder."

THE END.

INDEX.

www.ingramcontent.com/pod-product-compliance
Lightning Source LLC
Chambersburg PA
CBHW031405020726
47499CB00005B/1473